NEW ARRIVALS ON WEST INDIA DOCK ROAD

THE WEST INDIA DOCK ROAD SERIES BOOK 1

RENITA D'SILVA

Boldwood

First published in Great Britain in 2025 by Boldwood Books Ltd.

Copyright © Renita D'Silva, 2025

Cover Design by JD Smith Design Ltd

Cover Images: Shutterstock and Stephen Mulcahey

A CIP catalogue record for this book is available from the British Library.

Paperback ISBN 978-1-83617-266-6

Large Print ISBN 978-1-83617-265-9

Hardback ISBN 978-1-83617-264-2

Ebook ISBN 978-1-83617-267-3

Kindle ISBN 978-1-83617-268-0

Audio CD ISBN 978-1-83617-259-8

MP3 CD ISBN 978-1-83617-260-4

Digital audio download ISBN 978-1-83617-262-8

This book is printed on certified sustainable paper. Boldwood Books is dedicated to putting sustainability at the heart of our business. For more information please visit https://www.boldwoodbooks.com/about-us/sustainability/

Boldwood Books Ltd, 23 Bowerdean Street, London, SW6 3TN

www.boldwoodbooks.com

For my children.
You are my reason.

It is during our darkest moments that we must focus to see the light.

— ARISTOTLE

PROLOGUE

1938

West India Dock Road is slightly crooked, like, some say, those who inhabit it. But, its residents stubbornly maintain, this is what adds to its quirkiness, its otherworldly charm.

There's a microcosm of the world to be found here, in this street that resonates with the swell of the Thames. Clip-clopping carriages, an amalgam of languages from all parts of the world, exotic and mysterious. The siren call of the froth-topped water churned by ships coming in to dock, reverberating with their foggy, yellow boom, these vast vessels that have sailed tropical seas, carrying tales of uprisings and triumphs in faraway places, loaded with strange goods and stranger people. The air here is thick with mist and intrigue, every gentle caress of it infused with the briny, hops-and-spice scent of different, more exotic lands.

At the junction where East (India Dock Road) meets West (India Dock Road) is the tall and imposing structure that is The Eastern Hotel, standing guard majestically over the goings on in its street, turning its nose up at the unsavoury characters to be found at the Sailors' Palace Hostelry run by the British and

Foreign Sailors' Society opposite and even worse, The German Sailors' Home down the street.

On either side of the road, an eclectic array of businesses ply their wares. A Jewish shop nestles nose to nose with a butcher's. A sailmaker's and ship's chandler's nudges a shop advertising clothing for 'sailors and other nautical types', a Chinese hostelry sits happily beside a lodging home for 'Asiatics and Africans'. A snatch of music wafts from a music hall, brightly exuberant, mingling with resounding cheer and the scent of hops and smoke from the public house nearby.

Seagulls call, loud and plaintive and the air tastes of yearning, ache and nostalgia.

Men of all colours and hues carry on their dark, drawn faces the imprint of their travels, their longing for home etched into the weary lines of their faces, their rugged sailor's hands clenched into fists holding a cherished memory of a long-ago time in the place they belonged without question or antagonism.

Divya stumbles and a deep voice carrying haunting echoes of old chants from foreign lands asks her in a thick accent if she's all right.

An arm as brown as her own rights her, gentle, gold eyes bright with concern.

And for the first time since she arrived in this strange land, Divya experiences a flicker of belonging.

PART I

1

BOMBAY PORT, INDIA, 1938

The ship is huge. So loud and busy and noisy – even more so than the port, which is crammed with passengers and porters and carriages and animals, the alleyways leading off it spilling with vendors sitting on the mud beside towering hills of carpets, silks, intricately woven tapestries, guavas and papayas, jackfruit and watermelon, onions and chillies, coriander and mint, mounds of lethal red chilli powder and bright-yellow turmeric, tomatoes and coconuts, and fish, dead eyes and gleaming scales glinting bright silver, dancing monkeys, performing bears, sweetmeats sticky with sugar, perfumed with rose water and dripping syrup. The air smells of brine and spices, is thick with moisture, swirling with grains of sand and salt, and carries the hazy red sheen of dust. A lean-to fashioned from a bright-purple sheet stretched across four tree trunks acting as posts does brisk business, selling steaming tumblers of tea, thick and milky, flavoured with cardamom and cinnamon. Another makeshift tent beside it, this one with an incandescent-orange awning, sells parathas and potato curry. Yet another, treacly sweets layered with nuts and honey, oozing nectar.

Brown-skinned coolies carry huge trunks onto the ship upon their heads – effortlessly it seems, not even breaking out in a sweat as they follow in the wake of their white, hatted and suited masters, who are perspiring in the sweltering heat, their noses quite pink, beads of sweat trembling upon their formidable moustaches. The coolies converse jovially with their fellows, who pull huge trolleys packed with teetering trunks and hat boxes in danger of falling off the ramp and into the sea. They are followed by dainty white ladies in printed sundresses, their faces cast in shadow by their enormous matching hats dotted with artificial flowers and fruit, a legion of flies buzzing hopefully around them, vigorous strokes of their small fans barely displacing the heavy, humid air.

Everyone seems to be in an enormous hurry, the din ear-splitting – ships tooting, dhows dotting the dirty, yellow water, the bare-chested men manning them grinning as they call out to each other, their voices musical and hypnotic, their muscles gleaming chocolate, teeth glittering yellow in leathery, brown faces. The air sizzles, tasting of ghee and cumin, salt and saffron, burnt sugar, caramel gold.

Hawkers circulate the ship decks, selling, via baskets slung around their necks, everything from wilting flowers and over-ripe mangoes to colourful bangles glinting silver bright in the sunshine, and toys: dancing puppets, leering cloth dolls, little tin soldiers.

'For your charges,' says one, thrusting a one-eyed monkey sporting an evil grin at Divya.

She waves him away, busy soothing the baby, who's crying, hot and drowsy but unable to sleep with his face tucked into the crook of Divya's shoulder – she's hefting him on her hip while keeping a firm hold on Master James, the toddler, who's also sniffling, quite overwhelmed by the chaotic activity around them.

Why is the cloth monkey blind in one eye? Divya wonders, musing as to what child would enjoy playing with a one-eyed monkey, which looks so scary, even she had flinched when it was summarily pushed at her.

She's lost sight of Mrs Ellis, two women cutting in front of her, clothed in voluminous dresses, pale pink and vivid green, that dance in the frivolous, salt-infused breeze, matching wide hats and parasols inclined at a rakish angle.

'Is it true the governor of Mysore is on board?' gasps one breathily.

'I heard he's travelling with the crown prince of Putana. Word is that they've commandeered the best suites in first class.'

An arc of errant spray slicks Divya's face with briny caresses.

Divya is tired and as overwhelmed as the children after the long journey from the town to the port, suddenly finding themselves right in the midst of this hive of frenzied activity.

She will be glad to get a moment to herself in her cabin once she's settled the children into theirs in first class.

* * *

The Ellises' – Divya's employers – suite is plushly spacious and luxurious. And blessedly peaceful after the noisy mayhem outside.

A study, two bedrooms – one master and the children's room – a drawing room, all equipped with, what appears to Divya's inexperienced eye, state-of-the-art furnishings.

But Mrs Ellis is not impressed. 'I was expecting something bigger. And the children's room is shockingly lacking. I shall complain,' she clucks.

From outside drifts the trundle of trolleys and the call of porters as they transfer luggage to the cabins, followed by the click-clack of heels and the thud of boots, the feminine trill of a voice raised in question and an answering masculine rumble.

Through the portholes, Divya spies the sea, tumultuous green, dotted with dhows and swelling with frothy caps.

The ship's gentle sway and the sudden calm after the commotion outside means the baby has finally fallen asleep on Divya's shoulder, his hot breath warming her neck.

The toddler is tucked against her, chewing the pallu of her sari, which he does when he's nervous, overawed by and unsure of his surroundings, his huge eyes taking everything in.

'Find your cabin and come back soonest before the baby wakes,' Mrs Ellis, *Memsahib* to Divya, says just as the quiet in the cabin is shattered by the most almighty toot, causing the baby to startle awake and the toddler to whimper.

And then, with a jerk and a jolt accompanied by a rousing cry from above board, the ship starts to move in earnest.

Divya rocks the baby, kissing his downy head, while at the same time soothing the toddler and gently leading him towards the porthole.

Now that the ship is moving, there are no dhows in sight and the water is turquoise, glittering diamonds in the sunshine. Birds alight briefly upon the waves, their wings displacing rainbow fountains as they skim the surface and fly away, dark, shadowy stains upon the blinding gold firmament.

Endless blue water lies ahead of them and Divya is suddenly struck by an urge to run, beset by pangs of intense longing and homesickness for the village she called home for the first eighteen years of her life. Nerves and trepidation make her stomach cramp as she embarks on this voyage to a new country thousands of miles away from all that is familiar, the full-bellied cries of her charges so different from the gnawing, stomach-cramping, hungry keens of children in her village, clothed in mud.

She aches for the open skies, white sun, humidity and orange earth of her village, red rice coated in curry so spicy, it scalds your mouth so you forget how little of it there is. Home. Harsh as the relentless sunshine during the drought, the torrential onslaught of the monsoons but beloved all the same, like the scaly fish riddled with bones which stabbed your mouth, stuck in your teeth but oh my goodness was its flesh so wonderfully, sweetly delicious.

Her mouth tastes of salt and yearning.

2

1920 – 1937

Divya was an only child, a girl at that, but her parents never once made her feel less, not enough, like the other villagers did. They never said, like everyone else, '*Hai*, you're only a girl, a drain on your parents. They have to arrange dowry for you, for when you get married, work hard and thanklessly and save endlessly. A son would have brought in wealth in the form of dowry, and help in the guise of a daughter-in-law to look after them in their old age. You, on the other hand, will marry and go away and then, what will they do, your parents, rendered poor by giving all they have as dowry for you?'

On those occasions when Divya's parents heard the villagers' lament, they swooped in and stopped it with a sharp look or a cutting retort. 'Do not speak about our daughter this way. She's precious and perfect. The gods' and goddesses' gift to us. She's worth a thousand sons.'

'That's all well and good,' the villagers huffed. 'But who will look after you both in your old age when she's wed and gone?'

'I will care for my parents, whether I'm married or not,' Divya would maintain.

'So, if you look after your parents after you're married, who will look after your in-laws then?' the villagers would snort, shaking their heads at Divya's foolishness.

Divya never considered not getting married – it was a woman's duty to do so. The only women in the village and beyond who didn't marry were those cursed with disfigurements and ailments. They were shunned by all and sundry, considered a huge burden on their parents. 'They must have committed great sins in their previous lives,' the villagers whispered, 'to be born that way.'

Divya's parents went both at once, drowned in a flash flood while travelling into the next town to meet with the matchmaker who had found a potential groom for their beloved daughter, at seventeen already in danger of becoming an old maid; most of the girls in the village were married off by fourteen and had at least a couple of children by the time they were Divya's age. Her parents' death – a double loss to Divya, orphaned in one fell swoop. But at least they were together. Now they wouldn't have to worry about there being no one to care for them in their old age, once Divya married and left home. It was scant solace but Divya repeated it to herself often, in those shell-shocked days after, as she tried to comprehend and come to terms with her great loss, the end of her life as was, the beloved centre of her parents' world.

Of course, the villagers blamed her. The fact that her parents were the only casualties of the flash flood – everyone else was rescued – underlined their conviction that Divya was somehow responsible for her parents' demise.

'You are bad luck. It was because of you they died. If they hadn't aspired to engage the services of a matchmaker to secure for you a groom from the next town – someone educated, working in an office – always aiming above their worth and yours, they would have been hale and hearty and well. Who did they think you were – a queen? What did they think was wrong with the boys in our village, the boys you grew up with, whose parents were known to them? They would be farmers, not office workers. So what? Nothing wrong with hard slog instead of "working" in an office, pushing paper while pandering to the whims of and bowing down to the white Sahibs.'

The villagers, who had watched Divya grow from the time she was conceived, whose children she had played with, attended the missionary school with, now ostracised her, just when she was at her lowest, grieving for her parents, her family gone. But the villagers were afraid that associating with her meant the bad luck they had decided she was cursed with would visit them too.

Divya's parents had set out to the next town with such hope, to meet the matchmaker who would introduce them to the eligible boy who would provide their cherished only daughter with a better life than theirs.

'He works as a clerk in a white Sahib's office. A man of education. He will keep you in luxury,' they enthused to Divya. 'He is the only son of parents who own a brick-and-mortar house in town, a far cry from our mud hut, leased to us by the landlord in exchange for working his fields.'

Divya's ma and baba had blithely ignored warnings of the storm the village guru predicted was looming, the glower of clouds collecting above, casting a slur on the sun's bright-gold glow, giving truth to his prophecy.

'We will be back by the time the storm breaks. Sealing this match is more important. We want to secure this groom for you before somebody else with an eligible daughter swoops in.'

Afterwards, Divya chastised herself endlessly for allowing them to go. Why had she not gone with them too? Then at least she wouldn't have to endure this pain, her life spooling emptily, directionless, in their absence.

But they hadn't wanted her to accompany them – 'Ritual dictates that this first meeting must be conducted between the elders.'

When she bid them goodbye, why did Divya not have any premonition, an inkling of what was to come?

After her parents died, the match fell through: 'We don't want a girl tainted by bad luck.'

The villagers shunned her.

The landlord swooped in and claimed the hut back now that Divya's father was not there to work his land in return.

Seventeen years old, orphaned, homeless and desperate, Divya had bundled her meagre belongings into an old sari and walked into town – the very town that her parents had been bound for that fateful day they lost their lives.

But on the day Divya set out, the sun shone harsh as the villagers' glares boring into her back as she walked away, their hissed murmurs of, 'Good riddance – now that she's gone, taking her cursed luck with her, the Gods will bless us,' following her.

All Divya had with her were her mother's saris, her father's lungis – the traditional loincloths favoured by the men in the village – she couldn't bear to part with them – and a few paltry coins: the meagre contents of the coconut shell scoop hidden at the bottom of the rice pot, where her parents had kept any money they were able to spare.

The sun was at its zenith and she wiped her sweaty face with her sari pallu as she trudged up the mud road and out of the village where she was born and had lived her whole life. Once she had left the village well and truly behind, she took refuge under a tree whose scrawny branches barely offered shade, and gave in to the tears of upset and sadness she'd been holding back.

'What will I do now, Ma, Baba?' she sobbed.

And there, the mud road shimmering in the relentless sunshine, dust rising off it in an orange haze, a rat snake undulating languidly, a weaving slither upon grainy red, and disappearing into the bushes opposite, a miracle occurred.

She heard her parents' voices, gentle and comforting as being enveloped in their arms, felt their presence, sandalwood and caramelised onions and love: 'You will be all right, our precious. You will be just fine. Go into town. Knock on the doors there. You will find a job and a place to stay before sundown.'

She wanted to stay there forever, under the scraggly tree, listening to her parents' voices, but they'd said all they had to, and her stomach was cramping with hunger, her throat dry and hoarse with thirst – her parents might be of the next world but she was still in this one, suffering from the limitations of the human form. And so, she hefted the sari bundle containing all her worldly possessions upon her back and walked into town like her (deceased) parents, briefly but magically returned to her just when she needed them most, had advised.

3

1937

The town was divided into sections based on hierarchy. The outskirts, on the very far reaches, which Divya came to first, were for the untouchables, the shudras who cleaned the toilets and did all the unsavoury, menial jobs eschewed by the higher castes.

Next, circling the town, was the native settlement – the upper-caste Hindus who worked for the white rulers. This was where Divya's parents had been heading, to meet with the matchmaker, when the river burst its banks and took their lives.

Now it snaked around town, placid and calm, a twinkling, silver expanse dotted with boats, under a wide, white sky, looking harmless, benign, beautiful. Boatmen calling to each other, one collecting sand from the sandbank in the middle of the river. A man washing his buffalo on the riverbank.

The town centre and its immediate surrounds were the province of the white Sahibs. Wide, residential streets with tall and sprawling brick mansions each enclosed within their own vast, high-walled compounds.

Hefting her bundle of possessions from one shoulder to another, wiping her face free of perspiration with her slightly smelly sari pallu, Divya boldly walked up to the gate of the first of these mansions that she came to.

The gatekeeper looked her up and down, barring her way. 'What do you want?'

Divya swallowed, the relentless sun burning her head (although it was demurely covered by her sari pallu, as was the custom in the presence of men), sticking her hair, damp with perspiration, to her scalp, rivulets of sweat dripping down her body, her sari moist with it, making her feel itchy.

She channelled her parents, hearing once again their voices in her head, a miracle just when she required it most, and lied, 'I'm the new hire. They're expecting me up at the house.'

'I wasn't told about it,' the gatekeeper muttered but he opened the gates anyway, nodding at her to go through, grumbling all the while under his breath about how he was expected to do his job if nobody told him anything.

And Divya walked through the gates, a skip in her step at her own boldness, glad to be rid of the man's sour breath in her face, his scent of stale sweat and festering grudges (he had stood too close). Thinking, *I'll worry about what to say if I don't get the job and have to encounter this man again on my way back later.*

The drive went on endlessly, it seemed, fruit trees flanking manicured and well-watered lawns, bright-red hibiscus and glorious cascades of orange and purple bougainvillaea basking in the heady sunshine. When she arrived, finally, tired and breathless, at the imposing mansion, Divya took a deep breath, and, before she could lose her nerve, knocked at the front door.

The snooty butler did not even look at her, glancing severely at her dusty feet as he pointed her in the direction of the servants' entrance.

The gardeners sniggered loudly as she made her way around

the house – it took ten minutes at least, it was that huge – to the back door.

The maids employed in the thankless job of sweeping the courtyard (for even the smallest gust of spice-sprinkled breeze served only to scatter the dust they'd so religiously swept aside all over the clean area, smacking pebbles and grit into their faces) had straightened up as Divya walked past, glad of the respite, their pallus tucked into their waists, saris glimmering red-gold in the sunshine, staring unabashedly at Divya as she knocked, at the right door this time, this one not as grand, paint chipped in places, and waited for a response.

The man who opened the door yelled at the maids, 'What are you staring at? Get to work.'

Divya had a glimpse into the kitchen, vast and busy and bustling. She looked longingly at the maids sniffing as they chopped a mountain of onions, others peeling baskets of potatoes and great big nodules of ginger, one grating carrots, another coconuts, yet another plucking feathers off of two fat chickens, very different from the scrawny specimens pecking listlessly at the dust in the natives' section of the cantonment.

Although Divya was prepared to do any work at all, and would be grateful for it, she hoped she would be hired to work in the kitchens. She loved to cook, having learnt the skill, her ma proudly declared to the villagers, who, once they sampled Divya's cooking, came back for more, 'On my lap as an infant.'

In fact, Divya's very first memory was of sitting beside an earthen pot, watching it hiss and bubble with great absorption. She had thrust a curious palm out to touch it and her mother had pulled it back, gathering Divya in her arms, kissing her cheeks while whispering, 'No, my heart, it is very hot. Look at the twigs I've set alight *under* the pot. That is fire and you should, by no means, touch it. Look.' Her mother gently angled Divya towards the orange-topped twigs which spat and fizzed with furious venom. 'Even from here, you can feel the heat it generates.'

Divya had stared, fascinated, at the dancing, performing, bright-red tongues of fire. She had been too mesmerised by the sounds the pot made, the frothy goo splattering down its sides to notice the dramatics under the pot.

'Heat is what makes the rice cook. Before then it's raw, like this, look.'

Her ma had set Divya down and dug in the gunny sack beside her, plucking a few grains of uncooked rice and handing them to Divya.

Divya put them in her mouth. They were very hard, like tiny pebbles. She spat them out. Her mother laughed and tickled by her mother's mirth, Divya giggled.

'See, you don't like raw rice. It needs to be cooked to make it edible.' Ma scooped some boiled rice out of the pot using a ladle fashioned from one half of a coconut shell, and after blowing on it to cool it down, fed it to Divya.

Divya munched happily on it, smiling.

'This is the same rice that you didn't like when raw. How much tastier and softer and plumper it is when cooked, no?'

Divya nodded and clapped her hands.

Some of Divya's happiest memories were of cooking with her mother, Ma praising her when she produced a dish that she deemed, 'The best I have ever tasted.'

Divya loved the alchemy of food preparation, how mixing of the right kind of spices and flavourings transformed even the blandest dish into something exquisite. Ma and Baba were proud of her ability to make, they said, 'Something out of nothing. Even in the midst of ravaging drought, even if there are only one or two ingredients, you will create something tasty, somehow. You know instinctively what spices go with what vegetable. You combine ingredients we would never have thought of and the result is outstanding. Your cooking made even old Laxmi smile,' her parents would marvel.

Laxmi was famously curmudgeonly. Rumour had it that she had not smiled since her husband ran away with her sister.

'But you managed it.' Her parents beamed. 'And have you noticed the villagers have been dropping by when you start cooking, hoping to be invited to join in our meal, for the fragrant scents are irresistible? Even the village dogs gather outside our hut angling for scraps when you are cooking.'

Now, Divya prayed to the Gods, and to Ma and Baba, 'Please, I hope I get to work in the kitchens here.' It would be an absolute delight to cook in such a well-stocked kitchen with such fresh and bountiful ingredients.

An older woman stirred a huge saucepan bubbling upon the biggest stove Divya had laid eyes on, using a wooden ladle. The scent of roasting spices, sizzling oil, frying garlic and stewing milk making Divya's mouth water, her hungry stomach groan. All she'd had to eat was half a chapati before she left the village, which she'd made from the last of the mealy, worm-infested wheat scraped from the bottom of the gunny sack. She might be a good cook, and even though she'd added herbs and medicinal leaves plucked from the bushes in the courtyard to the meagre dough, they could only go so far.

'What do you want?' The man at the door, the head chef, Divya guessed, was impatient. 'You are wasting my time. That lot won't do anything properly without my supervision.' He gestured behind his shoulder at the maids, who hid their scowls behind their veils, attacking their work with renewed gusto, propelled by fury at their supervisor no doubt.

'I... Is there any work going? I'm a hard worker and happy to do anything at all.'

'Well, as it happens...' The chef began, but almost immediately, the older woman, who had been waving her ladle, coated with a thick, vermilion sauce, at the maids gawping at Divya, came to stand beside him.

She peered closely at Divya and her face changed, becoming grim as she whispered loudly in the head chef's ear. 'It's that cursed girl whose parents died in the flash flood. My sister Bhanu was one of their neighbours – I would see her when I visited my sister. What a tragedy – the daughter's bad luck causing the parents' death. Bhanu is devastated; they all are in the village. They have kicked her out. If we employ her, we're inviting bad luck.' Making sure Divya overheard like she was meant to, the woman's punishing gaze pincering her.

Of course, Divya thought, despair blooming in her chest, chasing away the momentary peace she'd experienced upon hearing her parents' voices, everyone in town would know too, for this was where her parents had been headed.

The head chef's eyes hardened to set cement and with a clipped, 'No work for the likes of you here,' he shut the door in her face.

The sweepers' and gardeners' titters followed Divya all the way out of the compound, scalding more than the sun battering her head, scorching her body.

And yet, even as she was turned away from subsequent houses, the sun unleashing gold-tipped arrows of burning ire, she was loath to give up – for what would she do, where would she go? The bitter bile of desperation gnawing at her empty stomach, chipping away at her dogged belief: *Ma and Baba promised I'd get a job before sundown.*

4

The next house Divya decided to try her luck – *her luck, ha!* – was even more enormous than the ones before. The compound going on for miles it seemed. A fruit orchard. Manicured lawns. A vegetable garden. A tennis court. A paved courtyard surrounding a gushing fountain, water cascading in kaleidoscopic rainbows in front of the entrance to the grand, multi-storeyed mansion.

As she walked round to the back of the house, profuse with purple and bright-pink bougainvillaea and orange marigolds gilded by sun – she had learnt her lesson by now – she heard a child's cries, mournful and tragic, at odds with the burbling, celebratory song of the fountain.

The cries pricked Divya's eyes, spawning reciprocal grief, but before she could give in to it, she heard her parents' voices again, for the second time that day: 'Turn around, Divya. Go, knock on the front door.'

'I'll only be told by the severe butler to try my luck at the servants' entrance,' she protested to her dead parents in her head.

But they were insistent: 'Knock on the front door.'

And so, she retraced her steps, walking around the fountain, the child's mournful cries following her.

When the butler opened the front door, the child's wails were louder, heart-rending.

'I'm looking for work,' she managed, her voice wilting as the butler looked her sternly over, doubting her wisdom for heeding her deceased parents' imagined voices in her head.

'Go round the back,' the butler barked in a clipped voice and was about to shut the door in her face when a woman's voice called, over the sound of the child's wails. 'Who is it, Ganesh?'

'A woman looking for work, Memsahib,' he said in English.

'Does she have experience with babies?'

The butler paused, turned, looked at Divya, one eyebrow raised.

And Divya, whose experience of babies was holding her neighbour's newborn once, for a couple of minutes before handing him to her mother, afraid she'd drop him (she'd found him slippery and floppy as a fish), nodded vigorously, meeting the butler's assessing gaze, hoping he wouldn't read the lie writ large upon her face.

'Bring her up to the nursery,' the woman called.

Only a minuscule pursing of the butler's lips gave away what he thought of the idea, even as he held the door open and inclined his head to indicate to Divya to step inside.

Thank you, Ma, Baba, Divya exalted in her head as she entered the mansion – through the front door at that, taking what felt like her first proper breath since her parents died.

As she reached the head of the very grand, lushly carpeted staircase in the wake of the butler, the baby's cries steadily getting louder, a small body lurched from an open door and out onto the landing.

'James, come back here at once,' the same voice that had

instructed the butler to bring Divya upstairs, called sharply. All the while, the baby cried, abjectly mournful.

The little boy intently charged ahead, hands stretched out, his face scrunched up in absolute delight, presumably at running away from his mother. He was wearing a vest, a bulky cloth nappy and booties which must have once been white but were now soiled reddish yellow, and he was weaving along on little sausage legs.

As he approached Divya, he stumbled, his pudgy hands flailing as they vainly gripped at the air to steady himself, and she bent down, all instinct, managing to catch him just in time, lifting him up in her arms. He was unbearably soft; he smelled of baby powder and innocence. He regarded her solemnly with wide eyes the colour of the sky at dawn, the creamy blue of promise. His face scrunched up preparatory to crying and then, inexplicably, he decided against it and smiled instead, a wide beam of pure, unadulterated joy.

It lodged right in Divya's broken heart, warming it.

With a fisted and grubby hand, the little boy patted Divya's face. It felt like a blessing, benediction.

'He likes you.'

It was the woman, hefting her crying babe in her arms. She was tall and imposing, but appeared as utterly exhausted as the wailing, red-faced and tear-stained infant she was trying and failing to placate.

Divya, utterly absorbed by the little boy, had not realised that the woman and the baby were now beside her.

'Set James down please and see if you can settle Hugh,' the lady said.

'Yes, Memsahib,' Divya said, but when she tried to gently lower James to the floor, he refused, clinging to Divya.

And this innocent cherub's wholehearted affection, uncomplicated, unconditional, freely given, assuaged, in a small way, the giant wound that was Divya's heart, shattered by her parents' deaths and the rejection and animosity of the villagers and everyone else she had encountered since.

He doesn't think I am bad luck. He likes me.

'James, come let's go get something to eat, shall we?' the woman said.

And finally, James slid down Divya's body but tugged at her hand.

'He's taken to you. You might as well come along,' the woman said. 'What's your name?'

'Divya Ram,' she said, even as she thanked the nuns at the free missionary school she had attended for her passable English.

'Very well.' The woman nodded. 'The nanny took ill last week and went home and hasn't returned. We got a letter from her today informing us that the doctor suspects black fever. I doubt she'll be back. Here, try soothing Hugh.'

The child was thrust at her, James tugging at her sari.

Divya patted the baby's juddering back, cooing to him and rocking him while wiping his nose with her sari pallu.

And for the first time since her parents died, in trying to soothe this hot, dearly upset little babe, Divya experienced a very small easing of her own grief.

Gradually, as they made their way past several ornate rooms, the baby's sobs quieted.

By the time they arrived in the dining room, where the woman – 'I'm Mrs Ellis, but Memsahib will do nicely' – imperiously ordered tea for herself and warm milk for James, maids obsequiously rushing to do her bidding, the infant had exhausted his tears, his small body going limp in Divya's arms, warm breaths escaping his face which was tucked into the crook of her neck.

The breeze drifting in from outdoors scented with roses, tart and spiced with raw mangoes, green peppercorns and unripe bananas, deposited piquant kisses upon Divya's face.

'You have a way with children,' Mrs Ellis observed, as she and James tucked into ginger cake and pistachio barfi, almond puffs and creamy gulab jamuns swimming in golden syrup, plump raisin and roasted cashew studded kheer, pineapple upside down cake, tropical trifle with custard, milky rasgullas and nutty pedas, a huge platter of juicy watermelon, mango, papaya, jackfruit and guava, all washed down with tall glasses of lime sherbet, clinking with ice cubes – James had eschewed his milk in favour of the cool drink.

Divya's stomach rumbled embarrassingly loudly at the abundance of food she – as mere help – was not welcome to partake in, and she hoped Mrs Ellis didn't hear. She felt lightheaded with hunger and tiredness – she was still standing holding the child; she had not been invited to sit.

Once he had eaten and drunk his fill, James came up to her, threw his arms around her sari-clad legs and grinned up at her, his cheeks stained with the juice from the mango he'd just eaten.

'Will you stay?' Mrs Ellis asked.

5

Divya quickly became a fixture at the Ellises': their boys' ayah.

They were desperate. The baby was teething and the nanny, taken very ill with black fever, did not return, as Mrs Ellis had predicted. The nanny's bad luck proving lucky for Divya (an irony given how she'd been hounded out of her village – the only home she'd known – for her supposed bad luck), who knocked at the Ellises' front door on the day they received the news that their nanny was unlikely to return.

Divya had no experience with babies. But when she held the crying infant and rocked him, soothing his desperate sorrow, she experienced a minuscule easing of her own sorrow. When she lay the baby, tired out from crying and asleep on her shoulder, very gently back in his crib, the toddler had come up to her and touched the tears on her face that she hadn't even been aware of shedding and looked at her curiously. In the company of these children, their unconditional acceptance of her, her heart had finally found a little solace.

While the children accepted her wholeheartedly, the other servants in the Ellis household were wary of her, her reputation as the 'bad luck' harbinger having preceded her. The servants ate together, curries prepared from leftovers from the feasts concocted daily for the Ellises, but Divya could not join in as she was busy with the children and she got the sense that it suited the servants just fine. They took care to leave some of the curry and rice for her and they were pleasant enough, but they never dropped their guard, never touched her, or even ventured close to her, as if she was a pariah, as if her supposed bad luck was catching.

Divya had wished, given her love of cooking, to offer to cook for the servants, once her charges were in bed. How wonderful it would be to work in a fully-equipped kitchen such as the Ellises'! She had eaten the mixed-vegetable curry her first evening there (beef was avoided as the Hindus wouldn't eat it and the Muslim staff would not touch pork so the food was mostly vegetarian to cater to all tastes) gratefully and with gusto. But even as she was eating, she was coming up with ways to improve it, perhaps with a touch more coriander powder, a sprinkling of fresh herbs, a dash of pepper to give it a kick. As for the rice, she'd thought it would be so much more fragrant and complement the curry that much better if tossed in ghee flavoured with cumin and cardamom seeds and cinnamon bark. But then the little one woke up and started wailing and Divya shoved the last few morsels of rice and curry in her mouth and ran to attend to her charge. In any case, it was just as well she didn't offer to cook for the servants for she would no doubt have been rebuffed, given how they avoided contact with her, making sure to stay at arms' length when they encountered her. But... every time she passed the kitchen, saw the maids chopping and stirring and peeling and dicing, she experienced a pang, her fingers itching to create magic with food again, like she had when her parents were alive and all was well in her world.

And then, six months on, just as Divya had settled into the job and managed to get the boys into a routine, Mr Ellis came home with the news that he had resigned from his post as Lieutenant-Governor. The uprisings in India were getting worse, he said, the natives' pig-headed drive for independence was out of control. Didn't they see they were better off with British governance, with those in the know telling them what to do? How on earth would they govern themselves when they were killing each other with their communal riots? He had enough of this blasted country, heat and spices, mosquitoes and insects and tropical illnesses, snakes and monkeys and beggars and dirt and dust and mayhem everywhere one looked. More and more he missed, and longed for, the cool and civilised climes of his beloved England. Which is why he had decided that they were going home to Mayfair.

'Well, I can't possibly manage the children on my own on the voyage over. Can you find a travelling companion, a nanny to accompany us?' Mrs Ellis wanted to know.

But there was no English nanny to be found at such short notice. For, once Mr Ellis had made up his mind, things moved very fast indeed – the house packed up, room by room into trunks, bound and ready to be shipped to England.

And so it was that as the day of the passage drew near, Mrs Ellis looked speculatively at Divya, and disappeared into the library – where she never usually set foot – to talk to her husband.

And not long after this meeting, Divya herself was summoned into the library.

It used to be an impressive room, tall shelves replete with books, scented with knowledge, windows open so the baked dust-and jasmine-tinted breeze lovingly stroked the spines and ruffled the pages of ancient tomes.

Now it was bare, shelves gaping empty, a mere shell, only the ink and musk, nostalgia yellow fug that hung heavy in the room, sighing with the memory of what was, hinting at its purpose, dust motes suspended above sparkling like jewels in the nectary sunshine angling through the window.

Mr Ellis looked Divya severely up and down while Mrs Ellis gazed speculatively out of the window.

Divya swallowed. She'd known this was coming. The idyll was at an end. She would miss the children dearly. She'd grown very fond of them.

She'd been very lucky – boarding and food supplied with her position. But because of this, her pay wasn't much – the Ellises weren't the most generous of employers, the boarding being a mattress in the children's room, which suited Divya fine given she'd shared a mat with her mother in their one-roomed hut, her father snoring beside her mother on the other side. She'd been intensely lonely after her parents' deaths so sharing a room with the children was a blessing. Divya had liked listening to them sniffle and sigh in their sleep.

And now she was back where she started when she arrived in town. No place to stay. No job.

But... she had more money to her name, knotted securely in one of her mother's saris. Not much. But more than the few paltry coins she'd had before – all that was left in the coconut-shell scoop: the sum total of her parents' savings.

'If you are agreeable, then I'll book your passage,' Mr Ellis was saying.

What? Divya jerked back to the here and now, pushing her musings aside. Had she heard right? Was Mr Ellis suggesting...?

'So will you travel with us?' A hint of impatience colouring Mr Ellis's voice, his lips set in a thin, rigid line.

Oh! She wasn't losing her job. Instead, they were asking if she'd accompany them on the voyage to England. *Oh!*

She had nothing here. No family. No home.

But England... So very far away. The other side of the world! She could neither picture nor imagine it, this land her pale employers hailed from, that they spoke about so fondly, their eyes softening, expressions wistful, voices soft with longing.

Divya swallowed, found her voice. 'But what will I do once in England?'

Mr and Mrs Ellis exchanged looks. Then, Mr Ellis: 'Well, once we are settled at home and have found a nanny for the boys, we will pay for your passage home.'

Why not, thought Divya. It would be an adventure if nothing else. She had nobody waiting for her here, no demands upon her time. She was attached to the boys and wasn't ready to part from them yet.

And not only that but she would be seeing the world, gaining more experience. *And* she would also be making money, growing her savings, which would help when she returned and had to start afresh, look for a job, make a new life.

Ma, Baba, what do you think? she asked, in her head.

She waited a beat, two, but her parents were silent.

Mr Ellis however was not, having reached the end of his – very small – reserves of patience. 'Well?'

Divya took a deep breath. And on its exhale: 'Yes, I will join you.'

'Good girl,' Mrs Ellis nodded – her only contribution to the discussion. 'You can go to the boys now. They will be waking up from their naps.'

'I'll book your passage,' Mr Ellis said.

And so it was agreed. Divya, who had never travelled beyond the confines of her village until her parents passed, was going to England!

6

EN ROUTE TO ENGLAND, 1938

And here Divya is now, en route to England, swaying with tiredness even more so than the ship is doing, having barely slept on the train journey to the port, with both children unsettled and fretful. She is completely out of her depth in this huge vessel – she cannot even begin to fathom its size – which will carry them across oceans to her employers' homeland thousands of miles away.

What would Ma and Baba have made, she wonders, of their only child, at eighteen years old, journeying across the world in a container that holds hundreds, that is enormous beyond belief, but is nevertheless jostled this way and that at the mercy of the waves.

She aches to hear her parents' voices again like she did when at her lowest, cast out of the village that was her home.

But they remain silent.

The sea stretches to infinity, green-blue waves undulating, dancing to the tune of the gods' merry making, merging, at the edge of beyond, where the gods come out to play, with the skies, pearly gold, glimmer and glitter, blessing and benediction.

Divya missed the last glimpse of her homeland as the ship set sail but, in any case, it wasn't a place she recognised, the busy port, packed with hawkers and coolies, gentlemen in suits and kurtas and women in saris and dresses, holding on to their hats and veils as the blowsy breeze flirted with their hair. English-women waved dainty handkerchiefs in goodbye as their impassive husbands stood straight and stiff beside them, hats in place, suits untouched by the red dust that coated everything else, that blew sand and grit into faces, the tang of spices and drains, jasmine and fish entrails. Scrawny dogs weaved between legs, horse-drawn carriages and bullock carts. A man with a dancing monkey drew a crowd under a dazzling sky. A sadhu with matted hair and orange robes squatted on a rock facing the sea, meditating despite the mayhem surrounding him. Men bathed in the yellow water, unmindful of the dhows that weaved around them. Vendors hawked toys and sweetmeats, lurid-yellow, deep-fried snacks that looked inedible...

The sea air stings Divya's face, balmy and salty. Tears of homesickness stab at her eyes.

Stop it. There's nothing waiting for you at home. And what will you do there anyway – your hut has been requisitioned by the land-lord, leased to a new family. Nobody wants to marry you or be associated with you, seeing as you're considered bad luck and shunned by all and sundry, even those who've known you since you were a bump growing in your mother's stomach.

Grief pincers with sharp ruthlessness for Ma and Baba, a life that once was, despite her inner self's sharp remonstrance.

'Hey, look out! Mind where you're going,' a voice calls, jolting Divya from her melancholy musing.

Having settled the boys down for their nap, Divya has been walking blindly along the ship, trying to locate her third-class cabin that, the Ellises have informed her, she will be sharing with two other ayahs. But, she must admit, she is well and truly lost.

She looks up into smiling eyes the colour of coconut oil, crinkling pleasingly in the corners.

'I... I'm trying to find my cabin,' she says.

Laughter, like the syrupy jalebis which she and her mother would prepare together, deep-fried, nectar-filled tubes of golden delight.

'You're going the wrong way. These are the bowels of the ship, ma'am.'

Ma'am. Is he being sarcastic?

But no, his gaze is earnest, eyes sincere.

And the sorrowful ache of missing and yearning for her parents eases briefly. She smiles.

7

'I'm Raghu, one of the lascars on board this ship,' the man says.

She can only nod, mesmerised by his eyes the colour of flowing gold.

'You seem lost, ma'am.'

Ma'am. It feels so good to be addressed thus. Until now she's been 'girl' and 'ayah' to the Ellises, 'witch', 'demoness' to the villagers, and before that, 'our star', 'our heart' to her parents.

In the overheated engine room she has erroneously stumbled into, machinery and oil and busy activity, she is struck by how far away she is from home, bound to a strange country on the other side of the world, at the mercy of strangers. She shivers.

'Are you all right, ma'am?' Concern in those golden eyes.

Someone pushes past her, bumping her shoulder roughly.

'Out of my way, what are you *doing* here?' A man hefting a huge box on his head.

'Hey, watch out.' Someone else is coming on the other man's heels, rushing past Divya, sour sweat and garlic breath.

She's trapped, claustrophobic. She cannot breathe.

There's a gentle hand on her arm, leading her out of the stuffy engine room, and up some steps, until they are in the open.

Fresh sea breeze, moist and rife with salt, caressing her face. The sky above, wide and endless and incandescent, dotted here and there with fluffs of clouds.

The water sparkles silvery blue, surge and swell, rippling and gleaming, like a beam in a lover's eye, like the necklace that was her mother's pride and joy: 'It will be yours one day.'

She drowned with it.

Divya shivers again.

Sea brine stabs at her eyes, inciting moisture which she wipes away.

A seagull swoops low and flies off, a blue-grey scar upon bright-white canvas of sky, a fish flapping in its beak, scales glinting. It is oppressively hot and humid. The sea, she imagines, would be velvety warm were she to touch it.

The man who led her out of the engine room, Raghu, chats with crew who are splashing water onto the deck, presumably to clean it, steam rising in swirling wisps as the cool liquid makes contact with the burning surface.

He throws his head back and laughs at something they say, his mirth syrupy silver.

He turns to her. 'Feeling better, ma'am?'

She nods.

'Your first time onboard, is it?'

Again, she nods.

'It can get overwhelming,' he says kindly.

He waves to someone walking past, hefting a trunk upon his head, who grunts hello in return. He appears to know everyone, this man. He is so comfortable in his skin, an easy smile on his rugged face. And his fingers, she notes, are chapped – he's no stranger to hard work. And yet, although his body is packed and strong, he was so gentle with her.

'Where are you headed?' he is asking.

She swallows and finally finds her voice. 'My cabin. It's in third class.' She shows him the entry pass Mrs Ellis had given her, with details of her cabin and berth number and the section where it is located, despite which she has got hopelessly lost.

Speaking of which...

Mrs Ellis will be expecting her very soon indeed. She barely has time to change and freshen up.

But she doesn't want to leave this open space and make her way inside, experience, once again, the choking feeling of being trapped with no way out.

'Ah,' he says, when he has perused Divya's entry pass. 'I know exactly where it is. Come I'll take you there,' he offers.

'Your work...'

'It can wait.' He smiles.

He has a beautiful smile, she thinks, *like hope. The promise of rain after an interminable drought.*

'What is a lascar?' she asks the question that had bloomed in her head when he introduced himself as such.

'Oh, we lascars are responsible for the smooth running of the ship.'

'Ah,' she says. Then, she can't help adding, 'You better get back before the ship runs into trouble.'

He laughs, and she revels in his joy, like the tumble of the stream in front of the hut Divya shared with her parents – no longer theirs now – when replete with monsoon abundance.

'Now here's your cabin. If you need anything else...'

'I won't, thank you kindly.'

He smiles, unperturbed. 'Just in case you do, ask any of the lascars for Raghu.'

She nods.

And with another beguiling grin, Raghu disappears and Divya turns to peruse the cabin she will be sharing with two other ayahs, both of whom aren't here, but their cases are. She has been assigned the top bunk in a room so narrow that if she stretches her hands, she will touch all sides. There's barely space to move – it is neither luxurious nor spacious like her employers'.

How will the three of them sleep in here?

It is claustrophobic. No portholes. No view of the sea.

She gasps for breath, feeling nauseous.

And quickly freshening up in the tiny sink in the corner, she rushes back up to first class, this time following the signs, determined to find her bearings, not rely on anyone, not even her dead parents' voices in her head, which, in any case, she hasn't heard since the fateful day when she walked out of her village and into this job that has now led her here to this moving mansion crossing oceans, circumnavigating the world.

You are on your own now, an independent woman. You must behave that way.

PART II

8

ENGLAND, 1938

Divya's first impression of England is of mist and fog. A thick, grey blanket hovering over the docks, obscuring everything.

She shivers, feeling premonition rock through her. She is not usually given to flights of fancy, does not hold with feelings and hunches but now, she's beset by an apprehension of unease causing goosebumps to erupt on her body.

A chill of warning.

She shrugs it away.

She is cold, that's all it is.

She is wearing her sari and another one wrapped around her like a shawl, covering her ears which seem to be the most vulnerable part of her body where the cold is concerned – the frosty wind whooshing through them and wrapping itself around her very bones, it seems. In addition to the saris, she's also wearing an old coat of Mr Ellis's, one he never wears but nevertheless very reluctantly handed down by Mrs Ellis when, after Aden, the further north they headed, the chillier it became, and Divya was shivering although she had wrapped her sari pallu tightly around herself and used another sari as a shawl.

'Didn't you realise England would be cold?' Mrs Ellis had sniffed.

Nobody told me. I thought it would be like India: warm and humid, Divya wanted to say but she wisely kept her mouth shut and her thoughts to herself.

The coat swamps her – it is too big – but she is glad for it. She snuggles inside it as they wait for land to appear.

The first time she wore it and carried the baby, he appeared puzzled.

A question in his wide eyes, lips wobbling in preparation to crying as he didn't recognise this stranger wearing a dark and stiff cloak in place of his ayah with her soft, cotton saris.

The toddler had stared askance at her.

'Dada?' he asked tentatively.

She laughed. 'I'm Ayah, Chote Sahib.'

And at her familiar voice, both of her charges were reassured, chuckling along with her.

Thankfully, although Divya has felt nauseous at times, and homesick often, has been overwhelmed by the sheer size of the ship, she has not been seasick, unlike some of the other ayahs, who have been ill throughout the crossing, their faces peaky and grey, confined to their cramped cabins with a bowl handy, retching constantly, unable to look after their charges, which has, according to Mrs Ellis, inconvenienced their employers no end.

'Mrs Rouse, in particular, is at her wits' end,' Mrs Ellis had sniffed, fanning herself vigorously. They were yet to cross Aden, sail into cooler climes. 'Mrs Rouse employed the ayah to help with her children and ease the crossing, but instead she's had to look after the blighters herself, poor dear, with no help from the ayah at all. The ayah says she's ill – if you ask me, and Mrs Rouse agrees, that it is an affectation to get out of working, Thank goodness you're not so inclined.' Mrs Ellis crimped smugly, one-upmanship in her voice, as if Divya was her own personal posses-sion, chosen wisely and well, even as she graced Divya with a severe look as if to say, *Don't get any ideas.*

'Mrs Rouse is getting rid of the ayah the moment the ship docks. She will find someone who actually does what she's paid to,' Mrs Ellis said.

'Oh.' Divya's hand crept up to her heart, even as she hugged the baby closer to her, the toddler playing at her feet. 'But the ayah... what will she do?'

'She'll go home on the next ship, that's what,' Mrs Ellis said.

It's not her fault, Divya wanted to cry, *that she's seasick.* But it was futile to try and reason for she'd heard Mrs Rouse complain to Mrs Ellis: 'She should have thought of this before she came on board the ship.'

She didn't know, none of us did, how the ship would be like, Divya wanted to protest. *We couldn't imagine, before we set foot on it, how it would make us feel: claustrophobic despite being so huge, and scary, a floating mansion adrift on high seas taking us far away from home.* There was only water all round, the surge and swell of the sea, deep and fathomless – how did those steering the ship know where to go? How did they know to get to England? What guar-antee that they wouldn't end up somewhere else instead, if they ever reached land that is, for it felt to Divya like they never would. How could the Sahibs and Memsahibs put their trust in these few men, believing they were taking them in the right direction when there was only greenish-blue expanse, sometimes placid, often stormy, all round?

We didn't realise that the ship's sheer size and motion would occa-sion actual illness in some of us, Divya wanted to cry. *We were used to tropical fevers and snake bites and insect stings. We knew how to, if not cure, then at least ease the pain and sickness with medicinal herbs and potions, but this... constant nausea and illness we had never encoun-*

tered before. And in any case, where would we find medicinal herbs and potions in this floating house? Most of us had not left our towns before now – we couldn't even begin to imagine a ship this size. All we'd seen were the boats crossing the rivers in our hometowns and villages.

Instead: 'But will Mrs Rouse pay for her ayah's passage home?' Divya asked.

'Why should she?' Mrs Ellis snapped sharply. 'She hasn't done her job.' Warning in her voice: *this will be your fate too if you don't step up to what's expected of you.*

Divya shivered, although it was warm, feeling chilled by the callousness. 'How will the ayah go home if she doesn't have money?'

'That is not Mrs Rouse's concern,' Mrs Ellis said coolly. 'Now it's time for the boys' supper.'

It is sheer luck that I don't suffer from seasickness, Divya thought as she fed the baby, made sure the toddler ate his fill. She'd learnt from Mrs Ellis that that's what the disease was called. Seasickness didn't seem a strong enough name to convey the suffering Divya saw wrought on the faces and bodies of those who were plagued by it.

She knew it was the cowardly way out, but she just couldn't bear to face Mrs Rouse's ayah again knowing her fate, that she would be stranded at the port when they came to England, abandoned in a strange country, ravaged by illness, with no job, no money and no means to return home.

9

Now land has been sighted – England – the ship's captain and crew came through after all, bringing them safely to the promised land. How, Divya cannot even begin to fathom. Her charges are enjoying their siesta, a habit instilled in India during hot, drowsy afternoons when the whole household, from the cooks to the sweepers and gardeners and punka wallahs, snoozed after lunch, the breeze that drifted in through the window screens scented with earth and sun-kissed mango, sour tamarind and spicy peppercorns, hot and humid and gritty yet delicious.

Divya suppresses the longing for home which feels so very far away. She cannot envisage heat when she is so cold, even wrapped up in Mr Ellis's coat. She never thought a day would come when she wasn't warm – it was always hot even during the monsoons in India, a fact of life, taken for granted, like the sun. Now both are a luxury, she understands, for it is the middle of the day and there is no sun, no heat, only cool fingers of mist and fog and frosty breeze which inveigles itself into Divya's very bones.

Stop ruminating. You will be back home soon. For now, enjoy this new experience. Embrace it, her conscience chides. *You are lucky. You are with the Ellises, who will take you to their home, and provide for you until the boys are settled with a new nanny and then they will arrange for your passage home. Unlike Mrs Rouse's ayah who will be abandoned here, sickly and weak, an alien in a strange land, and have to fend for herself, find somehow, a passage back home...*

Divya shivers, hugging the coat to her.

She has just put her charges down for their nap and has come up on deck to find Mrs Ellis to tell her that the baby is sniffling a little, possibly coming down with a cold. He was up more often than usual the previous night, and clingy with it, wanting Divya to hold him and rock him to sleep, waking as soon as she put him down. Divya thinks it must be the change in the weather – it is warm in the children's cabin yet still, he must be susceptible to the change in climate outside. He was born in India after all – he has never known anything else; in that respect, her charges are like Divya herself.

Mr and Mrs Ellis, like the other Sahibs and Memsahibs, are giddy with anticipation for their first glimpse of their homeland, although of course they, with typical British restraint, try and hide it. The men stroke their ties or fiddle with their cufflinks, their women beside them, one hand holding their hats in place, the other upon their hearts. They might appear sedate but their eyes are alight with anticipation as they stand side by side, their gazes fixed in the direction of land – although all you can see is a swirl of thick mist, grey as the sky above. Every so often it parts briefly, affording a hazy glimpse of shore and there is a small sigh or gasp from the observers, quickly hushed.

'We left India at just the right time, my dear,' Mr Ellis says, moved by the sight of his beloved, rapidly approaching motherland, to smile at his wife – a brief lifting of his thin lips under his moustache. 'Colonel Knight was telling me the uprisings and riots in India, natives fighting for freedom from British rule, are increasing in frequency and number. Good luck to them, I say. They will struggle to run the country in the event they do get the independence they dearly want. Why they can't even stop fighting among themselves!'

'But Lady Dwyer was saying there's rumours of war with this Hitler annexing land all over Europe. Another war!' Mrs Ellis shudders, pulling her shawl closer around her shoulders.

'Stuff and nonsense. It will be nipped in the bud. Chamberlain will defuse the situation, mark my words, my dear. There's nothing to worry about.'

Mr Ellis puts his arm around his wife just as another restrained cheer rocks the gathering as the mist parts to offer up another small slice of land.

This then is England, Divya thinks, cold and grey and mysteriously obscure, a land that holds its secrets tight and close, revealing very little of itself, much like its people, reserved and remote, neither crying nor laughing openly with all of their hearts, guarding their emotions fiercely, hugging them to their chests.

When the baby cries as if his world is breaking, when the toddler laughs with delight and wonder, Divya ponders as to when they learn to hide, dissemble, suppress their emotions? When do they acquire that impeccable, formidable reserve that has enabled the English to rule over all of India?

'Memsahib, it's time for Master Hugh's feed. Is it all right to give him some of the medicine Dr Lester prescribed with it in case he's sickening?' Divya asks and Mrs Ellis, without tearing her gaze away from the direction in which land is occasionally sighted, nods her assent.

First class is silent, all the adults up on deck watching for their first glimpse of the motherland.

Every so often from the cabins wafts the haunting lullabies of ayahs, singing to their charges, or the chime of anklets as they walk up and down soothing fretful babies.

All is quiet in Mr and Mrs Ellis's cabin. Their trunks are lined up neatly by the door, packed by the cabin steward, waiting to be collected by the lascars. In the boys' room, both of Divya's charges are asleep.

The toddler lies with his face down, limbs splayed, still in repose, although his sheets are bunched indicating activity even while asleep.

The baby is on his back, chubby arms thrown up on either side of his face, legs folded, angelic face scrunched up, hindered breaths escaping in loud, snuffly gasps.

Divya pauses at the door to watch them, these children who will now be thrust, like her, into a different world to everything they've known and are familiar with, just as outside, the quiet is shattered by trolleys being dragged, trunks clunk clunking, lascars calling to each other, cries of, 'We're docking soon.'

The baby stirs and starts to cry.

The toddler sits up, startled, his face scrunching in preparation to wailing, stilling upon seeing Divya, who crouches down beside him.

'It's all right, Chote Sahib. It's okay. Come, let's soothe your brother.'

She gathers the baby in her arms and gently rocks him, giving him the bottle she's prepared, the milk laced with the medicine prescribed by their doctor before they set off for just this eventuality, while his brother clings to her legs, frightened by the noise outside.

There's a knock at the main cabin door.

Clasping the baby to her chest, the toddler holding on to her, Divya makes her way to the door.

'Come to collect the trunks, ma'am,' grins a very familiar face. 'The steward who should be doing it is otherwise occupied, so I'm here instead.'

She's seen the lascar, Raghu around and has smiled at him when he has nodded and waved but they haven't had a chance to converse since that first day when he showed her to her cabin.

His bright smile stands out among the lascars – she's caught a glimpse of it across the crowded dining room during the children's breakfast when the musical voices of Indian ayahs and the crisp tones of the British nannies provide background music to the chatter and cries and chuckles, the sobs and tantrums of their charges.

Raghu appears to be constantly working but also always smiling and the sight of him has warmed Divya's heart for he somehow reminds her of home, back when her parents were alive and their faces would light up at the sight of her.

She's barely seen the ayahs she shares her cabin with. The children have not adjusted to their unsteady new home that sways and rocks at will. They do not quite settle at night and their wailing disturbs Mr and Mrs Ellis, who complained that the suite they'd been assigned was too small and cramped, but, 'We couldn't get another as some maharaja's close relative has booked up most of the bigger suites.' Mrs Ellis's mouth pursed and voice tight to show just what she thought of that.

And so, Divya has spent her nights with the boys in their room, bedding down on the floor next to their beds on a makeshift mattress formed from her saris. She would not recognise the other ayahs in her cabin even if she bumped into them.

She knows they are Indian ayahs, like her, from the sari one of them had draped on her bunk and the small statuette of Lord Shiva, smelling of incense, that the other ayah had laid reverently upon hers. Will they stay on in England with their charges or will they too, like her, be let go, sent back to India once their charges have adjusted to their new lives with a new nanny in place?

10

'So, here we are, about to disembark,' Raghu says.

Divya nods, even as she rocks on her feet to soothe the baby and smiles gently at the toddler.

She does not want to encourage Raghu to be too familiar – a lesson drummed into her from childhood by her parents and the village elders: 'A good, dutiful girl does not talk to men; she does not even look at them. She keeps her head covered, veil in place when she encounters someone other than her brother or father.' In the village and surrounds, a girl's reputation was her everything. 'It is the greatest gift you can give the man you will marry, worth so much more than dowry. In fact, if your reputation is tainted, even if your parents can afford a dowry of a million rupees and enough gold and jewellery to keep the prospective groom in comfort for life, he might still say no, preferring a girl with a good reputation instead. By being dutiful and maintaining your reputation, you are upholding not only your good name and that of your parents, but also that of the entire village.'

Silly really, but even though she is now on the other side of the world from her village, in a ship just arrived in England, even after the villagers have shunned her so summarily, even after her parents are gone, she still feels the need to follow their decree. For Divya's parents might be dead and gone but that doesn't mean she cannot continue to behave in a way that would honour their values, uphold their reputation. She pictures them smiling at her, beaming radiance, eyes glowing with pride and love: 'Our precious, beautiful, wonderful girl. Our light. Our Divya.' Her heart aches with missing.

'This is goodbye then,' Raghu is saying and for a minute, she is confused, her parents in her thoughts – whom she never got to say goodbye to properly.

She focuses her wandering mind back on him, this lascar who has been kind to her. A friendly face during this unfamiliar, disorientating journey. Lack of sleep, nights spent soothing the children and days running after them, making sure they're all right, rendering it even more so. She's giddy with exhaustion. The sway of the ship, the endless sea, spanning in all directions, vast and fathomless, glimpsed through the portholes, the cold insinuating itself into her being uninvited, making her feel odd, restless, unsettled. Raghu is the one familiar presence, a glimpse of his smiling face providing calm reassurance, like the giant peepal tree in the village, so huge that its trunk alone could have accommodated the entire village, under which the elders would settle disputes. The tree that had been there for several generations past and would no doubt outlast them all and their descendants' descendants too. Divya would sit under the peepal tree on those rare occasions while her parents were alive when she needed solace that her parents couldn't provide. Its very girth, its wide awning of branches, the bulbuls and mynahs and parrots that nested amongst its foliage chittering above, sunshine angling through the leaves, showering dappled gold-green blessings, would instantly settle her, give much needed pause to her troubled mind.

And Raghu has been so to her during this voyage.

But...

She is a good girl, and even though she has no parents now, she has her virtue. She has heard tales of women being caught out by smiling charmers. She will not allow anything of that sort to happen to her.

And even if her heart tells her Raghu is a good man, she will be guarded. She is all alone in the world – she doesn't have anyone to look out for her. So although she likes this man, she will not give him any indication of how much he has meant to her.

She will do the job she has travelled to this country on the other side of the world from home to do. She will settle the children at their new home, and once the Ellises find a new nanny, she will make sure they are comfortable and at ease with her and then she will return to India, the Ellises paying for her voyage back as promised.

The thought of saying goodbye to her charges stabs her heart – she loves them dearly and she will miss them immensely – but she has no place here. This land is not her home and the Ellises have made it clear that they will only have her stay until they've employed a new nanny.

Once home, she will find work in town and in time, once the stigma of her bad luck has faded from memory, she will ask a respected matchmaker to arrange a match for her. Or, if she is brave enough, she might even try finding work and a matchmaker to arrange her marriage in a completely new town where she doesn't have to contend with the associated stigma of bad luck at all.

'Most likely I won't see you again,' Raghu is saying.

Her heart falls at the thought. For he has been something of a talisman for her, this lascar, bringing good cheer during the times she has caught a glimpse of his smiling visage, a friendly face while on this voyage into the unfamiliar. But she makes sure not to show anything of what she's feeling on her face.

'I will be at the West India Docks for a few weeks until I find work on a ship going back to India,' Raghu says.

Perhaps he will be on my ship homeward, she thinks and her heart jumps at the thought, despite her sensible conscience's practical plans and cautions.

'Is this West India Docks where our ship is docking now?' she asks.

'No, it is docking at Tilbury. The East and West India Docks were getting cramped so now the bigger ships dock at Tilbury. But until I find work on a ship bound for home, I am usually at the West India Docks as the chances of finding work unloading and loading ships and at the factories are better over there.' He pauses to smile warmly at her. 'So, if you need anything—'

'Why will I?' she cuts in, more out of fear than anything else, thinking of poor Mrs Rouse's ayah's fate. *Don't think of it.* 'My Sahib and Memsahib will pay for my voyage home.' She says it firmly, confidently – it is the truth. They have promised and they will keep their word. Why is she worrying?

It's because Mrs Rouse's ayah's fate has brought to her attention, sharply, how precarious her fate is. It rests in the Ellises' hands, it is dependent on them carrying out their promise to her. And they will. *They will.*

'I've heard...' A cloud briefly chases away the ever-present smile from Raghu's face.

'What have you heard?' Her voice is prickly, argumentative, as if issuing a challenge.

Picking up on her mood, the baby starts to grizzle and the toddler tugs at the hem of her sari.

'Never mind.' He is grinning again. But is it her imagination or is it not as bright as before? 'I'm sure you'll be just fine. But just in case you do need something, anything at all, ask at the West India Docks for lascar Raghu. Or if I'm not around, ask any of the lascars for help; tell them you're my friend.'

Friend. Her heart warms. He might just be saying it without meaning it in the true sense of the word, but nevertheless, she's touched and she will take it at face value. Her first friend since she was ostracised from the village after her parents died.

She smiles even as she moves the baby from one hip to another, gently jogging him so he settles against her shoulder. 'I won't need anything,' she says with more conviction than she's feeling. His reaction, what he began to say and then stopped, smiling not as brilliantly as before, has caused a dark fluster of unease, adding to the doubts she already had but was trying to push away.

No, *no.* She will not entertain them. The Ellises promised to pay for her voyage back. That was the sole condition of her travelling with them.

The baby, always sensitive to her moods, starts wailing. Divya soothes him while patting the toddler's head, for he's snuffling in preparation to crying. And suddenly, worried about what is to come, and sad about saying goodbye to this kind man who has called her his friend, the first nice thing someone other than her charges has said to her, done for her since her parents died, she wants to wail right along with them.

'Of course you won't, ma'am.' Raghu grins. 'You will be just fine and probably back in India before I am.' Raghu's voice is reassuring now. 'But I've grown to like you, you see.'

She blushes, looks down at the toddler, at her hand patting his tousled hair, to hide her confusion. *He likes me.*

Be careful, her conscience warns.

We're saying goodbye, she counters to the voice in her head. *Sahib and Memsahib will pay for my voyage home and I won't see him again.*

Nevertheless, it pays to be careful, her conscience parries.

'So let me have this,' Raghu is saying. 'The hope that I *might* see you. If you need anything at all, ask for lascar Raghu at the West India Docks.'

She nods.

'Goodbye Ma'am, it was nice meeting you.'

She's tempted to say, *You said we're friends, so you can call me Divya*. But, with her conscience screeching warning loud as the parrots that colonised the mango tree in the courtyard back home, she doesn't say anything at all.

He holds out his hand, like the Sahibs do, grinning cheekily.

Don't talk to men other than your brother or father. And of course, no touching them, her conscience cries in the cautioning tenor of the village elders.

Raghu is unfazed when she does not shake his hand. He grins, shrugs. 'I thought I'd try it.'

She can't help smiling.

'You have a beautiful smile,' he says.

And she blushes again.

His laughter follows her all the way up the steps from the first-class cabins onto the deck, a glorious tumbler of syrup, golden bright like sunshine, which is not in evidence. The ship pulling into port, gloomy and grey, shrouded in mist which coats her, slimily cold, depositing moist caresses upon her face.

England is a moody, damp screen, frosty and remote. A wall that projects, *Do not cross. You are not welcome.*

Stop being so negative. You're not here long. Open yourself up to this new and exciting adventure, something poor Mrs Rouse's ayah will not be able to experience, Divya chides herself. *You are lucky, despite what the villagers decreed. You are fortunate to have this opportunity.*

She'll settle her charges into their new home and make her way back to her home, India, which feels so distant, elusive as a butterfly, turquoise gold.

When she was being derided and scorned for bringing bad luck, she couldn't wait to get away from home.

But now she misses it with an intense, almost palpable ache, the relentless heat and white-gold sun, drought yellowing the fields one minute and stormy clouds frenziedly unleashing tempestuous monsoons that incite the trees into a wild dervish dance the next, warm people and nectary fruit, juice dripping down chins, red rice and lime pickle, spicy sweet, smiles and superstition, snake bites and healing potions, curses and wise men and gods galore.

PART III

11

The Ellises' chauffeur is waiting for them when they depart the ship at Tilbury Docks.

He doffs his hat, bowing smartly, 'Welcome to England, sir, ma'am, young sirs.'

His gaze skimming Divya even as he smiles and winks at the baby whom she is holding in her arms and the toddler hugging her sari skirt.

Divya's heart is heavy from having said goodbye to the lascar, Raghu, who had addressed her as his friend. And he had been, of sorts, she realises now, too late – for she had associated him with all that was familiar: home when her parents were alive. Perhaps it was because he treated her with respect, calling her 'ma'am' although she was but an ayah. With him, she felt accepted, without anything being expected of her – and the only other place she had felt so was with her parents.

Mr Ellis claps the chauffeur on his back, saying, with an uncharacteristic and, for him, a very wide smile, 'Rogers, my man, how are you?'

Divya, holding the baby in her arms while gently coaxing the toddler, who is shy and overwhelmed and clinging to her sari skirt, turns round for one last glimpse of her lascar friend.

But Raghu is lost amongst the milieu spilling from the ship, women in colourful dresses, holding on to their hats with one hand and their handkerchiefs in another, flanked by suited men, smiling and greeting their relatives and chauffeurs as porters trundle their luggage behind them.

The baby, fretful at this change of scenery – again – finally falls asleep on Divya's shoulder, as the Ellises sleek car transports them to the Ellises' house. With her arm around the toddler who is tucked against her side, Divya looks out avidly at England. Even travelling in a car is an experience – Divya has never been in one before – and she marvels at how smoothly it drives, how fast!

'It has been in my family for generations,' Mr Ellis declares about his home in Mayfair, English reserve making him sound stiff, but Divya notes his pride in the quiver of his moustache, in the softness that tempers his gruff voice.

She notices how he leans forward in his seat, his foot tapping in impatience if a carriage or hansom cuts in front of them – he is eager to return home; he cannot contain his anticipation. It warms Divya to her rigid, remote employer, this rare glimpse of entirely human, but to his mind, no doubt 'common' excitement, albeit tightly reined in, but even so, very obvious if you know what to look for.

Divya had learnt the word 'common' and what it implied, from Mrs Ellis, who used it often. For the Memsahib, being or acting 'common' was right up there with the worst transgressions. Mrs Ellis uttered it with a disdainful sniff, contempt dripping from each syllable. That is how Divya always pictured it – in Mrs Ellis's voice, her mouth puckered as if she was munching on something unpalatably bitter when she had expected something sweet.

Red brick buildings rise up to the sky, burnished stone, impressive and formidable. *So this then is London, the capital of the world!* She was expecting something different – more spectacular, more flamboyant, more loud, just... more. But of course, she should have known that, like the English themselves, it would be understated, reserved, displaying a solemn, quiet gravity. Here everything is coated in grey mist, a far cry from the ubiquitous orange dust of India.

Ah, now, this is more like it... Shops with colourful awnings, church spires, sombre bronze chime of bells, lush green rectangles of gardens in front of quaint cottages just like in the picture books Memsahib tried to get Master James to look at but which he was more interested in chewing the corners of.

Women hefting covered baskets, hands clutching toddlers, babies on their hips, older children skipping up ahead, tousled locks, toothy grins. *Are these women nannies, or mothers themselves?* Divya wonders even as she watches them pushing prams with precious blanketed bundles, their heads covered in scarves against the blustery wind, gossiping with each other as they queue at the greengrocer's (displaying produce Divya has never seen before), and the butcher's (cuts of meat, bright red and bloodied, hanging from hooks, making Divya's stomach turn). Their charges play hopscotch on the road, jumping out of the way of the car just in time, gawping at the sleek vehicle with bright-eyed admiration, just like the urchins in Divya's village jumping out of the way of the odd bullock cart. They would, without fail, be followed by a menagerie of stray dogs and cats, chickens and cows. They would play with sticks and stones and whatever else they dug up in the rubbish-strewn ditches, right in the middle of the mud road, grinning cheekily when a bullock cart ambled past, the farmer manning the cart threatening the whip he was using on his bullocks on the children if they didn't scatter right then.

Tears sting Divya's eyes, as much from the wind that nips with frosty fingers, freezing the parts of her face not covered by her sari pallu that she is using like a scarf, as from homesickness for a home that no longer is.

Suited and hatted men march briskly past, their polished shoes click-clacking on the pavement. Young boys, filthy toes poking out of torn shoes, tattered shirts, caps slung low on their heads, hooded eyes with jaded expressions too old for their years in grimy faces, hawk newspapers at street corners, a pile of news sheets sitting high beside them, calling out the day's headlines in clear voices that break with the jarring croak of imminent adolescence on the last, valiant note.

Men with hopeless eyes and faces scored by desperate lines sit beside rusting railings, hats upturned beside them, holding placards that read:

Homeless. Will do any job.

A cemetery, rows and rows of headstones smothered by wilted flowers and cracked pots, neatly spaced dead slumbering under marbled grey skies.

A woman bent at a headstone, polishing it to a shine gently with a cloth. Fresh flowers lie upon the stone, the bright yellow of hope, the blinding white of promise, the glorious violet of remembrance.

Whom has she lost? Divya wonders even as she thinks of her parents, whose bodies were never recovered. She has no place to go to pay her respects. And even if she had, she is now too far away.

We are always in your hearts, they whisper, she imagines, soothing her even from the other world.

But, unlike when she had heard their voices on the day she was chased out of the village that had been their home and hers, it doesn't provide the solace she craves. It can't take the place of their physical selves, warm and tangible, their eyes glowing with love for her, so she had felt anchored, knowing without a doubt that she was cared for, the centre of their world.

The woman tending to the headstone of her lost loved one turns and despite the distance separating them, her eyes, shimmering blue and fathomless as the sea Divya had just parted ways with, meet Divya's.

Divya smiles, feeling for the woman, empathising with her grief.

But the woman, far from smiling back, recoils as if Divya has flung slurs at her and turns away abruptly. And the tears Divya has been holding back find release, dropping silently down her face, wetting the baby's cheeks so he flinches in his sleep.

12

Mr Ellis's ancestral home is tall and imposing, much like the man himself.

Framed paintings of his grim-looking ancestors line the walls of the hall, the heavy curtains open but, despite the white, lace screens covering the windows, hardly any light. The paintings of Mr Ellis's relatives seem to be absorbing all the luminescence, so the room is dark and grave much like the ancestors themselves.

'You should really be using the servants' entrance but since the children are asleep, I suppose you can come in the front door, this once,' Mrs Ellis sighs, reluctantly allowing Divya to stagger inside in her wake, carrying the snoozing baby in one arm and the slumbering toddler in her other. The toddler had fallen asleep just as the carriage pulled up outside Mr Ellis' home and he said, with restrained self-satisfaction as he gazed upon the house, 'Well, here we are,' and the butler came to meet them, saying, sombrely, with a bow, hat in his hands, 'Welcome home, sir, ma'am. Masters James and Hugh.'

Like the chauffeur, the butler's gaze too sweeping over Divya, not worth mention nor acknowledgement.

And it's been so ever since. She is ignored by the staff, who look straight through her in the event they cannot avoid her, come face-to-face with her.

'What were they *thinking*, bringing a coloured home, expecting us to pander to her?' she hears when she goes to help herself to some lunch once she's settled the children for their afternoon nap.

The other staff eat together in the kitchen and she hears them, jovial and friendly, sharing stories of their day, gently pulling each other's legs.

Even the butler, who gives the impression of being remote and stiff, joins in.

But they neither include Divya nor leave food (porridge and toast with marmalade, pies and mash, soup served with great big hunks of bread and cheese) for her, like she's seen them do for the gardeners, or the maids too tied up with their duties to join the others for meals, falling silent when she enters the kitchen, staring at her, their damning gazes boring holes into her back, looking away when she tries to make eye contact.

In many ways, it is almost exactly like it was at the Ellises' household in India, but there, at least, the servants would leave meals for her. They would smile at her if they saw her, not look away or pretend to look right through her, although of course they would avoid touching her, in case they caught her 'bad luck'. There, she was shunned for her supposed bad luck. Here, it is her colouring that turns the other servants off.

Divya's first evening here, tired and disoriented and feeling nauseous and unsteady to be on solid ground again after the swaying confines of the ship, when she had gone down for supper, after putting the boys to bed, the servants were all gathered in the kitchen, sitting with hot cups of cocoa, the butler, the cook and the maids. The rich scent of chocolate spiced with cinnamon caused Divya's stomach to rumble with hunger even as she felt queasy again, lightheaded with exhaustion.

The servants had stopped talking when she knocked and had looked askance at her.

Divya had thought that as a gesture of friendliness, she could offer to cook for them one day – they might quite like Indian food, perhaps, something different?

But... 'Um... I...' Her words had dried up in the face of their coolness. Their hostile glares. It felt as if they were collectively judging her and had found her wanting. Her English, which was quite good to begin with, thanks to the nuns at the missionary free school that she had attended in her village, and which had gotten better during her months of employment, suddenly drying up, so she had scrabbled to find the words she wanted. *Help me, Ma and Baba*, she had pleaded with her dead parents in her head.

But again, as they had been since that day when she was kicked out of the village that had been her home and got the job with the Ellises, her parents were silent.

'I was told my supper...' she had managed, somehow finding the words in her addled brain, pushing them out of her dry mouth where they fell flat, sounding weak and nervous in the stultifying silence.

The cook had set her mug down and stood up, huffing, and with a frown, cut two slices of bread from a loaf, poured a glass of cold milk and set it down at the table at the other end of the room from where they were all grouped, wordlessly, albeit with another loud huff.

Divya had thanked the cook, which she did not acknowledge, and sat down at the table. She had forced the food down her uncooperative throat, which was plugged by a salty lump. The bread was dry but she managed to push it down as quickly as she possibly could, with the aid of the milk, which was freezing, like the glares of the posse gathered at the other side of the room upon her back – she was turned away but aware of them all the same – spearing her with frosty icicles.

She had washed her plate and glass and dried it with the tea towel, all the while aware of the pairs of eyes upon her, watching her every move.

It was only once she left that she had heard them speaking again.

'The cheek of her,' she had heard. 'A darkie, wanting to eat with us.'

After, that she took her daytime meals in the nursery with the boys. They at least did not discriminate. They enjoyed her company. They wanted, needed her. They did not see colour. They did not think she was bad luck. They saw her with their hearts, saw *her*, and loved what they saw. They did not find her lacking. They loved her, simply, completely, unconditionally.

It was a blessing and a gift.

Since that first evening, she has been subsisting on slices of bread, plain and stale, taking her supper up to her room in the attic once the boys are asleep in the nursery directly below, down one flight of stairs. If they wake in the night, she can hear them, go to them.

The other servants share rooms next to hers, ignoring her completely on the rare occasions she crosses paths with them. She makes sure to stay out of their way, spending all her time with the boys. Divya loves her charges, enjoys being with them, but she hopes it will not be too long that she has to live in this hostile environment, that the Ellises find a suitable new nanny soon and book her passage back home.

At night, as she lies awake on the narrow pallet that passes for bed, she hears the other servants' laughter, their murmured shared confidences, their easy companionship, wafting through the thin walls and she feels lonelier than ever, the frost-harangued wind howling and rattling against the window, one ear peeled for the baby's cries – for even though she is in bed, it is her job to tend to the boys. The chill never leaving her bones, no matter how deep she burrows under the thin sheets, piling all her saris on top and Mr Ellis's old coat for good measure, thinking with longing as her stomach cramps with hunger of the food she and Ma cooked together: red rice and mango chutney flavoured with coriander and mint, prawn pickle seasoned with mustard tempered in oil, sour sweet mango curry, onion pakoras with tamarind chutney, mackerel marinated for hours in a masala made from cumin and coriander and mustard and vinegar and red chillies and green chillies and peppercorns and shallow fried in spitting coconut oil served alongside deep-fried gram flour coated chilli peppers stuffed with spiced potato.

13

'We won't be requiring your services any more,' Mr Ellis says.

Divya has been expecting this.

They've found a nanny. White. Someone who gets along with and is accepted by the servants. In fact, she is treated with deference by them as she is a cut above them – no room in the attic for this nanny. She is in the room next to the nursery. The boys, with the ease and innocence of children who go to anyone who showers affection on them, have taken to her.

They don't need Divya any more.

Divya knows the time has come to say goodbye to the boys and to England, although she will part from the boys with a heavy heart.

So when Mr Ellis summons Divya into his study for a meeting, and summarily informs her that he and the Memsahib are letting her go, she is not surprised.

It is what her employer says next that renders Divya speechless...

'But Sahib, you promised...' Divya is shocked, moving her

weight from one leg to another even as she squeezes her palms together in upset. Unable to comprehend what she has just been told.

As she tries to process what Mr Ellis has said, Divya's eyes flit about the room.

Mr Ellis's study is impressive, dark and sombre, shelves lined with books, weighty with knowledge, a cabinet with brandy and the whisky that Mr Ellis prefers.

Mr Ellis spends most of his time when at home in his study and Divya, who has been summoned here this morning, her first time inside this room, can see why.

It is a big room but snug, redolent with the must and ink scent of books, overlaid with the amber nectar aroma of the whisky Mr Ellis drinks. There's a settee and side tables arranged by the fire-place that envelops the room in a warm, smoky glow, red-gold flames cavorting playfully, every so often an ember spitting orange-tipped blue. An armchair opposite a polished walnut desk with an antique lamp behind which Mr Ellis is seated, playing with his pen and summarily clearing his throat after delivering his pronouncement.

Divya has not been invited to sit, of course. She is standing beside the armchair, wringing her hands as she tries to process what her employer has just said.

'As I made it clear already,' Mr Ellis says, his lips curled with impatience at having to liaise with mere help when he has several more important things to do, 'we won't be requiring your services any longer.'

'Sahib, I knew I would have to leave once the boys got used to the new nanny.' Divya bunches her hands into fists, nails digging into the tender skin on the underside of her palm. The pain of it allows her to focus on the here and now, taking her mind away from the heartache of having to part from her charges. She loves them but she knows, has always known that she would have to say goodbye to them one day.

She swallows past the lump in her throat. 'But Sahib, you said you would book my passage back to India.'

Mr Ellis steeples his fingers and looks gravely at her. 'I do not recall saying any such thing. Here's what you're owed.' He holds out an envelope. 'Please leave by the end of the week.'

He takes off his glasses and pockets them, as if to signal an end to the conversation.

'But Sahib, my passage home...'

'As I said, you'll have to take care of that.'

'But when you asked me to join you on your journey here, you said...'

'I'm sure there's enough in your pay packet to cover your passage back.'

'But...' She bites her lip to deny the tears stinging her eyes access.

She had hoped to use this money to get herself settled once she returned to India. She would rent a small place in town, either her own or another one where she was not known to anyone and thus not dogged by the supposed 'bad luck' attributed to her, she'd imagined. And whatever was left would tide her over until she found a job, she'd hoped. Once she started working, she would set any money she earned after rent and housekeeping aside to pay for a matchmaker to arrange her marriage – to someone who worked in an office, like her parents had wanted for her. She didn't know if it was what *she* wanted – marriage, children, but what she *did* know and wanted very much was to realise her parents' dreams for her, in the process of doing which, they had lost their lives.

But now those aspirations her parents had for her will have to be postponed even further.

She hears the village matrons' voices in her head: 'mind you don't end up becoming an old maid. The further you travel on the other side of twenty, the less grooms you will find; after twenty-five, it is only widowers who will deign to give you a second glance and even then, they will have plenty of younger girls to choose from.'

She takes the money Mr Ellis is holding out.

It is less than half of what she was expecting.

'Sahib, I've worked for twelve weeks, taking into account the sea voyage, but this is less than six weeks' wages...'

'We paid for your passage here. England is not cheap and living costs have gone up tremendously since I was here last. Your food and board while here have been provided for by us. We've taken that into account while settling your wages.'

'But Sahib... there isn't enough here for my passage back.' Divya had seen how much her passage had cost on her cabin entry pass and had been shocked at the amount they were charging for a small bunk bed in a cramped cabin even as she understood that what they were paying for was the miracle of crossing seas, being transported halfway across the world.

Now, she feels despair claw at her throat as the desperation of her situation slams her. She is all alone in an alien country. What if she cannot go back? No. *No.* She tries to push the worry away but it stabs with sharp-taloned claws. She doesn't know anyone here. How will she manage? In India, she understands the ways of the people and even if she is ostracised, shunned because she is deemed bad luck, she is among people of her own skin colour and she can cope, find a way. But here... Here she is ostracised *because* of her colour...

Tears once again prick at her eyes.

Her employer shrugs. 'I'm sure you'll find a job to make up the money for your passage home. We will give you a good reference. That should help.'

'Sahib.' She swallows, her throat hoarse. 'I've loved your sons and looked after them with care.'

She has worked so hard, staying up night after night settling them, soothing them, as they struggled to get used to England, so she is swaying with exhaustion, dizzy and lightheaded with lack of sleep.

Mrs Ellis saw the children twice a day, for half an hour at most – as soon as the boys started getting crabby or restless, she would ask Divya to take them back to the nursery. Divya understood that this was the way of the Sahibs and Memsahibs but even so, she wondered, especially when the baby's face lit up when he saw Divya or when the toddler plucked a flower from the garden and presented it to her with a beaming smile and she felt warmed, weren't the Ellises missing this? Didn't they mind? Would they regret that they had farmed their children on to help, later, when the boys were grown? Or perhaps, most likely, it would not occur to them at all, for they too had been raised by nannies. When she had children, Divya wanted to be with them every minute if possible, so she wouldn't miss out on any of their milestones, their heartfelt gifts of smiles, their effusive affection, their joy and their innocence. Like her parents had been there for her.

Now... 'Please, Sahib.' The words bitter as they leave her mouth. She hates having to beg. But if that's what it takes, she will. 'Please make up the money so I can book my passage home.'

But Mr Ellis is standing up to indicate that this interview is over, his voice clipped and taut with impatience as he says, 'I expect you out of here by Friday.'

* * *

She goes to Mrs Ellis.

'Memsahib, please, I haven't been paid what I was promised and you did say you would book my passage home once the boys were settled here in England.'

Mrs Ellis does not look up from her knitting. 'I don't look after the money side of things. You've to bring it up with Mr Ellis.'

'I have and he—'

'Well then,' Mrs Ellis says in a tone of voice that suggests she has said all she's going to on the matter.

'But I've looked after your boys—'

And now her voice sharp. 'It was your job for which you've been paid.'

'Not well. You promised to—'

'That's enough. We will give you a good reference with which you can find a job elsewhere. Now I don't want to hear from you or see you again.' And with a crisp, 'Goodbye,' Mrs Ellis stands up and sweeps out of the room without a backward glance, her knitting discarded on the cushion beside her, a mess of multi-coloured yarn.

On the passage over, Divya had felt sorry for Mrs Rouse's ayah, abandoned in England, having to fend for herself, find enough money for a passage home.

Now Divya finds herself in the same unlucky situation.

No, it is not the same. You at least have some money saved. You are not weak from seasickness, only weary from sleepless nights and long days. Think of the positives, her conscience chastises.

But, scared and feeling all alone and abandoned in an unfamiliar land with its harsh weather, unforgivingly cold, Divya finds it increasingly hard to do so.

All she can think, despairingly, is that she is superfluous to requirements.

Unwanted. Dismissed with not enough money to go home.

She is a stranger in a strange country.

What will she do?

14

Friday morning and Divya is unemployed, clutching her meagre possessions in a cloth bag – her mother's saris that no longer smell of her mother but only of Divya's own sorrow and grief. Her father's lungis. Her payment – six weeks' salary for twelve weeks' work – is in the pocket of Mr Ellis's old coat, now hers, along with the reference the Sahib and Memsahib have provided.

She is heartbroken having said goodbye to her charges.

The baby had flashed a toothless grin and the toddler had waved a chubby hand before going back to playing with his building blocks.

They did not understand that this was goodbye forever. She wanted to hold them to her, plant kisses on their gummy cheeks, but their new nanny was looking on impatiently, waiting for Divya to leave so she could get on with the structured timetable around which she planned their day and which, Divya knew, had impressed Mrs Ellis greatly.

Divya had overheard the Memsahib telling her ladies – wives of the Sahibs Mr Ellis socialised with at the club – who came to tea with her every Tuesday, 'My boys' nanny used to be governess to the Viscount Ashbourne. She has proved herself invaluable in a matter of days. She is extremely efficient, and already has the boys following a strict routine.' Then, lowering her voice slightly, 'I was worried they'd gone native. Their ayah spoilt them rotten, you see. That's the trouble with Indian ayahs. They don't know the meaning of discipline. But Nanny Forster is a godsend. She comes highly recommended, from Lady Highbury no less, who is, as you know, terribly hard to please.' Mrs Ellis's voice smug with pride.

Divya had left with one last look at the boys, no longer her charges, saving their likeness in her mind's eye to take out and cherish later. It was better this way, she told herself, them not knowing she was going for good, even as her arms ached to hold them one last time. *Better this way*. But oh, how it hurt. There had been one too many goodbyes.

The Ellises live on a wide road, encased in the gilded hush of wealth and exclusivity, the houses all forbiddingly tall and similarly imposing, although, in her short time here, listening to Mrs Ellis and her friends talk, Divya knows that they would be severely upset if they were told that their mansions were, in any way, *similar*. They fancy their homes unique and each better than the other – comparing and one-upmanship, albeit in a civilised and understated way, seem to be the order of the day at Mrs Ellis's gatherings, with each lady trying to outdo the other, discreetly of course.

Divya did not take note of where Mr Ellis's family home was situated in the context of the great city of London – she had not expected to get out and about herself. When the time came to leave England, she had naively assumed that the Ellises would make arrangements for her to get to the port. Why had she accepted their word at face value? Why hadn't she questioned it more before she left India? Then, she wouldn't be in this situation now, marooned in a city and country she doesn't know, at all. For Divya has not left Mr and Mrs Ellis's house since she arrived in a blur of first impressions, to a house as reserved as Mr Ellis himself, formed from a brief, rushed glance of the elegant building, before she stumbled across the threshold while burdened with her sleeping charges, the butler looking down his nose at her and Mrs Ellis none too happy about her using the main entrance and not the servants' one behind the house.

Divya might be in England but apart from the wind howling at her attic window and the cold seeping into her bones, both from the weather and the frostiness of the people she has encountered, she has not really seen much of the country except for the port and whatever she managed to absorb on the car journey to the Ellises' home.

But now she sees that the Ellises live in an exclusive place. Divya had overheard Mrs Ellis crowing to the other ladies she had socialised with on board the ship that Mr Ellis's home was in the centre of London, Mayfair, don't you know, her voice smug, especially when the ladies sat up straighter and fingered their pearls, eyeing Mrs Ellis with newfound respect. It might be in the city but it appears the city is not allowed to encroach in here, wealth rendering it a rarefied air of otherness.

There is nobody about. Divya walks along the wide, empty street and encounters only the odd carriage or hansom or motorcar.

Bravely, she knocks on the doors of neighbouring houses, the knockers fashioned in the shape of a lion's head here, a silver-fanged snake there, their boom reverberating deep in the annals of the impressive residences – all those floors for one family, their vast retinue of servants relegated to the attic.

It is just like the time she knocked on the doors of the white

Sahibs in the British cantonment in town after she was kicked out of her childhood village.

Here too, stony-faced butlers turn her away. No 'ask at the back door.' Although she does know there is a servants' entrance here too. But she is not welcome even there.

They look at a point above her head when they say, tightly, 'No jobs for the likes of you.'

'But I have a good reference...'

The doors slam in her face.

When Divya tries to hail a carriage, they don't stop, ignoring Divya, looking right through her as if she isn't there, like the servants did at the Ellis residence.

The long, exclusive road comes to an end, finally, and she turns into another – this one with fewer trees, more houses – less grand, closer together, and with more carriages than motorcars. More people out and about.

But again, none of the carriages want her custom, even as she tries to flag them down. 'Please. I just want to get to the port. I will pay.' Wondering even as she says this, how much it will cost her and how it will eat away at her meagre earnings. She isn't sure how far the port is from here. A considerable distance away, she imagines. The journey to the Ellis mansion in Mayfair from the Tilbury Docks had felt interminable, but she cannot gauge if it was because it really was far or because she was exhausted and disorientated to find herself on solid ground again, after the constant motion of the ship, the children irritable and weepy and clingy for the same reason.

The carriage grooms shoo her away with the horses' whips, eyes flashing.

'Who do you think you are, the king's consort? No custom for the likes of you.'

She shivers, pulling Mr Ellis's old coat, now hers, tighter around her, their laughter ringing cruelly in her ears.

This then is England. Cold. Wet. Smoggy. Unwelcoming, judging from the mocking and loathful looks she gets.

It is very different to when she was with a white family. While in the Ellises' patronage, she was protected, to an extent, their whiteness compensating for her colour (except when she was out of sight of her employers; then the other servants ignored her or mocked her). Now that she is alone, she is fair game for catcalling and scorn, her dark skin a brand that damns her, rendering her different, other, unwanted.

But she has no choice but to walk on, enduring people crossing the road to avoid bumping into her. Insults flung at her, slurs of *blackie, coloured, sooty hag* and worse, along with, 'What are you doing here? Go back where you came from.'

She tries knocking at more houses and businesses, looking for jobs, but everywhere she's turned away.

Her colour is all anyone sees and it is an impediment. A scourge.

Divya walks for what feels like forever, until the roads narrow even further and there are more signs of life and activity. The city finally seeming like a city. Smoke spilling from chimneys in great frothy swirls, colouring the grey sky smoggy navy. A train's shrill whistle from very close by making Divya jump. An iron-monger's, ammonia and rust, fire and clang. A cobbler's, the meaty reek of leather. A greengrocer's, vegetables in neat piles, the proprietor haggling with a woman, her hair tied in a scarf, a covered basket upon one arm, a toddler hanging off the other inciting in Divya a fresh stab of ache for Masters James and Hugh. A butcher's, whole carcasses of sheep dangling from hooks in the ceiling, the butcher wielding a hatchet with a wide smile, apron dotted with blood. A seamstress at a sewing machine, head bent over a gown, cream silk rippling in an elegant cascade, surrounded by her creations, lace and taffeta gowns, almost too beautiful to wear.

The smell of smoke and earth and iron and caramelised sugar and industry.

Children play in the street, skipping games and others with balls made of scrunched-up newspaper, jumping out of the way when trolley buses and tram cars trundle past, narrowly missing the swishing whips the grooms of carriages use on their horses. They point at Divya and laugh, giggling and whispering among themselves.

She arrives at a railway station, the sign reads, *Liverpool Street Station*, busyness and crowds. Great big beasts of engines belching monstrous balloons of steam, hissing and creaking and groaning as they pull a dizzy procession of carriages laden with goods and people.

Divya stands shivering, shifting from foot to foot as she hesitates, debating whether to take the train to Tilbury Docks? But will it cost more than a carriage?

She takes a deep breath and is about to enter when she is pushed away none too gently.

A portly man frowning at her, face florid and scrunched up in a hellish frown. 'Can't you read?' he cries, pointing to the sign above him, which says, *No Blacks or Coloureds*. 'Your entrance is that way.' He points a distance away.

People beside and around him tut, shaking their heads, some gawping, others flinging insults and slurs at Divya.

Clutching her bag containing all her worldly possessions, Divya walks away, trying to keep her head up high. But it droops upon the weary stalk of her neck.

Divya's stomach rumbles. She did not have breakfast before leaving the Ellises' residence – she didn't know if she was allowed, and she was too downhearted to brave the hostility of the servants one last time. Now she regrets it.

Her feet are sore and blistered.

She cannot feel her fingers. They are numb from the cold.

She comes to a hostelry. Ah, at last. Perhaps if it is not too expensive, she can stop here for the night.

But again... *No Blacks or Coloureds*, the sign reads.

Divya sighs. Too defeated to reignite the fire of anger that has burned since the Ellises summarily dismissed her, with not enough money and no place to stay in a country not her own thousands of miles from home.

Yes, she was shunned at home for bad luck, but at least she understood the language, the body language, the expressions, the customs, the food, the money. What they said and didn't say but implied.

Here, everything is strange and nobody wants her. Her colour shutting doors as effectively as poison taking a life.

15

It feels to Divya like she has been walking the streets of London forever. How big is this city?

'Out of my way!' She jumps away just before the woman whose path she was supposedly blocking – although the pavement is empty and she could have just walked around Divya if she really wanted to – shoves her. 'You don't belong here.'

How many times has she heard the same refrain? Too often to count and yet still it hurts just as much as the first time. Her status, she understood within an hour of leaving the Ellises' home, because of her skin colour lower than the wastrels, the street dwellers, the drunks and lowlifes – they might be barred entry from certain places but they don't have to use separate entrances and exits, like she does.

Everything is a poisoned dart, seeping pain, bleeding hurt. And she allows it to skewer her. Perhaps the villagers were right in claiming that she was unlucky, that her bad luck brought about her parents' death.

Stop thinking like that. Her parents' faces looming before her weary eyes. She was loved. The centre of their world. She channels them and they give her the strength to trudge determinedly on.

She is so cold. And more than a bit the worse for wear, having traversed the better part of the city looking for a means to get to the port, for work, and as evening draws near, a place to stay for the night, the spitting rain which seems to be a feature here leaving her wet and bedraggled, her hair sticking in clumps to her face, her coat dripping from a day's worth of damp showers.

She appears to have arrived in a not very salubrious, in fact, downright seedy part of the city: taverns alive with brawls, spilling with drunks; more littering the alleys with begging bowls; gaudily dressed, scantily clothed women with dead eyes; rough sleepers with desolate gazes.

She feels that same desperation clawing at her with anxiety-sharp talons. Dusk is falling and she needs somewhere to rest, so she is not at mercy of the outdoors, the weather not as bad as leering men who look at her with question and speculation in their eyes.

'You're pretty.' A bedraggled man grins at her, yawning cave of mouth with several teeth missing, eyeing the bag containing her worldly belongings that she's clutching to her chest, reading the despair upon her face. 'Come with me darlin'. I know a warm, comfortable place to stay.' The first person who's called her something other than *blackie, darkie, soot face* or something else along those lines since she left the Ellises. Who has actually talked to her rather than insulted her.

But he has an ulterior motive, evident in that lecherous shine to his eyes as they travel greedily down her body.

'No thanks,' she says, jerking her hand from his slick-fingered grasp, feeling dirty, soiled. She walks away as fast as she can – not fast at all given her blistered feet, exhausted body – back straight, trying to ignore his calls, his mocking mirth.

'When you can't find anywhere else, you know where I am.'

She tries not to make her fear evident, show how far out of her depth she is. And yet when a train rattles overhead, a shrill whistle, hiss of steam, she flinches, startled, sure he is behind her, his sour breath on her neck, and a mad-eyed woman rocking under the bridge points at her and laughs and laughs, as if Divya is the biggest joke she's ever heard.

Her throaty, phlegm-coated cackles follow Divya for quite a while, above the clip-clop of passing carriages, the hawking songs of street vendors, the neighing of horses, who look better fed and cared for than the beggars on the street.

Dusk has arrived, cloaking everything in shadow. Divya is hungry and spent, having walked for the entire day. She comes to a park and lies down on the grass, dark with shadows, swaying in the frost-needled wind that bites and stabs, that teases and insinuates into Divya's very being, making itself too comfortable, the chill seeping into her bones, her teeth chattering non-stop. She is too tired to move, the undersides of her feet scored with welts, sore and aching. Her clothes damp. Her shoes from India, which she had bought with her wages for the journey here – in India, she had never worn shoes – not suitable to walk these cobbled streets. They are ruined, moisture seeping through them, wetting her socks so they stick damply to her blistered feet, and into her body so she shivers uncontrollably, unable to get warm, even as she gives in to the tiredness pulling her eyelids closed...

16

'Divya, our precious.'

She hears her parents' voices. Like she had at her lowest when leaving the village after their death.

'Divya, love. Please get up. You need to move, find a place to stay.'

Then, she had found the strength to heed them. To forge on ahead, despite losing everything. Her home. Her family. Her life as she knew it.

Now it has happened a second time. But this time, it is in an unfamiliar country thousands of miles from home.

This time, she cannot find the strength to go on.

'My dear,' she hears. 'My dear.' A gentle hand on her arm.

Her mother? Come to fetch her, take her to wherever they are, Ma and Baba?

Please, I want nothing more. Take me to you.

'My dear?'

The arm is around her now.

Summoning all her willpower, she opens her eyes. They hurt. Everything hurts. She is so very, very tired.

Her blurry eyes finally focus.

She looks up, into the face of an angel.

Kind and white and aglow, ringed by a halo.

Has she died? Gone to the heaven that the English believe in?

It makes sense. She is in their country after all.

'My dear.'

The angel is speaking to her, her voice gentle, as soothing as Divya's mother's embrace.

The angel is followed by more. They gather her in their celestial arms, tenderly, as if she is something precious and she feels rocked, comforted. This is how she must have felt in her mother's womb, she thinks. The pain, although there, peaking and prodding as she is jolted in the angels' soft embrace, although they take care not to jostle her too much, is bearable precisely because they are taking such care of her.

I'm going to heaven.

But if I go to English heaven, will I be reunited with my parents?

I'm sure I heard Ma and Baba's voices but I don't any more. Is that a good or bad sign?

Please let me meet my parents even if I go to English heaven.

Please gods, goddesses, Jesus. I want to be reunited with my ma and baba.

It is her last thought before she gives in to the gentle rhythm of being hoisted in soft arms, scented with roses and solace.

17

Divya dreams of home, her mother's comforting touch, her father's rumble of a laugh. Cooking with her ma, melt-in-the-mouth samosas and spicy potato pakoras, onion kachoris and fluffy puris with mint chutney, red rice and fish curry, okra fry and aubergine masala, ginger drops and cashew barfi, coconut puffs, pineapple sheera, milky rasgullas and nutty pedas, watermelon, mango, papaya, jackfruit and guava, masala tea, sweet and salted lime sherbet, and if that wasn't enough, goblets of cardamom-infused lassi.

Her mother plants kisses on her cheeks. Her father looks on, smiling proudly. 'Our precious girl. Our pride and joy. Do not heed what the others say.' Her ma gently wiping Divya's eyes, reciprocal tears gracing her own. 'You are enough. You've always been enough. You bring us joy. You complete us.'

Divya's father vigorously nodding assent, saying, sharply, 'I've told them they're wrong. That they can keep their opinions and their prejudice to themselves.'

Baba coming to Divya and putting his arm around her too,

like her ma is doing, so she is ensconced in her parents' embrace, their scent of sweat, spices and love.

Is this heaven?

'My dear...'

Divya wakes to the tantalising aroma of toasting bread and warming milk.

Her whole body aches.

Light pincers her eyes, bright white.

I'm not dead for if I am, would my body hurt so? And where are Ma and Baba? I thought they were with me...

'My dear?'

But there are angels hovering over her, pale faces, orbs of dark haloes.

She must have spoken out loud, for the angels smile and shake their haloed heads gently. 'We're nuns, my dear. You fainted in the common by the church, right outside our convent. Lucky for you that we were out on our constitutional. You would surely have caught pneumonia if we hadn't found you in time,' they cluck softly.

They fuss over her, helping her sit up, bringing bread and milk. She lets them. It's nice to be cared for, looked after. The last time was when her parents...

The wounding agony is worse than the physical pain hounding her body, all her limbs aching to the very bones.

She'd thought she had died and was with her parents. She had believed so completely and for a few brief hallucinatory hours, she was happy. Even now, if she closes her eyes, she can feel their love-filled embrace, hear their voices, see their faces glowing with pride and love for her. And so now the pain of loss hurts twice as much, for she has to accept that they are well and truly gone all over again, that what she experienced was just a fever-induced mirage...

Her parents are gone. And she is here, in a strange country at the mercy of these kind nuns, the Ellises having reneged on their promise to pay for her passage home.

Desperation assaults. She is so weary. She wants to lie back down, sleep her worries away.

But... they won't go away. You're not a child. Your concerns will still be here when you wake.

Tears sting her eyes.

'Whatever it is, prayer will help, child. God will help,' the nuns say softly.

They press something into her hands.

A Bible. 'Yours to keep,' they say, smiling gently at her. 'Read it when you hurt. Set your worries at Jesus's feet. He will show you the way forward.'

The missionary nuns in the free school they'd run for the children in Divya's village, which Divya had attended, had taught their charges to read and write and converse in English using Bibles.

But those books were much used, battered and worn.

This one is pristine. The newest thing Divya owns. She runs her hand over the cover. 'Thank you,' she says. 'For this. For tending to me when I was ill.'

Although a part of her wishes she had died. Then at least she would be with her parents, no longer having to worry about what to do next, where to go, how to go on.

And now, she hears her parents' voices in her head. *Don't think that way. Your life is precious. You are precious. We are with you, always.*

'Don't thank us,' the nuns are saying. 'We are only doing the will of Jesus. He brought you to us. Thank Him.'

And they kneel beside her and begin praying, their eyes shut tight, exalting their god. 'We have among us a child who's found her way to us. Bless and help her, oh dear Lord.'

Divya wishes she had even an ounce of their faith.

And again, she hears her parents' voices in her head. *Your life is precious. You are precious. We are with you, always.*

She may not have faith but her parents have faith in her.

And as the nuns start singing a hymn, 'The Lord Will Provide,' Divya thinks, *I will not give up. I will come up with a plan to earn enough money for my passage home.*

The nuns reach the crescendo of the hymn, the music reverberating all around Divya, haunting and uplifting. And then, miracle of miracles, she sees her parents in front of her, their faces that were fading from memory perfectly clear, eyes bright with love, soft with pride as they exult, *That's our girl.*

18

Divya says goodbye to the convent and the nuns – albeit very reluctantly as they are so kind and non-judgemental and accommodating – as soon as she is feeling well enough, not wanting to encroach upon their hospitality longer than strictly necessary.

Truth be told, she had not wanted to leave the cosy, warm confines of the convent where she was accepted just as she was. 'God welcomes everyone, child, regardless of colour, race, class or nationality.'

She had been moved to ask if she could stay on and work for them until she had earned enough for her passage home.

But, 'We do all of our chores ourselves, my dear,' they said gently. 'It is how we serve the Lord, through worship and through serving ourselves, each other and the community.'

She had been disappointed but she had always known, even as she asked them, that she couldn't stay, that this sojourn, although much needed and wonderfully rejuvenating, was temporary. With the nuns, her bruised and battered soul, wounded and shrivelled by the setbacks she had encountered, had recovered somewhat.

'I want to find a job, earn enough to go back to India,' she told the nuns, even as her entire being shrivelled and shuddered at the thought of knocking on doors only to be rejected, over and over.

'Here,' the nuns said, tucking a piece of paper into her hand. 'Go to Paddy O'Kelly's boarding and lodging house on West India Dock Road. Ask for Charity. We named her, you see. And that lass has proved true to her name. Tell her we sent you. She will see to you, we promise.'

West India Dock Road. Where had Divya heard that street name before?

And then it came to her: an image of a smiling face, eyes the soft gold of sunflowers revelling in sunshine. The lascar from on board the ship who had addressed her as 'Ma'am'. Who had called her his friend. 'Just in case you do need something, anything at all, ask at the West India Docks for lascar Raghu. Or if I'm not around, ask any of the lascars for help, tell them you're my friend,' he'd said earnestly as he and Divya were parting ways.

And she had felt warmed.

West India Dock Road.

It was a sign.

'How do you know the Paddy O'Kelly Boarding and Lodging House? Have you stayed there?' Divya asked the nuns.

'No, child. Charity's mother, Moira Kelly, used to be one of us,' Mother Magdalen Clare said gently.

'One of you?' Divya was puzzled even as she recalled what the nuns had said... 'You said you named Charity.'

'Yes, my dear. We did.' Mother Magdalen Clare said, she and her fellow nuns smiling enigmatically.

'How was Moira Kelly one of you?' Divya asked, even more confused now.

'Moira Kelly used to be a nun,' Mother Magdalen Clare said, her gaze wistful.

'Oh?' Divya tried to hide her surprise. 'But you said... she's Charity's mother?'

'Yes.'

'She's no longer a nun?' *Of course she isn't, if she has children*, her inner voice chastised.

But Mother Magdalen Clare was patient.

'Sorry, my dear, I'm not telling this right. You see, Moira, when she arrived from Ireland, was a little lost. Back home, she was part of a big family and had grown up in Ballinagree in Cork where everyone knew everyone. All her life, she wanted to escape her small village and so as soon as she could, she got on a boat to come here. But once here, she was desperately lonely. So she turned to the one thing that was familiar. Religion. She had been brought up a staunch Roman Catholic. And she was desperately missing being part of a community, a family, and so she joined us.'

'Ah,' Divya said, for now she understood.

'She didn't have a calling, you see, our Moira. And our profession is hard enough even for those with a calling.' Mother Magdalen Clare smiled. 'And so our Moira quickly realised that being a nun was not for her.'

'Ah,' Divya said again.

'Paddy used to attend our church regularly every Sunday. When he got a job at the docks and started attending the church there, Moria missed him something terrible.' Mother Magdalen Clare's eyes twinkled softly.

'Turns out Paddy missed Moira too. He came to us to ask for Moira's hand. We prayed about it. Consulted the Bible. And the answer was that they were meant to be together, Paddy and Moira. The Lord works in mysterious ways. Who were we to stand in the way of His wishes? We gave them our blessing.' Mother Magdalen Clare said and all the nuns beamed, their eyes glowing.

'We were there when they opened their boarding house, we prayed over it and Father O'Donnell blessed it. We were there for the christening of each of their children. We named their first-born Charity,' Mother Magdalen Clare cooed. 'And she has lived up to her name, that gel, running the boarding house as soon as she was old enough. You see, Paddy came back from the war a ruined man. He ran the boarding house for as long as he could but...' Mother Magdalen Clare sighed, and the other nuns joined in, a collective deep, burdened exhalation.

'And all that trouble with poor Moira.' Mother Magdalen Clare sighed again and the nuns shook their heads sadly, their wimples which, Divya in her feverish state had taken to be haloes, dancing, eyes bright and shiny with empathy.

'We are praying for her, for Paddy, for the whole family.' Mother Magdalen Clare said, the others nodding assent.

Divya knew instinctively not to ask about what the trouble with Moira was. The nuns seemed very upset.

'But Charity, bless her, is managing the best she can, with the help of all the great and good at West India Dock Road.' And then, smiling gently at Divya, 'Paddy, Moira and their brood found their community in West India Dock Road. You will too.'

Divya wished with all her heart that Mother Magdalen Clare was right.

'You will find a job there,' she added with firm conviction.

I hope that's the case, please, Jesus, Hindu gods and goddesses, Ma and Baba, Divya prayed.

'And until you find your feet, you will lodge at the O'Kellys' boarding house. Charity will look out for you, just you wait and see, our girl.'

It warmed her heart, Mother Magdalen Clare's steady promise. And she hoped, with all her heart, that it would come true.

'It will,' Mother Magdalen Clare said, as if she had read her
mind. 'We are praying for you.'

As Divya leaves the convent, she tries tentatively to reimburse the
nuns for their hospitality, for looking after her when she was ill,
for letting her stay and taking care of her. But they won't hear
of it.

'We were only doing our duty, child,' they insist, refusing to
take the money she holds out. 'You save your coins. You will be
needing them.' And, 'Can you read English?' they ask.

'Yes.' With difficulty, but she can. She has the nuns at the
missionary school in the village to thank for that. Homesickness
stabs with knives of intense longing for a home no longer hers.

The nuns must notice the shadow that crosses her face.
'When you are lost or lonely or feeling down, read the Bible we
gave you, child.'

'Thank you.'

'It will offer you solace. God will show you the way,' they
promise, smiling at her. 'After all, God, in His immense mercy,
brought you to us.'

She nods assent, but secretly she thinks, *knows*, that it is her
parents' doing as much as Jesus's. They had made sure she
collapsed right in front of the convent just as the nuns were on
their walk. Divya could have given up, given in, anywhere but she
did it there, in a safe place, where she would be taken care of –
her parents looking out for her, like that day when she was kicked
out of her childhood village.

'Your former employers live among the nobility,' the nuns tell

Divya. 'Somehow, you've ended up here, at our Ursuline convent in Forest Gate, several miles from Mayfair. Now, to find Charity at the Paddy O'Kelly Boarding and Lodging House, you need to go to the East End of London. I think you'll find yourself more at home there.' They smile.

At home? she wonders. Nothing in this country so far has made her feel at home. The nuns are welcoming, kind, but they too are other. Different.

'Trust us.' The nuns smile, divining her doubts.

She does, which is why she is headed there now.

19

'You are now in Forest Gate. You need to walk downriver along the Thames to get to West India Dock Road. Keep the river in your sight and you won't go wrong,' the nuns had advised, giving Divya a packet of sandwiches and the Bible. 'We will pray for you, child.'

And that is what Divya does. The river is never far away, a grimy, muddy yellow expanse. As she walks, Divya notices how different these streets are to Mayfair, where the Ellises lived.

That area was ensconced in an aura of wealth and privilege, remote and inaccessible. Removed, distant from reality. Inhuman almost.

Here, all of life is in the streets.

A shoe-black man has set up shop beside a train station, looking hopefully at anybody walking past, calling, desultorily, every so often, 'Shoes shined to perfection. So polished, you can see the street reflected in 'em!'

A teenage boy, haunted eyes in a drawn face, walks past wearing a billboard slung around his neck. He must be paid a few meagre shillings, Divya would bet, not enough for a decent meal, let alone lodging and livelihood to walk around all day wearing that. Divya looks at his legs, shoes scuffed and torn, toes peeking out. Then she sees what the billboard advertises, and she is shocked speechless. It is an advertisement for soap:

Guaranteed to clean a black face white.

'Ye need one of these.' The boy smirks, catching her looking.

A couple of children wrestle on the road while their mothers tell them off.

'Eddie, you stop that this instant!'

'Jack, how many times must I tell you...'

The boys ignore them while the other children stop their own mischief to watch, riveted, and to cheer them on.

'Clear orf the road,' a man approaching on his horse snarls, his magnificent beast bucking and neighing, its mane, a glorious amber waterfall, swirling secret messages in cursive loops.

And finally, the boys stop, their clothes dishevelled, ducking agilely from the clips on the ear their mothers were poised to deliver, to more cheers from the other kids.

'Just you wait until we get home,' their mothers grumble as they tuck their baskets closer to their hips and shuffle forward in the butcher's queue.

The shop next to it stinks of cow dung. *Cow dung, here? Inside a shop?* And then Divya sees that it is a dye shop, the legend in bold in front of the shop reads:

We dye to live.

Perhaps they use cow dung to dye things? If so, this is the first she's heard of it.

A sudden squall brings with it the icy rain that is such a

feature of England, she is learning. Mr Ellis's thin coat is not warm enough. She is always cold here in England. Except when she was with the boys. Holding them, tending to them was when she was happiest, their love, their warm affection pushing away all frostiness, the harsh inhospitality of this new, unwelcome place, where the servants too looked down on her.

The nippy September air tastes of ice, and Divya pulls her coat closer around her. The merrily teasing gurgle of the Thames as the murky yellow water froths and fumbles against the pebble and dirt festooned bank is at odds with the inevitable slurs and insults tossed at her, the crossing of the street to avoid contact with a 'coloured' as if the shade of her skin is an infectious disease. It is just like when the servants at the Ellises household in India would avoid touching her as if her bad luck was catching.

A carriage comes clip-clopping by, and she is afforded a glimpse of the extravagantly dressed couple inside, the woman in a glittery gown the velvet violet of the midnight sky, sequinned with twinkling stars, her gloves the pale cream of breaking dawn, the man in a top hat and suit the navy of secrets, his head angled towards the lady. A beggar, who was squatting too close to the road, jumps out of the way of the carriage wheels which were in danger of running him over.

'Watch out!' the groom yells indignantly, the horses neighing and arching, the woman's pink mouth a shocked 'O', the gentleman's lips pursed in disapproval, the beggar's bowl overturning, the few meagre coins scattering on the road, set upon by the urchins who've appeared as if from nowhere it seems, the beggar joining the fray, crying, 'Get away! Those be me day's earnings,' his voice desperate.

The carriage disappearing down the road, only a whiff of the lady's rose perfume left behind mingling with horse manure and the muck and slime and dank mulch scent of the river.

If you are poor, your life is worth nothing. And if you are dark-skinned and poor with it, then that's even worse than nothing. The rich and privileged are kinder to their pets than to the homeless who, Divya has overheard Mrs Ellis and her friends deride, 'litter' the streets with their filthy, ragged faces, their hunger-caved stomachs, their illness-ravaged desperation.

A train chugs on the bridge overhead, a fug of smoke, the scent of coal and the humid heat of billowing steam momentarily easing the chill that has settled into Divya's very bones since she has been in England.

A beggar lies prone under the bridge, on the dirty ground on the banks of the Thames, his bag of possessions clutched to his body which, she realises to her horror, as she gets closer, is stubbornly still. Chest neither rising nor falling. A couple of street urchins hover nearby, gawping, their eyes on his bag of possessions.

'E's dead as a doornail.' One of them sniffs.

'Reckon 'e'll 'ave much?'

'A sixpence'd do nicely,' the first one remarks, rubbing his stomach.

Divya intervenes just as the boys reach for the bag. 'He deserves a burial, not to be burgled while he's not even cold.' Her voice trembling as much as her body, from sorrow for this poor man, the grief of her parents' death, who had drowned in the floods caused by a river overflowing on the other side of the world, still raw, assaulting afresh even as she wonders, *Will this be my fate? Nobody to bury me, nobody to care, abandoned, unclaimed like a bag of rubbish.*

She is jolted rudely from her melancholy ruminations by the harsh laughter of the boys. Jarring and sharp as the ice-edged wind. 'What planet are you on, darkie? Do you think anyone cares for the likes of 'im? Go back where you came from. Perhaps they've burials there!'

These boys, just children, their voices not broken yet, but, for all their bravado, their eyes raw and stark, too old for their years, having seen too much, the worst of humankind, their innocence stolen by their circumstances. She understands why they mock her – with her, they can feel superior. Otherwise, they are lowest on the social scale but here, they have a chance to lord it over someone like the upper classes do to them.

Despite their obvious differences, these street urchins none-theless remind Divya, with a pang of ache and missing, of James and Hugh. Will they be scornful of people of her colouring, when they are the age of these children? Or will they retain an inkling of memory, a fondness in their hearts, an impression of the dark-skinned ayah who loved them and sang them haunting lullabies in a language that seems familiar but that they cannot access, and be better disposed towards those different from them? In colour and circumstance?

Someone jostles her and she startles, nearly stumbling. A heavyset man, cap sitting rakishly on his head, smile leery, smoke from his roll up obscuring his leathery face.

'Lookin' for a good time, darlin'?'

She ignores him, walking faster, clutching her bag of worldly possessions to her chest.

The man follows her, whistling languidly, the silt and sewer reek of the Thames, a barrow boy pushing a handcart. The man's gruff voice, smoke and snigger, 'I can show you a good time, luv.'

She hastens her pace, her worn shoes struggling to keep up. They were ruined when she got caught in the rain the day she fainted near the convent, and she has patched them the best she can with newspapers. Their headlines are alien to her, whether international:

A brilliant aurora borealis, "a curtain of fire", amazes people across Europe; the light display visible as far south as Gibraltar.

Three hundred swimmers are dragged out to sea due to freak waves at Bondi Beach in Sydney; lifesavers perform heroically, saving all but five people.

National:

War unless Britain is strong.

Even local, for that matter:

Missing cat found in chimney, was white now soot black but well otherwise.

Woman, aged twenty-five, dies in house fire.

Divya had paused in the act of patching up her shoes, momentarily fascinated by the advertisements for products she will never use: Bulmers Champagne Cider, Ronuk Sanitary Polishes for Bright and Healthy Homes, King Six Cigars, Euthymol Toothpaste for Sweet Breath and Pearly Teeth.

Her father would drink toddy, made from palm-tree sap, and smoke hand-rolled beedies. No Champagne or cigars for him. They had cleaned the floor of their mud hut with cow dung, a fresh coat every morning, and their teeth with mango leaves. They washed in the lean-to by the well beside their hut which Baba had constructed from coconut frond plaited mats, with water drawn from the well and tipped into the brass pot which was heated with kindling, flavoured with smoked wood, scented with lime and mango and earth. When the well dried up in the drought, they would bathe by the lake where they went to wash their clothes which they dried upon the rocks and shrubs on the banks.

Now these alien newspapers in an alien country where she is stranded for the foreseeable future, until she earns enough money for the passage home, stuff and patch up the holes in her worn shoes, which she'd had to get used to wearing before travelling to England.

But just when she needs the shoes to step up, they trip on the uneven cobbles and the man's grimy hand whips out and clasps her arm, his blackened fingers clamping her wrist in a painful vice. His face too close, breath sour and pungent, eyes the dark blue of stormy waves.

'Come away with me, wench.'

'Let me go,' she cries, trying to wrench her hand away.

But his grip is strong.

Blackly scowling clouds mar the late-afternoon sky, leaching it of whatever weak light it had half-heartedly produced thus far. Divya had wanted to get to the guesthouse recommended by the nuns before it got dark.

Tears bite but she pushes them back.

'Let go,' she says, loud and firm.

The children playing hopscotch on the road stop skipping to nudge each other and point.

The newspaper boy, his toes poking out of the holes in his shoes, his pile of papers set down by the railings, stops calling out the day's headlines in a clear voice, mouth open, scratching his head beneath his threadbare cap as he watches what's going on.

The air smells of ice and fear.

Divya tries meeting the eye of a woman passing by, her basket covered by a cloth, a loaf of bread peeking out, her hair covered by a scarf to stop the wind assaulting her ears.

Please help, Divya conveys with her desperate gaze.

Divya is a dark-skinned girl, out of place here, no business being in this country. She deserves all she gets. That's what the woman is thinking, Divya is sure, as she averts her eye and quickens her step.

There is a public house up ahead, the smell of vinegar and rowdy laughter. The rousing foghorn of a ship coming into harbour.

'Help,' Divya cries, desperation bitter in her mouth, for she knows that it is futile. No one is coming to save her.

The children have gone back to playing.

Over by the river, the water laps the shore in frisky waves, dirty brown, children mudlarking for treasure on its banks.

The man grins at her, showing grubby, yellow teeth, eyes flashing with lusty desire.

He bends towards her and she aims her bag containing all of her possessions right at his shins while at the same time lifting her foot and aiming a kick.

'You bitch,' he screams, loosening his grip upon her as he clutches at his shins and she uses the opportunity to pull away, escape.

She runs, the children's laughter echoing in her ears alongside the man's curses, a string of fiery expletives. She runs in her holey, patched up with newspaper, soggy and threadbare shoes, praying that they don't choose this moment to give way, past the public house, the men smoking by the sooty wall, who catcall as she whizzes past.

She turns a corner and runs right into a solid wall.

20

The wall is human, scented with lemon and musk, strong arms holding Divya up.

She is so tired of being hounded, of being afraid. She had had a brief respite with the nuns but once she left their refuge, she has been discriminated against, shouted at, people crossing the road to avoid her.

Or others like the man just now, propositioning her, thinking her fair game.

Even the street urchins barely older than her charges, James and Hugh, laugh and point and make fun of her just because the colour of her skin is of a darker shade than theirs. So what? Isn't the colour of the blood that runs within that outer covering the same? If she was split open, wouldn't she then look the same as them? Doesn't she hurt and wound and feel just as intensely as they do?

Why didn't she catch pneumonia and die that day in the park? Why did the nuns have to save her?

You are being ungrateful. You are lucky to be alive, to have been saved by the nuns, her conscience chastises.

But she is so very weary.

And so she rests against the human wall and allows herself to be held by those arms for a brief moment longer than necessary, giving in to instinct. A rare indulgence.

'Now then, what's this, eh? Got wild horses after you, miss?' A voice, warm chocolate, threaded through with laughter.

Miss. Since arriving in England, she's been *girl, darkie, soot face* and other choice insults, or not worthy of addressing at all. Nobody has addressed her thus, with respect, save the nuns and that lascar on the ship, Raghu, who had called her 'Ma'am'. His smiling face rises before her eyes and she pulls away from these arms.

She looks up into dancing eyes the colour of the parrots that used to screech in the mango and jackfruit trees at home and drive Ma crazy.

It is a shock especially when juxtaposed against the image of Raghu in her mind. She was expecting kind, brown eyes and a shock of black hair and instead, there's this tall, muscular man with green eyes and hair the yellow of sun-kissed hay smiling at her. And as far as she can see, the smile is genuine – there is no hint of scorn or ridicule.

'So, who's after you then, miss?' he twinkles at her.

'Ah... I...'

And then, the man who was haranguing her, whom she was running away from, is upon her, his pungent breath in her face, flinging obscenities at her, his hand clasping her arm in an iron grip, nails digging into her flesh. She can feel the skin tear and bruise, even as her eyes sting and her ears hurt from the force of his hate, men from the public house staggering after him, gathering on the road, the children skipping nearer and even a carriage slowing down to watch.

''Oo do you think you are, darkie, eh?' The man's sour spittle flecking her face. She tries not to recoil or to allow the hot tears stabbing her eyes and gathering on her lashes to overflow.

But before he can do more, the man before her is intercepting her attacker. 'Unhand the lady, please.'

In response, the man clutches Divya's arm harder and laughs, more spittle, pungent and smoky, mingled with dregs from his roll up flecking Divya's face. ''Oo are you calling a lady? This wench 'ere needs what's coming to 'er.'

The man Divya ran into says, without raising his voice, but the threat is clear, 'You will take your hand off the lady right now.'

And at last, her aggressor drops Divya's hand and takes a step backward. 'Taken a fancy to 'er yourself, eh? Didn't think she'd be your sort.' He smirks.

'I'd advise you to leave, go about your business or I am not responsible for what I might do,' Divya's rescuer says, quietly, conversationally but anyone can see that he means it.

The hecklers from the pub disperse.

The children snigger and the man who had set upon Divya, not one to step away from an opportunity to pick on someone weaker than himself, yells, 'What you looking at? Shoo!' Then he too shuffles away, whistling loudly.

'Are you all right?' the man Divya ran into asks Divya gently.

Divya can only nod, wiping her face with her hand, even as she waits for her heartbeat to settle. 'Thank you, sir,' she manages, through the salty lump in her throat.

'Ah, it's nothing.' He waves her thanks away. 'Men like him...' He shakes his head, a muscle working in his jaw, his mouth a thin, grim line. Then, 'Where were you headed, miss?'

His gentle tone, the 'miss' said with such respect, moves her and perversely makes her even more tearful. She swallows down the tears, clears her throat. 'I...'

She pulls the note the nuns gave her, with the address of the lodging home, from her pocket. It is creased and she smooths it. It is precious. 'The Paddy O'Kelly Boarding and Lodging House on West India Dock Road.'

'Ah, Charity's place.' The man smiles.

Dimples dance in his cheeks like the clouds playing hide-and-seek with the sun.

'You know it, sir?'

'Very well indeed. Come, I'll take you there.'

When she hesitates, he says, looking right at her, 'Miss, you can trust me.'

She realises as she looks at his earnest gaze the bright green of monsoon-bejewelled fields that she does.

She follows in his wake, feeling already different, not hounded by gazes, but, in his protection, safe, able to set down briefly, the burden of otherness that has followed her like a dogged shadow even as darkness settles soft and grey upon the London streets. But it is never fully dark here, lamp light twinkling, cries of children and calls of mothers, scents of dinners being prepared, the ripple and swell of the Thames, the clip-clop of carriages, the hiss of steam and the whistle of the trains, sour hops and inebriated laughter from public houses. And yet, she is not scared, for this man is with her.

21

Divya walks beside this stranger, whom she instinctively trusts, and who has promised to take her to the Boarding and Lodging House the nuns recommended. A trolley car trundles past with a rattle and a rumble, its lamps setting the road aglow. The few passengers inside looking variously weary, bothered, burdened, indifferent. It overtakes and nearly pushes a horse-drawn carriage out of the way, the groom brandishing his whip at the driver and, once the bus is past, murmuring soothing reassurances to his horses, as gentle with the animals as he was fierce with the bus driver.

Dusk is falling over East London and the Thames appears shadowy grey, shimmering docilely beneath the blue-black awning of sky pierced here and there with valiant beacons of stars.

Ships and barges rock gently, looking dreamy in the murky gloom settling softly over the river. A steam hooter emits a shrill whistle. The scent of silt and hops and sizzling onions. Mothers calling for their children to, 'Get over 'ere, come on 'ome for yer tea'. The rumble of handcarts and the increasingly urgent call of street market vendors hawking everything from toffee to spices to wilting vegetables to scarves, as they pull their awnings closed, shutting for the day.

Divya and her rescuer pass a crowded eatery from wherein wafts the deliciously smoky scent of grilled meat and sizzled onions. People spill from the shop, some standing about as there's no place to sit, tucking into steaming portions of... 'Saveloy and pease pudding, just what I fancied tonight,' a young woman says, closing her eyes as she brings a heaped and steaming forkful to her mouth. Divya's stomach rumbles. She hopes her companion doesn't hear.

The lamplighter walks up and down the street lighting the gas lamps and they sputter and glitter as if they have secrets they are struggling to keep to themselves. The mudlarking urchins skip past, clutching their treasures in their fists and torn pockets, excitedly making plans. 'We'll hawk these tomorrow and will return in search of more after spending our pennies on a treat. Sweet caramelised chestnuts or even ices perhaps.'

The man beside Divya, laugh lines around his eyes and gold stubble dusting his cheeks, walks easily, long, loping strides which Divya tries to match but she keeps falling behind. He notices and slows down, falling into step beside her.

The scent of boiled cabbage and frying meat drifts from houses they pass on the smoky air.

Men staggering home from public houses give them a wide berth, shaking their heads in disgust while muttering among themselves. Women clasp their children closer and cross the road to avoid the mismatched couple.

Low whistles and catcalls follow them.

'What you associatin' with 'er for? Plenty of our own kind for you,' someone sniggers loud enough for them to hear, followed by the rumble of masculine laughter.

'Mind your own,' Divya's companion calls easily, seemingly unperturbed by their scorn and prejudice.

Suddenly, he comes to a halt mid-stride, causing Divya to nearly walk right into him once more. She stops just in time.

'What's the matter, sir?' she asks, alarmed. Perhaps he's changed his mind about accompanying her to the Boarding House?

'In all the commotion, I quite forgot to introduce myself. What must you think of me?' he says.

'Oh no, sir, please don't worry. I did not introduce myself either,' she says, relieved that he's not having second thoughts about offering to help her.

'Jack Devine at your service. Very pleased to make your acquaintance, miss.' He smiles at her and tips his hat, eyes emerald gems in the gloaming, twinkling to rival the stars piercing the grey gloom of sky here and there.

She returns his smile. 'I'm Divya Ram.'

Ram, her father's name bequeathed to her, along with his eyes and his wide forehead. The ever-present pang of pain and loss stabs afresh. But even though she doesn't hear her parents' voices, they are with Divya, every step of the way, helping her, she is sure. They orchestrated that she fall into a faint right by the convent just as the nuns were setting out on their walk. They arranged for her to bump into this kind, decent man who is treating her with respect of the kind she isn't accustomed to and has rarely encountered since her parents died.

'Thank you for your help just now, sir. I really appreciate it.' She can't help the shudder that rocks her, but manages to stop herself from rubbing her arm which throbs from where that man had gripped her.

His eyes darken and narrow, glinting emerald sparks. 'Some people take liberties. I'm sorry about him.'

'It wasn't your fault.'

But she can see that he is sorry.

'Thank you for taking me where I want to go. I hope I'm not putting you out,' she says.

'Oh, this is my home turf.' When he smiles, the lines around his eyes crinkle pleasingly and dimples dance in his cheeks.

'You live in West India Dock Road?' she asks.

'I grew up there and went to the local school. But then my pa's business took off and we moved to Essex.' A wistful look comes to his eyes, his voice taking on a melancholy chime.

'Ah, is it far?' Divya asks.

And now he twinkles at her and she is glad that she has unwittingly (for she genuinely does not know where Essex is in the context of where they are headed) caused the shadows in his eyes to disperse momentarily. 'It might as well be on the other side of the world for an East End lad, born and bred.'

'Ah,' Divya says, thinking, *I'm on the other side of the world from everything familiar and I'm sorely lost, pinning all my hopes on this lodging house the nuns have spoken so highly of.*

'You see,' Mr Devine is saying, his gaze far away, a mournful note jarring his voice again, 'I lost my ma very early on; I can't hardly remember her...'

'I'm sorry,' Divya says, thinking, *I know a thing or two about losing parents, but I'm lucky that I had Ma for seventeen years. I cannot imagine not having memories of your mother. Memories of cooking with my mother are what tide me through my darkest days.* But she's too shy to tell him all this. In any case, he must note the empathy in her voice for he nods at her, his shimmering gaze like stars reflected upon the fathomless ocean she had crossed to come to this country.

'I've no siblings; I'm an only child...'

Again, like me, Divya thinks.

'So the East Enders were my family. You'll soon find out, we all look out for one another in the East End.'

His conviction that she will not only have a place to stay but also be accepted into the East-End community warms her, even though, after what she's experienced, she doesn't quite believe it.

'I might have moved away but I can't stay away,' he's saying. 'At heart, I'll always be an East Ender.' He pauses, but Divya senses he has more to say, so she walks quietly beside him, waiting for him to continue.

'I never fit in in Essex. They looked down on me at the school my pa, in all good faith, sent me to. I wasn't good enough for them.' His tone hard, like chewing on a bitter seed.

I understand, she wants to say. *I don't fit in here. I'm not good enough.* But she keeps mum. One, because she's shy and two, well… his is a different kind of not fitting in – this is his country and he is white, he is just not the right sort for the people in Essex. It is like Divya in India, shunned because of her bad luck, and yet she knew that she *belonged*, India her country, her birthright, her home.

'I ran away whenever I could, back to the East End. I still am, even now I am grown, in my mid-twenties and running the business – it was roofing to begin with and now it's property – alongside my pa,' he says, grinning mischievously at her.

She realises that his tone, his entire demeanour changes when he speaks of the East End, his voice is lighter, happier.

'You are a good listener, you know,' he says, a smile in his voice. 'We've barely met and here I am baring my heart.'

She blushes, looking down at her feet in her worn, soggy, paper-stuffed shoes. She feels warmed by his compliment, fiery heat setting her face aglow.

'What about you? What brings you here then, Miss Ram?'

Miss Ram.

For a brief, confused moment, she's tempted to look around, see who he is addressing, before it strikes her that it is *her* name, her father's name. When uttered with such respect, in his clipped British tones, she didn't recognise it. It makes her sound like a British Memsahib. She is quite overcome.

After a moment or two, she finds her voice. Where to begin? How to answer his question? Should she give the long version or the short one, say she wants a boarding house for the night and nothing more? After all, he is a stranger. But he is being so kind, not to mention gentlemanly. He has gone out of his way to help her. And he has been so open with her too.

And so, she gives him the abridged version of the whole sorry tale. 'I was a nanny to two young boys...' her voice stumbles slightly as she thinks of James and Hugh, beset once again by longing and missing, '...and accompanied my employers here to England. Now they no longer need my services. They've found an English nanny...'

'More suitable for the boys,' Mrs Ellis had said.

'...so I'm looking for somewhere to stay until I can earn enough for my passage back to India.'

'Ah, a shame. I'm sorry.' Mr Devine is beside her, matching her smaller stride, which must be very slow for him. This too she appreciates immensely. He is a genuinely thoughtful man. Like before when he apologised for the man he had rescued her from, Divya once again sees that he truly *is* sorry. It warms her and touches her more than she can put into words, and so she is quiet, walking companionably beside him.

After a bit, 'How did you hear about the Paddy O'Kelly Boarding and Lodging House?' he asks.

'The nuns at the convent...'

'Ah, the Ursuline Sisters in Forest Gate.' A smile in his voice. 'You know them?'

'Ah yes. They would visit the school Charity and I attended, bringing treats for us kids.'

'Charity who runs the Paddy O'Kelly Boarding and Lodging House?'

'The very one.' He turns to smile at her.

'What a coincidence,' she's moved to say, even though in her heart, she thanks her ma and baba, for this too is surely their doing. *Ma and Baba, you* have *been helping me every step of the way.*

He laughs and it is like the stream weaving between the fields beside her childhood home, gurgling with joyful abundance when the monsoons arrived and it was replenished after being famished during the drought.

'Miss Ram, you will find that the East End of London is like a small village despite being a huge part of the sprawling metropolis of London. Everyone knows everyone here. We are all connected to each other, one way or another, either friends for life or sworn enemies.'

There's laughter in his voice and it makes her bold enough to say, 'And which one is Charity?'

'Well,' he chuckles, and his mirth colours the grey gloom rainbow bright. 'Charity should have been my enemy for life,' he is saying. 'I pulled her plaits when she first started at school – I was older and a bit of a bully.' His eyes twinkling merrily as he reminisces. 'But Charity, who was but a bitty thing, fought me. And, wait for it, she *won.*' He pulls a face, green eyes sparkling like beacons, his voice fond. 'I lost my status as top bully boy after that.' He is rueful.

'She sounds wonderful.' Divya chuckles.

'She doesn't take any prisoners,' he says, smiling.

Divya doesn't get it. What have prisoners got to do with anything? 'I'm sorry, sir?'

'Call me Jack,' he says easily. 'It's a phrase that means she gives as good as she gets. She will not stand on ceremony or be mild, just because she's a girl.'

'Ah. I suppose you need that if you run a boarding house.' Divya is surprised that she is speaking her mind to a gentleman, so at ease with this stranger she's just met.

'Yes, definitely,' Mr Devine twinkles at her and she feels warmed.

She is touched that he listens to her, gives her words weight. Makes it seem like her opinions count. This was not the case even in her village. Women were expected to be demure, mute and meek, hide their faces behind veils in the presence of men. It was different in Divya's own home. With her parents, when nobody else was around, she could be open and opinionated. But elsewhere in the village, women did not, could not speak their mind. In fact, since her parents died, she's not spoken her mind at all. If she had been sure they would listen, and take her opinions into account, she would have had something to say to the Ellises.

But now, this man is listening to her. He answers her questions, considers her opinions.

It is novel. A gift.

And it takes her mind off the vitriol directed at her, the looks of scorn and loathing she attracts.

Her companion is laughing. 'Charity O'Kelly is a character for sure. But steady and loyal with it. You are in safe hands with her.'

Exactly what the nuns had said. And now, despite people glaring as they see her walking with a white man, chatting to him, crossing the road when they see her approach, she relaxes even further in this man's company.

He is easy to talk to. Silent when he senses she wants to be quiet, content to walk beside her, whistling a merry tune.

The river thrums gently, a tugboat emits a shrill whistle, a steam train rattles and chugs on the bridge above and a trolley bus trundles past.

The wind whispers frosty confidences even as it stabs with icy fingers.

She is cold and hungry, but nevertheless, she experiences a slight easing of the burden, the worry about what she will do next. She feels, for the first time since Mr Ellis summoned her into his study and told her she was being let go without enough money for a passage home, hopeful that perhaps there will be a way she can forge ahead. Until now, she has been trying to convince herself, telling herself she will do so, but not really believing it.

Now she thinks that perhaps it is possible.

She has the nuns' reassurance. She has this man validating the nuns' promise that Charity, who sounds amazing, will give her a room to stay. She will bed there overnight and tomorrow, at first light, she will go about finding a job. She will brave the slurs at her colouring. She will persist. This man has not cared that she is of a different colour to him. Neither did the nuns. And she has a feeling that neither will Charity.

And that offers her hope that there will be others who will look past her colour and employ her. She will not rest until she finds them.

She will not give up.

A kindling of hope ignites through the miasma of despair that had descended upon her, bright as a ray of sunshine piercing through clouds, golden iridescence.

And for now, it is enough.

22

They are walking past the docks now. Dock cranes silhouetted against the grey smog like skeletons of giants, glowing eerily with a shiny, silver light.

Barrow boys pull handcarts, cheekily hawking the last of their wares to any lingering passerby who has the misfortune of crossing their path. 'You ne'er gonna see this price again. 'Ere lookit, where else'll 'e git this treasure so cheap?'

Factories belch smoke into the overcast sky, navy balloons smudging the determined shine of the intrepid stars that have managed to push through the frowning clouds.

The East End buzzes with life and energy even in the evening, unlike where the Ellises lived, the sombre, red brick mansions looking upon the wide, empty streets with grave satisfaction. The Ellises' part of London might have been cloaked in the hushed opulence of obscene wealth but it was, Divya thinks, cold and unwelcoming unless you were of a certain class of society.

The cobbles here in the East End are grimy and soot dusted, and so are the tenements sandwiched between factories and businesses, leaning into each other as if eavesdropping on secrets, crumbling bricks testament to the humanity passing through them, reverberating with the sounds of lives being lived inside, laughter, chatter, the scent of meat and cabbage and potatoes mingling with the ammonia reek of the outhouses, buzzing with flies.

Men of all colours, white, brown, yellow, black, Divya notes with wonder, although their faces are all uniformly grimy, congregate by the tenements beside a rubbish bin overflowing with rotting vegetables, stinking of dog pee. They smoke and chat among themselves, their muttering interspersed with the occasional guffaw and nudge and wink, with each potent exhale of their roll ups – the fiery fug causing Divya to cough as she passes – shrugging off the tensions of the day just gone. Workers change shift, wearily patting each other's shoulders, those going on shift looking as tired and exhausted as those coming off it, the same hangdog expressions mirrored upon their faces, whether black or brown, yellow or white.

A steam train rattles past with a screeching whistle on the railway viaduct above, making the tenements shake and judder dangerously, coating them in a smoky miasma of coal-dusted steam, Divya revelling in the welcome burst of heat.

Many of the men walking past raise a hand or call a cheery greeting to Divya's companion. They look at her with curiosity instead of disdain or scorn. They do not cross the road – such as it is, just a narrow strip between the tenements – to avoid her and it is another gift, warming her already warmed heart.

A heavyset woman polishes the front step of her shop until it shines, her whole body jiggling with fierce industry, and opposite, another woman, her hair covered in a scarf, uses her broom and pail to do the same. They both raise their hands in cheerful hello when they see Divya's companion, the heavyset woman resting on her haunches and puffing as she gasps for breath to say, 'Jack Devine, as I live and breathe. Back again, son?'

'Can't get enough of you, Mrs Thompson.' He winks.

She waves her cleaning cloth at him, laughing. 'Go on with ya.' And, to the lady opposite the road who has gone back to cleaning her front stoop, 'You missed the corner.'

She waves her broom at Mrs Thompson. 'Mind yer own,' she grumbles and Mrs Thompson cackles like a witch, turning her beady eye at a teenage girl wiping a shop front window. 'Not clean enough, love. Still can't see my reflection in it.'

'That's cause you're squatting down,' the girl says without missing a beat and the woman chuckles.

'Don't be cheeky now.'

Mr Devine whistles cheerily beside Divya and the breeze that strokes her face tastes of the sea, salt and sugar and smoke.

Divya marvels at how different it all is to the Ellises' remote and lifeless street. All life is here on *these* streets. She throws her head to the heavens which are darker still and have split open to spray them with the ubiquitous, mildly spitting moisture so common in England, Divya is learning, the clouds unable to decide if they want to divest of their burden or not, settling for something which could, at a stretch, be classed as rain.

Shop owners call to each other in an incomprehensible tongue as they close up their businesses for the day, pulling the shutters, locking them.

'I thought I was beginning to understand all the different accents in this city – even if I can't make out everything when spoken very fast, I can still guess at what is being said. But this accent I can't understand at all. It can't be an East-End thing because I understood Mrs Thompson and the others just now.'

'Ah,' Mr Devine smiles at her, his eyes glowing. 'They're Jewish and speak a different language altogether.'

'Oh?' *How wonderful*, she thinks. Different colours, different languages, all here, mingling freely.

'Yiddish, it's called. Don't worry, you'll get used to us East Enders soon enough,' Mr Devine assures.

'I think I'll like it here very much,' Divya says, meaning it, even as she hopes that everything will work out, that Charity will have a room for her.

Mr Devine beams at her, his eyes sparking gold, and she feels warmed despite the drizzle that is now picking up force.

23

They are passing the factories now, belching smoke, machines cranking and clanking, men grunting as they heft gunny sacks and planks of timber, grey dust settling all around them. Divya is assaulted by an amalgam of scents, guessing from the aroma as they pass each one what is manufactured there. Cloying perfume of nectar and caramel from the sugar factory, pulped fruit from the jam factory, baked sugar and rising dough from the biscuit factory, ginger and cardamom and cinnamon from the spices factory, damp, woody nuttiness form the timber factory, the gagging reek of old meat from the leather factory, the wet hay and earthy scent of grains from the grain factory, the scent of smoke and potency from the tobacconist.

Fog swirls over the river, grimy yellow.

A boy perches at the street corner, wearing a too-big coat, much like Divya is, wet and soggy and buttoned-up wrong, swamping him, weary lines too old for his years dragging his face down. He hawks the evening paper, and Mr Devine digs in his pockets for a coin and buys a copy, patting the boy on his head, sending his cap awry.

The boy grins wide, displaying a crooked mouthful of teeth, righting his cap. 'I say, thank 'ee kindly, mister.'

The East End with its busyness and hustle reminds her of the port when she boarded the ship to come here, Divya muses as she takes in everything avidly.

'Here we are,' says the man beside her.

Walking alongside him has given her comfort – she was shaken by her encounter with that man who had followed her more than she can put into words, shivering every time she thinks of it.

'The West India Dock Road,' he says, smiling at her, his eyes crinkling pleasingly, glinting in the gathering dusk like warm secrets.

PART IV

24

The Paddy O'Kelly Boarding and Lodging House is two doors down from the public house, from whence drifts the pungent scent and merry laughter harking of a good time. It is a thin, tall building wedged between a Jewish tailor and a communal wash house, women emerging from it carrying baskets of scrubbed clothes, the scent of soap and clean linen.

Mr Devine knocks on the front door, once, then again, harder, and when there's still no answer, he tries the door knob and, turning to grin at her, says, 'It's open. Come on.' And when Divya is hesitant, 'I promise Charity will want us to wait indoors, out of the cold.'

The entryway is dark and narrow, a stairway leading directly upstairs and doors opening off it on either side. There's a small desk in an alcove which Divya notices once her eyes adjust to the darkness – it's dusk outside and even darker here, and so quite an adjustment.

The house smells of boiled cabbage and there's absolutely no sign of occupation, although Divya hears faint voices and other more eerie sounds echoing down the stairs and ricocheting off the walls. The place has a lost-in-time feel so Divya is not quite sure where the sounds are coming from, whether upstairs or through the shut doors on either side.

Not for the first time, Divya is grateful for Mr Devine, who calls cheerily, 'Yoohoo, Charity O'Kelly, you there?'

When there's no response, he turns to Divya and shrugs, still smiling, appearing unbothered.

'She'll be seeing to her parents or one of the lodgers. She's definitely around somewhere. Yoohoo, Miss Charity, proprietress of the best lodging house this side of the docks, there's someone here for you.'

Once again, Divya is thankful that she bumped into Mr Devine. The nuns would say, guardian angels led Divya to him. Divya is convinced that in her case, the angels guarding her are her parents. She can't hear them, they can no longer talk to her, perhaps, but they *are* there, looking out for her. Sending help in the form of nuns and this Mr Devine.

The thought is a comfort and she smiles shyly at her companion.

In the darkness, his green eyes sparkle as he grins back at her.

Then suddenly and with no warning, there's an almighty thunderous clattering down the stairs.

At first it's only thud, thud, thud and children's uncontained giggles and laughter festooning the dark stairwell, colouring it bright with mirth, illuminating and swelling it with happiness.

Then they come into view: a child who appears to be newly adolescent and his two younger brothers. For it is unmistakable that they are siblings – they have the same colouring, the same lanky build, and similar features.

'Can't catch me,' the oldest boy teases, shrill voice on the cusp of breaking into the more gruff and growling timbres of adulthood.

'Bet I can too,' cries the youngest.

Their voices, high and happy and spirited, lending bounce and heft and life to this hitherto grim place.

'Now, now, boys, what's this, eh?' Mr Devine laughs as they bound down the last few steps and career into him, nearly knocking him over with the force of their unrestrained and enthusiastic descent.

'Mr Devine.' They grin happily, dancing around him. 'What brings you here?'

They all have laughing brown eyes and dark hair, too long and in need of a cut. One of them – the youngest – has riotously curly locks while the other two sport very straight, silky hair that gleams in the dark.

'Where's your sister, eh?' Mr Devine asks.

'Gone to the market to fetch groceries,' the youngest pipes up.

'It's evening and the market traders reduce their prices to get rid of their vegetables,' says the oldest.

'It will be vegetable soup again tonight,' grumbles the youngest with downturned lips.

'You're lucky to be getting that, you are,' says Mr Devine, affectionately ruffling the little one's curls.

He looks around Mr Devine and spots Divya. 'Oh, you've someone with you.'

'This is Miss Divya Ram,' Mr Devine tells them and turning to Divya, 'Miss Ram, may I present the O'Kelly boys: Fergus, Connor and Patrick.'

Three pairs of wide, brown eyes regard Divya curiously, even as the little one says, 'Everyone calls me Paddy, like my da. But they don't confuse us, for he's big and I'm small.'

She hides her smile by biting her lip and nodding gravely. 'Pleased to make your acquaintance, Paddy O'Kelly.'

He grins widely.

She turns to the other boys, 'And yours, sirs,' she says nodding at each of them.

'They're not sirs,' says Paddy, hands on hips. 'They're not old enough.'

'Speak for yourself, Paddy,' says his oldest brother, clipping him round his head.

'Ow, what was that for?' Paddy scowls at his brother, before turning to Divya. 'Have you come for a room?'

'Yes I have,' Divya says.

Her colour doesn't seem to matter to the boys – she was a bit worried, the reaction since she left her employers making her wary, despite the nuns' recommendation, and even though nobody batted an eyelid at her or crossed the road to avoid her, or made a comment upon their strange pairing when she walked beside Mr Devine once they neared the docks.

But she needn't have worried, for the boys nod easily.

Divya has been praying that Charity has a room for her ever since leaving the nuns, but now she wants it even more so, despite this building being so dark and gloomy. It is because of these boys. She has been missing her charges sorely. But even though she's only spent a few minutes with these children, that ache has eased a little. There's something about the innocence, the mischief-laced sweetness of children, their unquestioning acceptance that centres her, makes everything bearable.

'The upstairs attic room is free I think,' says the teenager, Fergus, officiously.

Connor appears content to let his brothers talk, quietly observing all that goes on.

'It is too,' Paddy nods earnestly, 'I hid in there just now which is why you couldn't find me.' Looking at his brothers and crowing smugly as he says this.

'Ah.' Divya can breathe now. There *is* a room for her, if Charity feels inclined to let it to her. Mr Devine and the nuns have assured Divya that Charity will do so. Nevertheless, Divya prays, *Please, Ma, Baba, let it be so.* She wants to stay here in this lodging house and be part of the mixed community she saw around the docks. Here, she is almost sure she will not be turned away if she knocks on doors at one of the businesses, looking for work. She is willing to do anything at all.

'Let's wait for your sister to confirm, shall we?' smiles Mr Devine.

He is good with the boys, Divya notes.

'Speaking of which, she's here I think,' says Fergus for the door rattles behind Divya and a young woman steps inside.

25

Charity appears to be perhaps a couple of years older than Divya. She looks exactly like her brothers with her dark hair and eyes. Her hair is longer and pulled back into a bun and covered by a scarf but curly black strands escape it to crowd her cheeks.

There are worry lines crimped into her face and shadows hollowing her eyes.

She's carrying a basket with wilted vegetables and a sorry-looking loaf of bread. 'Boys, look at the state of you. Those clothes you're wearing were freshly washed and now they are grimy again. What have you been—?' She stops short when she catches sight of Mr Devine.

Her face lights up in a smile and the lines disappear so she looks younger, like the girl she is, not much older than her teenage brother, Divya thinks, experiencing a flare of admiration for her.

This girl, her own age or thereabouts, appears to be running this lodging house.

What was it the nuns said? Ah, yes, that Paddy, Charity's father, had been ruined by the war. And her mother, Moira...

something was wrong with her, but Divya didn't know what as the nuns hadn't told her and she hadn't felt right to ask.

Up until now, Divya had thought of Charity only in the context of a room for herself at her lodging house. She hadn't thought of her as a person in her own right, except briefly, when Mr Devine mentioned how Charity had fought him, even though she was smaller, and won.

But now that she is here, in front of Divya, a slip of a girl, looking tired and harassed, Divya is completely in awe. This young woman, barely even an adult, is single-handedly managing this lodging house.

Anything is possible, if you have the will for it, or if you are left with no choice but to do it, that's what this girl is proving. If she can do this, run a boarding and lodging house so competently, I can find a job and earn enough for my passage home.

'Oh, hello there, Jack,' Charity is saying. She has the sweetest voice – clear and musical. Divya can picture her singing in the nuns' choir. Instead, she is here, hefting the huge burden of running a boarding house on her slender shoulders. 'To what do we owe the pleasure? Hope the boys are not bothering you?' One eyebrow raised mischievously as she surveys her brothers.

'Bother?' snorts the teenager.

'When have we ever been a bother?' cries the little one while, true to form, the middle brother, Connor, stands silent and serene, removed from it all.

'When have you not?' she sighs but fondly. 'Now shoo.'

'We were helping you,' Paddy cries, hands on hips. 'This lady needs a room and we said the attic one is free.'

Lady. Paddy called *her* a lady! Divya could kiss him.

Now Charity's gaze rests upon Divya and she smiles. Just like her brothers and her friend Jack, there is no judgement in her gaze, no difference because of Divya's colour, no flinching from it, no outrage at the daring of this coloured woman wanting a room at her lodging house, just warm welcome.

It is a relief and Divya's heart settles.

'Hello there,' Charity says. 'Give me a minute to set this basket down in the kitchen and I'll be right back.'

She opens one of the doors leading off the narrow hallway, which is feeling very crowded with all of them cramped in there. Divya spies stairs leading down, perhaps to a set of rooms – the kitchen and scullery, she thinks, based on the layout of the Ellises' mansion. Although this house is much smaller of course. But the servants' sections – the kitchen, scullery and pantry, will all be set out similarly in great big houses or small and will be grouped together for practical purposes anyway, she surmises.

While they are waiting for Charity to return, Mr Devine quizzes the boys on school, which they dodge expertly.

'One word for school,' drawls Fergus. 'Boring.' He drags the 'Bo' so it sounds 'Boooo'.

'Yes, boooring,' his youngest brother repeats.

'What are you, my echo?' Fergus challenges his little brother, while Connor giggles, slapping one hand to his mouth to control his mirth.

Please don't, Divya thinks. Those starburst chuckles are the only sound she's heard from the child.

'Is Mr Doyle still there?' Mr Devine asks, unperturbed by the boys' response.

'Yes, old as the hills he is and grumpy with it.' Fergus rolls his eyes.

Mr Devine laughs. 'He was old and grumpy when I was at school.'

'He is grumpier still now,' the teenager grumbles.

'And how would you know this, Fergus, seeing as you were but a babe in arms when I was at school?' Mr Devine asks.

And this is when Charity appears. 'Speaking of school,' she says sternly, fixing all three boys in her gaze, 'have you done your schoolwork?'

'Yes,' they mumble and, looking at each other, unspoken communication passing between them, they disappear, bounding up the scuffed linoleum stairs as loud as a herd of elephants and as if a pride of lions were after them, before their sister can persist in quizzing them further.

'Where are you off to, boys, in such a hurry? And do you have to make that great clatter going up them poor stairs – what have they ever done to you that you punish them so? And never mind that, you'll wake the whole house,' Charity calls but they're already up one floor and pretending they can't hear her.

Mr Devine laughs, even as the boys' quickly stifled giggles drift down the stairs.

Charity shakes her head and rolls her eyes. 'I bet they haven't even opened their books,' she sighs.

'Kids, eh?' Mr Devine chuckles.

Divya smiles. She is warming to this place the more she is here.

Now it doesn't feel cold and grim but welcoming even though it is just as dark. For the boys' mischief, Mr Devine's easy charm, the glow of Charity's wide smile make up for it.

'So, you are wanting a room?' Charity smiles at Divya, going up to the desk in the alcove next to where Divya is standing and pulling out a tall ledger and pencil. She opens the ledger and turns the leaves until she comes to the one she wants and moves the pencil three quarters down the page.

'Yes, I...' Divya is suddenly tongue-tied, for she wants this so very much. She takes a breath, finds the words she needs in her dry mouth. 'The nuns at the convent...'

'Ah the Ursuline nuns.' Charity smiles even wider, if possible. 'They visit Mammy every so often.'

'They recommended you.'

Charity beams and it is as if her whole body is aglow. 'Good, good. And how did you meet Jack here?'

'I bumped into her.' Mr Devine grins.

'Ah you did, did you?' Charity raises an eyebrow. 'Do you make a habit of bumping into damsels then, eh, Jack?' she teases, eyes twinkling mischievously, so she looks even more like her brothers.

'Miss Charity O'Kelly, you're getting too cheeky, I'll have you know.'

'I always was, if you recall, Mr Devine.' And turning to Divya, 'Now then, Miss...'

'Ram. Divya Ram. But please, call me Divya.'

'Only if you call me Charity.'

'First names already,' Mr Devine smiles. 'I think you'll be all right here, Miss Ram. I better get going.'

'Thank you for your help, sir.'

'No need to stand on ceremony with me. It was nothing,' Mr Devine says.

'It meant a lot to me, sir,' Divya says, shuddering inwardly as she thinks of what nearly happened with that other man. If this man hadn't come to her rescue – well, it doesn't bear thinking about.

'Please, call me Jack,' he says.

'First names already,' Charity twinkles.

'Ah, you stop,' Mr Devine smiles at Charity. 'Right then, goodbye, ladies.' And with a sweep of his hat, bowing extravagantly at the two of them, he is gone.

'Nice to meet you, Di...' Charity blushes. 'I'm sorry I... How do you say your name?'

'Divya,' Divya says.

'Divya,' Charity repeats. 'Beautiful name.'

'It is beautiful when you say it. Musical.'

'Ah the Irish lilt.' Charity laughs. 'I grew up here but I still have it thanks to Mammy and Da.'

She looks at her ledger. 'Now then, what do you know, Paddy was right. The attic room is free and yours for as long as you want it.'

'Thank you.' Divya says, But she doesn't allow herself to relax until she knows the answer to her next question. 'And how much will it cost, please?'

Charity tells her and Divya quickly tots up the numbers. She will have to find a job soonest to supplement the cost of the room. She doesn't want to think about what will happen if she can't and her money runs out. Her guardian angels, her ma and baba will surely intervene and prevent this. *Please.*

'It will be good to have a woman stay. It's all men here, decent people, I assure you – I make sure of it. They're mostly sailors who are stopping until they can earn a passage back.'

Like me, thinks Divya. *I too plan to stay until I can earn enough for a passage back.*

Does this mean the other lodgers here are from India? She thinks of the black and brown and Oriental men she saw on her way here. *Not only Indian, but men of different colours and nationalities, perhaps. I will be, like the nuns promised, at home here.*

26

'I too would like to get a job as soon as possible, so I can earn enough money for a passage home,' Divya is moved to tell Charity.

She is very down to earth and appears to take everything in her stride. Divya feels instantly at ease with her.

Charity nods, chewing her pencil as she considers Divya with serious eyes, her gaze bright and expectant. 'Do you know what job you'd like to do?' she asks. 'The men staying here walk to the docks each morning and wait, hopefully, for the callout.'

'Callout?'

'When work is announced and men are picked for it.'

'Ah.' Divya takes a breath. 'I came here as a nanny but I am willing to do anything at all.'

'I would do anything for someone to take my siblings in hand, Lord knows,' Charity sighs but Divya knows from her fond smile that she's joking and doesn't really mean it.

'Do you know of anyone who is in need of a nanny?' Divya asks.

Charity laughs ruefully. 'Not round here. None of us can afford it. We look after our own, you see.'

'Yes.' Divya nods.

'But you'll find somewhere, I'm sure.' Charity reassures but Divya notes that she doesn't sound too convinced.

Which makes Divya realise that Charity might understand where Divya is coming from. And so she feels able to say, 'I tried around where my old employers lived. But they all want white nannies.'

Charity nods. 'That's what those upper-class people, our so-called betters, want, someone who speaks proper and who looks proper too. We don't measure up.'

And the way she says 'we' and 'our' warms Divya's heart even more towards Charity.

'Now, as to your room...' Charity says. 'Mammy, Da, the boys and myself live downstairs. This floor and the floor above are given to lodgers. Your room will be in the attic up another flight of stairs. You don't mind?'

'No. I'll be all right,' Divya says. She is just grateful to have a room here in a place and with people she already feels so comfortable with.

'The communal sink is one floor down. And the privy is outside. Come, I'll show you round.' Charity smiles.

Divya pays her rent for the week, carefully counting out the money from the meagre collection of coins that comprises her earnings, and follows Charity up the stairs.

Her room is very small, a closet really, no space for herself and Charity both at the same time. Charity points, with an apologetic smile, to the thin palette of bed, a small cupboard with the door nearly falling off wedged beside it below a tiny window that lets in a draught, frosty wind howling like a banshee.

And even taking into consideration the small privy that stinks something terrible ('Men!' Charity sighs. 'I cleaned it just this morning') and the sink a floor down from her room, Divya has a strong feeling that she will be happy here.

'It's not much,' Charity sighs.

'It's a place to stay. Thank you,' Divya says sincerely and Charity smiles.

27

Divya wakes to noise outside her window.

A great big hubbub, an amalgam of voices, chatter, laughter, thuds and bangs.

Boots pounding on cobbles.

A man whistling out of tune.

The clink of milk bottles.

And behind it all, the swell and gush of the Thames, its salt and brine scent. Ships hooting, their foghorn boom telling tales of faraway lands, brimming with exotic produce and people even more so. Haunted-eyed sailors with hangdog expressions, each line on their rugged faces telling a story of the places they've been, the things they've seen, the hardships they've suffered, gather beside and wait on the docks for the day's callout, hoping for work, a chance to get on a ship that is travelling back to wherever is home for them.

High-pitched, young voices call as they tumble down the street with their wares.

Women cry, fond laughter threading through their voices, 'Go on with you, our Tommy. We don't be needing that today.'

Newspaper boys ring in the day's news:

'Rumblings of war in Europe!'

'Sport with Ireland winning!'

This to a loud cheer from the Irish contingent.

When Divya goes downstairs, after she has washed, best she can, in the sink down the stairs, and dressed, Charity is trying to make it out the door with a great big basket of laundry on her hip while juggling another in her free hand.

'Here, let me help.' Divya grabs a basket.

'Thank you.' Charity smiles at Divya. 'You arrived just in time.' Once she's out the door, she holds her hand out for the basket Divya is carrying. 'I can manage now. I thank the Lord every single time I do the laundry that the communal wash house is right next door.'

'I'll come with you,' Divya says. 'I'd like to help.'

'No, I can mana—'

'Please, I insist,' Divya says and Charity beams.

The air outside smells of jam and smoke and encroaching winter, cold with a bite to it, flavoured with toast and apples and washing soap as they enter the steamy and busy wash house.

A host of women, their stockings rolled down and sleeves rolled up, wash and scrub and laugh and gossip as they wring and rinse and scour and boil, arms and mouths working simultaneously. The room is hot and humid with it, although all the windows are open, and smells of clean clothes and human sweat. The army of women scrub on their boards and wrestle with the mangles and pull dripping sheets from boilers, some of them up to their forearms in sudsy water. And all the while they talk even though perspiration gathers on their lips and between their breasts.

Divya looks at them and aches for that easy camaraderie. She had not realised, when her parents were alive and she was part of the village, what a privilege it was. She had taken it for granted. Belonging. Having somewhere to call home.

Of course all that changed the moment her parents died, but...

She had had it just the same for a brief while and she hadn't treasured it. Hadn't realised what a gift it was. Will she ever find it again?

Standing there, watching the women banter and chat even as they sweat over their families' clothes, Divya vows to herself that one day, she too *will* have this. Belonging. A family of her own whose clothes she will be happy to wash and for whom she will be glad to slog, and vice versa. Where she will be accepted easily and completely and unconditionally. She will have many friends and an extended support group. In India, where her colour won't stand out, in a community where she will not be defined by her bad luck, she will start anew, a fresh beginning, and she will have this.

'Morning all,' Charity calls.

The women turn as one, pink-faced and rosy-cheeked from exertion, flaxen hair and brunette locks alike glued to their sweaty faces, damp and lank from the steamy humidity of the wash house. 'Yoohoo there, Charity, love,' they call cheerily.

They stop talking as they take Divya in.

Divya waits for their shocked gasps. Their anger and upset at her, and at Charity for bringing her along, a woman of colour standing among them.

But it doesn't come.

Instead, they smile kindly, warmly at Divya. Her colour not seeming to bother them one jot.

It is humbling and she is aware of hot tears stinging her eyes. Her emotions are all over the place.

Once again, she thinks, *the nuns were right*. West India Dock

Road seems far more accepting than the other places she's encountered in London – not many to be sure, but enough.

'Meet my new lodger. This is Divya Ram,' says Charity cheerfully. And, to Divya, 'And these are the women who run this street with an iron fist, keep it fed and washed and in clean clothes as you can see.'

'Don't be cheeky now,' says one of the women, shaking her fist at Charity. But she is grinning widely as are the others, as they say, 'Welcome to West India Dock Road, gel. You'll find us a friendly lot here, for the most part. Don't mind old Gladys, over there. She's a sourpuss to everyone.'

'Mind how you go, Maud,' grumbles a heavyset older woman, her hair tied back with a scarf, who Divya understands to be Gladys.

Most of the women speak with the same musical lilt as Charity – they must be Irish too, Divya surmises.

'Hello all,' Divya says, suddenly shy. 'Thanks for the welcome.'

The women smile, nod and go back to their washing. Divya turns to Charity. 'Can I help?'

'You already have, by helping lug the baskets here. Now I'm all set. There's bread in the kitchen. Please help yourself to breakfast.'

'I'd like to make myself useful,' Divya says.

Charity surveys her, hands on hips. 'None of the other lodgers have ever offered to help. You really mean it, don't you?'

'I really do,' Divya says.

'You'll regret you asked. You can take it back now, before you commit,' Charity says, warning in her voice.

'Go on.' Divya smiles. 'It can't be that bad.'

'Oh but it is.' Charity is grim. 'I will let you backtrack once you've heard what it is.'

'You're scaring me now,' Divya says, thinking, *How I love this banter. I've missed it even though I've never experienced it – not with a woman friend, and yes, Charity does feel like a friend. I've enjoyed a version of it with my parents, perhaps. How can I miss something I've never enjoyed before?*

'You should be scared,' Charity says ominously. Then, 'Look, my brothers go wild knowing I will be here a while. When I return, the kitchen will be a mess, like a bomb has gone off in there. If you can take it, and only if you have the patience for it, mind, like I said, you can backtrack...'

'You want me to supervise their breakfast?'

'Yes please, since you asked,' Charity says. 'But as I said, you can—'

'All right.'

She leaves the warm wash house to a blast of cold air smelling of the river, almost walking into a woman laden with laundry, to Charity's words at her retreating back, bright with relief, 'Don't feel you have to. Don't let them run rings around you. Feel free to be firm with them. Thank you kindly, Divya Ram.'

28

'Something smells good,' Charity says as she comes into the kitchen, hefting the bags of freshly washed laundry, Divya rushing to help her.

'I hope you don't mind,' Divya begins, as Charity sets the baskets down and stretches luxuriously, hands on her hips...

But Charity does not let her finish. 'Jesus, Mary and Joseph, am I dreaming! Is it really you, boys?'

Her brothers look up from their chewing to grin at their sister, Paddy nodding enthusiastically.

'What a glorious sight this is. My brothers all sitting quietly and eating up.'

The boys go back to their food, the music of cutlery on plates.

'You are a miracle worker,' Charity beams at Divya. 'They normally never sit down and I have to coax and cajole them to eat, but look at them now, they are wiping their plates clean.'

'This is delicious,' Fergus says, grinning at Divya. 'You make magic. Please can I have some more?'

He holds out his plate.

'This is a first!' Charity beams.

Divya glows.

'There's some for you too. Why don't you sit down and I'll dish you a plate?' Divya says.

To her surprise, Charity comes up to her and gives her a hug. She smells of washing soap and sweat.

Divya is overwhelmed. She cannot recall the last time she was hugged – perhaps when her mother was alive. Her father was not one for physical tokens of affection but he showed his caring through his actions – fixing the hay-topped roof of the hut so it didn't leak in the monsoons. Building a lean-to shed using coconut frond mats so his wife and daughter could wash in private. Building it beside the well so they didn't have to carry the heavy pots of water too far.

Divya wants to stay in this embrace forever. She has missed the comfort of human touch.

Charity, unfazed by Divya's colouring, treating her like a friend, which is what Divya already thinks of her in her head.

'Thank you.' Charity's eyes are glowing. 'This is the first time since Mammy and Da both fell ill that someone has offered to fix me a plate. But I have to peg the washing on the line...'

'I'll do that. Please. You eat up.' Divya tops up Fergus's plate and sets a heaped one in front of Charity.

Charity takes a bite and closes her eyes. 'I am in heaven, me. What is this, Divya? It is delicious.'

'I... Your brothers didn't want bread or toast so... I found some spices...'

'My goodness, they've been lying there since one of our Indian lodgers gave it to me – Munnoo, you'll see him around, he's an East-End institution, so he is. Speaks like the King; you'd swear he was of noble blood. Anyway, when he was staying here, he was a few bob short of rent and he supplemented it with the spices. He didn't have work so I didn't have the heart to protest.'

'I used them to season the bread before I fried it in the dripping.'

'It beats stale bread any day.' Charity is stuffing forkfuls in her mouth even as she speaks, grinning happily at Divya as she chews.

'We used to do it with rotis and chapatis that had gone stale, fry them with spices to lift them up,' Divya says, a wistful note in her voice as she recalls how she, Ma and Baba would sit under the mango tree and listen to bulbuls singing and parrots screeching as they ate spiced rotis, breeze redolent with guavas and secrets caressing their cheeks gently, whispering stories about the night just passed and the day yet to come.

'Something smells good.' One of the lodgers pokes his head around the kitchen door.

'If you give me half a crown, Mr Juma, Miss Ram here can make it for you,' Charity jokes. 'I must say it is delicious.'

'The scent reminds me of home,' Mr Juma says. He is darker skinned than Divya. He must be from the Africas. 'My ma used to make something similar. Here.' He digs around in his pocket, holds out half a crown to Charity. 'Please can I have some?'

'Well I was not ser...' Charity begins, but Divya is already coating bread in spices and heating up the pan, which is spitting with dripping.

As Mr Juma is eating, others follow, drawn in by the smell of spices – 'So aromatic' – and before Divya knows it, the bread is gone and all the lodgers have partaken of her breakfast, each of them paying Charity for the privilege.

'Divya,' Charity says, after. 'Please take this.' She hands the money she just earned from the lodgers to Divya.

'No, please,' Divya protests. 'I enjoy feeding people. It gives me comfort.' And it is a way of connecting with her mother, even, especially now she's gone. Watching the men enjoy what she had cooked, people of all colours, from the different corners of the globe that they called home, chatting away happily as they tucked into her food, asking for more, the air hot and flavoured with spices and conversation, voices with different lilts, accents harking back to countries and continents many thousands of miles away, all liberally seasoned with laughter. Afterwards, the men rubbing their bellies and saying, 'This has set us up for a long day of hard work in the freezing cold nicely. Thank you, Miss Ram.' It was reward enough.

Divya needs money, yes. But she had needed this more. Validation that she wasn't just defined by bad luck or dark skin, that she was more than that. That she mattered. Even here. In a country on the other side of the world from all that was familiar. That she had helped in some way. Given joy. Made a difference, however small, in people's lives.

It was like when she was with Masters James and Hugh. That same joy and comfort of being needed.

'Divya, are you still looking for a job?' Charity asks.

'Yes,' Divya says.

'Work for me. In the kitchen here. Feed the lodgers and us. And here,' Charity once again hands her the money. 'This is the rent you paid back to you with a little extra for the work you did today. And later, once I've finished my chores, I'll do the accounts and formalise this agreement, if you are willing of course and say yes to what I am able to offer. I might not be able to pay as much as your old employers did, mind. But you will get lodging, food and a salary. What do you say, would you consider it?'

Divya's heart glows. To do this, what she loves, every day, as a job. She hadn't even thought of cooking as one of the options available to her in this country with its different cuisine but, she realises after her morning feeding people, it is just what she would enjoy, love.

She doesn't have to think about it long. 'I would love that.'

Charity beams, giving her another hug. 'You'll have to get used to this,' she breathes in Divya's ear. 'I'm a hugger, me. The boys hate it.'

And Divya laughs even as she tentatively wraps her arms around Charity, hugging her back. This white woman who, in such a short while, has become her friend and her employer too. Who has solved her problems, giving her a place to stay and a job which she knows she will enjoy tremendously.

And thus, it is settled.

PART V

29

1939

It is nearly 6 p.m. and even though it's late spring, the air that strokes Divya's face while she queues up at the market, although fragrant with fruit and greenery, is nippy. The earthy, organic scent of wilting vegetables mingles with smoked kippers and coal fires from the smokehouse. The vegetable vendors bring down their prices at the end of the day, and so Divya has joined the other ladies of West India Dock Road waiting with empty baskets that they hope to fill with choice bargains. The veggies will be wilting after a day at the stalls but it is nothing a bit of spice won't be able to cure, Divya thinks.

Divya has been lodging and working at Charity's for a few months now. She has got used to waking to the boom of ships, their foghorn call and the swell of the Thames by which everyone leads their lives.

During her first weeks at the lodging house, once she had found her feet, she had asked Charity and the lodgers about Raghu, the lascar whom she had met during her voyage to England and who had been so kind and civil to her, who had called her his friend. For he was the one who had first mentioned

West India Docks to her: 'If you need anything at all, ask for lascar Raghu at the West India Docks.'

Charity and the lodgers were in accord: 'Munnoo will know.'

'Munnoo is staying at a lodging house in Limehouse. I'll find him for you.' Mr Benjamin Juma, who since that first breakfast was a huge fan of Divya's food (which was immensely gratifying), offered.

As promised, Munnoo arrived at Charity's with Mr Juma that very evening. Divya recognised him – he was the dapper man who had kindly helped her up when she stumbled on the cobbles the evening she first arrived, with Mr Devine, at West India Dock Road. He was dressed like a gentleman, in suit and tie, albeit one that had seen better days, and he spoke like one too. 'Ah, my dear, I heard young Raghu's working on a ship bound to Australia and has been contracted to do a few voyages with the company, so we may not be seeing him for a while. Word is he's doing very well and might be promoted to head lascar soon.'

Since then, Divya has enquired after Raghu a few times, but every time, the answer has been the same: Raghu is away.

Slowly but surely, Divya's pile of coins, secured in a knot in her mother's sari, is growing. At this rate, by the end of the year, she should be able to book a passage home.

If war is not declared before then, that is.

The displaced sailors from different parts of the world who, like Divya, are stopping at Charity's until they can earn enough for a passage to the faraway lands they call home, worry that in the event of war, passenger ships will be requisitioned for war work and it will delay them returning home even more.

Mr Devine, who is a regular visitor at the boarding house, is convinced there will be war. 'As sure as there is a nose on my face,' he'd said.

Connor, who never said anything if he could help it, asked, 'Where on your face?'

They all turned to look at Connor, nonplussed, unused to hearing his voice.

Mr Devine smiled, giving the boy a gentle clip on his ear, saying, 'Get away with you,' even as Connor hid his grin behind his hand, his eyes twinkling mischievously.

'Jack's keen on you,' Charity declares, often, eyes dancing as she nudges Divya.

'Stuff and nonsense,' Divya huffs. She cannot believe someone as handsome as Mr Devine, who has women falling over themselves to make a play for him, would want her. 'What does he want with me?'

'Have you looked in the mirror?' Charity asks, twinkling at her. 'You're beautiful, Divya.'

'Thank you, Charity,' Divya says. Even though she doesn't believe her friend, Charity's heartfelt conviction warms Divya's heart. Charity is true to her name: kind and generous. Seeing the very best in everyone.

The nuns visit every so often, bringing healing soup for Moira and Paddy, Charity's parents, both bedridden, a basket of fruits and Irish taffy for the boys and Charity. 'And now that you are settled here, for you too, Divya,' they say, smiling fondly at her.

The nuns sit with Charity's parents, praying with them, for them, and sharing stories of 'back home'.

It is the only respite Charity gets, Divya sees. For she does everything for her parents herself, uncomplainingly, including sitting with them, giving them time she doesn't have. But when the nuns visit, the worry lines crimping Charity's face relax a little.

'Da came back from the war a broken man,' Charity had told Divya.

They were sitting in the kitchen nursing cups of tea which Divya had brewed the Indian way, strong and spiced with cardamom and ginger. It was meant to be milky but there had never been enough milk when growing up – Divya's parents did not own buffaloes and the watered-down milk they received from Ananthappa who had three cows in addition to a buffalo, in exchange for Divya's carrot halwa which Ananthappa was partial to, was gone by midday. So Divya had got used to the stronger version which was just as well for late at night, here too, there was only enough milk for a few drops in each cup.

Everyone else was asleep, and once Charity finished the last of her chores, she had come into the kitchen for a tumbler of water to find Divya scrubbing the counters clean after having prepared the vegetables for breakfast – she planned to make upma, spiced semolina, the next morning.

'Ah, Divya, you aren't in bed yet?'

'I just wanted to have the veggies ready for tomorrow. The dock workers leave very early and need breakfast before then.'

'I should be doubling your salary. You are a gem, you are.'

'So are you. You look done in. Shall I brew you a cup of tea?'

'But you've just finished cleaning...'

'It won't take a minute.'

Afterwards, they sat side by side in the kitchen sipping the tea, the house settling around them, dream-infused fantasies of a slumbering household, of journeying to the faraway lands they called home and into waiting, welcoming arms the same hue as theirs, wafting on the cold night air thick with intrigue.

'This is strong and spicy, just what I didn't know I wanted.' Charity smiled at Divya.

In the quiet dark, her eyes glowed soft and wistful, and lines dragged her young face down so it looked old before its time.

'I worry about them, my parents,' Charity said, her voice

melancholy. 'My da has never been the same since the war. And Ma, well... After Connor, the doctor said she shouldn't have more children.'

'Ah,' Divya said, reaching across and patting Charity's hand gently, offering solace the only way she knew how.

Charity smiled at her, eyes shining. 'I love Paddy to bits. Cannot imagine life without him. But his arrival into the world did for Ma.'

Divya nodded, squeezing Charity's hand.

'Ma is always happier when the nuns come,' Charity said. 'And that makes me happy. I feel for her, bedridden while longing for home. She knows she can never go back and through the nuns, and their memories, she is able to visit home for a while. They bring Ireland to her.' Charity's eyes far away, soft with sadness. 'I wish she would be happy here, realise that this is her home now, here with her children. But I do understand. It must be horrible, stuck in a room, cared for by your daughter when she can spare a minute, hemmed in by four walls.'

They sat there, drinking their tea as life went on outside, regardless of the time, the street busy at all hours: the clanking of cranes, men walking past, boots pounding on cobbles, a burst of laughter, a shout, a lone dog's plaintive howl.

Divya has offered to help Charity with her parents but...

'No, Divya, it wouldn't feel right. It's my duty. I want to do it.' Charity smiling softly and squeezing Divya's hand. 'I so appreciate it. Nobody else has offered, ever. And you do far more here than is required or asked for anyway.'

'I...'

'You go above and beyond what is expected of you. You are so good with the boys and so good to me. It is appreciated, so very much.' Her eyes shining with love and gratitude. Then, softly, 'Ma was worse than usual today. I think she's sickening for her child-hood home.'

Divya can understand that. Although, for Divya, home is just a concept, intangible and undefined. She is not welcome at the village that she called home for most of her life. She will belong in India without question, her colour not a bar or a scourge, but she will have to start from scratch.

She lies awake at night worrying.

But, she thinks then, she will take it one step at a time. First, she will earn enough to book a passage back. Then, once she is in India, she will figure things out.

In fact, hasn't she managed well enough so far, even after the worst happened and she was stranded here, in a strange country with no place to stay and no means of returning home?

But, as for booking her passage to India at the end of the year, what if the war starts before then?

'But Chamberlain declared peace for our time. He signed the Munich peace pact with Hitler,' Benjamin Juma, one of the lodgers, who is from East Africa, says.

'Hitler will not heed it. Britain has pledged support to Poland in the event of an invasion. Shelters are being built. The Military Training Act has introduced conscription. All this indicates that the powers that be are getting ready for war,' Mr Devine, who happens to be visiting, says.

'No need for conscription,' Fergus, the oldest of Charity's brothers, only recently a teenager, declares. 'We will all sign up.'

'You need a clip on the ear, you do. You're too young,' Charity cries.

'We will fight for our country,' Charity's siblings chant as one.

'Away with you, shoo,' Charity huffs.

'The Royal Armoured Corps has been formed and Women's Royal Naval Service re-established,' Mr Devine is saying.

'Will you join the navy, Charity?' the boys ask eagerly.

'And who will run the boarding house? You lot?' she asks.

'But we will be at war. Like Mr Devine says, the government is already preparing for it,' Fergus cries earnestly. 'There's no shying away from it. There will be a war and we will all sign up.'

'Not another war!' protests old Mr Venables, who is deaf and blind on his left side thanks to shrapnel wounding him when he fought in the Great War.

The older men are tragic-eyed when they speak of the Great War, their women sighing, their gazes far away, shining with the memories of loved ones they have lost and all they had to endure. It is the young who have a skip in their step, the young who are too young to have memories of death and loss that have hollowed their parents' and siblings' faces. They speak blithely of fighting the Hun and driving them away and showing Hitler what's what, and their parents and older siblings tut and suck their teeth and turn away.

30

Each morning, Divya wakes in her small, functional room to the sounds of doors banging up and down the street and the thud of boots on cobbles as workers march towards the docks and surrounding factories.

The plaintive call of seagulls, the swell and surge of the Thames, clanks and bangs accompanying activity at the docks. The smell of smoke and industry and a crisp, cold new dawn.

Divya is used to the thuds and calls as men unload cargo and the booming foghorns of ships no longer startle her now. In fact, she sleeps right through all the noise and mayhem that carries on outside regardless of whether it's the middle of the day or the thick of night.

The breeze from the Thames, carrying the scent of spices and sawdust, angles into Divya's room through the small window, which somehow lets the cold air in even when it is shut.

And indoors, the patter of Charity's brothers' feet and their giggles as they, always up early, bound up and down the stairs.

Outside, the sky – once unfamiliar, grey and gloomy with sun struggling to pierce through, even in summer, now commonplace, so Divya doesn't bat an eyelid as she yawns, washes in the sink, and makes her way downstairs to the kitchen to begin preparing breakfast.

'Miss Ram, what are you going to cook today?' the boys call, beaming at her.

'I'm so hungry for your food,' Paddy declares, rubbing his concave stomach.

No matter how much she feeds them, they never seem to put on weight. They are balls of energy, running everywhere, getting under feet and in trouble.

'They were born with hollow legs,' Charity says fondly.

'Will you help me then?' Divya asks the boys and they nod eagerly, and although they make more work for her, spilling ingredients and creating mess, she wouldn't trade it for the world.

Charity will come in soon, yawning and bleary-eyed, to make porridge for her parents. Neither of them is an adventurous eater and they have stuck to their plain, milky porridge.

Divya will make breakfast for the boys and the lodgers and once the cooking and cleaning is done, she will start prepping for lunch. And after lunch, same again for supper. In between, she will make tea for any lodgers who are around and fancy it. She will make a pot the Indian way and another the English way and she will also prepare coffee for anyone preferring it to tea, whether Indian or English. She will serve snacks with it – cucumber and jam sandwiches, onion bhajis, potato pakoras, spinach parathas with mint chutney, carrot halva, milk cake, rice kheer.

When she has a spare minute, she helps Charity with what-ever needs doing and although Charity protests – 'You've enough to do without taking this on as well' – Divya can see she is grateful for the extra pair of hands, which equates to a few minutes shaved off an incredibly long day, a few minutes more with her parents.

'I don't know what I'd do without you,' Charity says often. 'You've taken over the kitchen and the daily trips to the market and that's two huge chores I can cross off my list. Every day, I would dread the inevitable task of coming up with something to cook that the boys would eat. But whatever I did, however hard I tried, they would complain and I would be at my wits' end. I wanted them to get their nutrition but I didn't know how. I am many things but not a cook. Now they actually eat instead of grumbling and protesting and moving food around their plate and they even ask for seconds! And I don't have to worry about their health as they seem to be eating more vegetables than ever before. As am I.'

'It's because Divya cooks them in such tasty ways. They don't taste like veggies at all,' Paddy says.

'I agree.' Charity beams. 'Thank you, Divya. You are a godsend.'

'Thank *you*,' Divya says. 'I'm doing what I enjoy for people I care about *and* getting paid for it. I love cooking and coming up with new recipes and seeing what works and what doesn't, what everyone likes and what only some do.'

'Well rather you than me,' Charity says and gives her a hug. She smells of exhaustion. 'You've changed our lives.'

'And you've changed mine.'

Divya enjoys the autonomy she has over the kitchen – she is in sole charge. Charity does not interfere but allows her to tweak recipes and menus as she sees fit, based on what is popular and tickles the boarders' and the boys' and Charity's fancy. Divya loves the challenge of buying the ingredients and creating a menu that suits a wide range of palates while also sticking to the budget that Charity has allocated for the week. She adores working alongside Charity, ensuring the smooth running of the boarding house; Charity rushing about, sorting this leak and that complaint, while Divya manages the kitchen and anything else that she can help with. Charity treats Divya like an equal and here, in Charity's company, at the boarding house, Divya feels useful, needed, valued and appreciated.

31

Divya's cooking is going from strength to strength. Its fame has spread. She concocts new recipes and tries them out on the lodgers and on Charity and her brothers, who tuck in enthusiastically. Others have started coming in, having heard of her cooking, wanting to try it.

The first time this happened was at the end of Divya's first month managing the kitchen, when Benjamin Juma turned up, one evening, with a man as dark and tall as himself. 'My friend Abdi has heard so much about your cooking that he'd like to sample some. Do you have a plate going spare? He's willing to pay for the privilege, of course.'

Divya had consulted Charity. 'I do have food going spare – you know I always cook extra just in case more people than usual ask for seconds.'

Charity waved the man's half-crown aside. 'Please join us.'

When he had eaten his fill, Abdi was effusive in his praise. 'I loved it so much. Benjamin is right, it is Indian food but the spices, they conjure up home for me. This is truly the first time that I have felt satisfied with a meal I have had in this country.

Thank you kindly,' he said to Divya, eyes shining. Then, to Charity, 'Please, I'd like to pay. For I want to come again, you see. Tomorrow, if that's all right?' His gaze hopeful.

How could they turn him away? Charity was too kind and Divya was moved by Abdi's heartfelt enjoyment of her cooking.

After that, more people came, friends of lodgers and *their* friends and acquaintances.

'Goodness, Divya, we're feeding the entire population of sailors from around the docks, it appears. I am doubling your wages, starting now.' Charity exalted after the first week when the dining room was busy all day, with people coming and going.

'It's all well and good and I like that the dining room is so busy and full. But how do I know how much to cook each day? I don't want food to go to waste in case I end up cooking too much and not enough people come,' Divya cried.

'Your food will never go to waste. I will eat anything that remains,' Fergus declared fervently.

'And me,' Paddy piped in, not wanting to be left behind.

Connor, as usual, just smiled, his eyes twinkling stars. But it was he who came with a plan. 'Stick a piece of paper at the door and ask the men to sign in if they are planning to come the next day and if so, for which meal. That way, you will know how many to cater for each day.'

'Goodness, Connor, you hardly speak but when you do, you come up with the best ideas,' his sister exclaimed, while Divya cried, 'That's exactly what I need, Connor, thank you.'

Connor blushed, turning away to hide his pleasure.

* * *

Connor's system has worked. Men sign up the previous day and if they know they're going to be coming for the whole week, then they make sure to note it. Thus Divya knows roughly how many to cook for each day and accordingly, she plans how much of each ingredient to buy at the market when she plans her menus. She always makes more than needed but no matter how much extra she makes, the food is all gone by the end of the day. The dining room at the lodging house is full to overflowing and bright and noisy with chatter and scents, accents from every part of the world.

Divya asks African sailors for their recipes from home and goes to the markets, and failing that, vendors just off the ships that have arrived from that part of the world and buys ackee and plantain and other exotic ingredients required for the recipes from them. She does the same for the Chinese and Nepalese lodgers and their friends, buying the Chinese ingredients from Mr Lee down the road, and the Nepalese vegetables and spices from the Indian market traders. And when she cooks their recipes, they are touched. They thank her profusely, eyes glowing with joy and homesickness. 'You do magic,' they say. 'You bring home to us.'

Every morning, after the exodus of the men south to the docks and the factories surrounding them, the women come out with buckets to scrub the section of pavement outside their front doors to a shine. They call out to each other merrily as they scour and polish until their knees hurt, each one determined to have her little slice of half-moon better and shinier than everyone else's.

'What are you cooking today, love? Smells wonderful enough to rid us of the stink of the Thames,' they laugh as they call to Divya.

'Yes, my dear, it surely does,' cry Mr Stone and Mr Brown. They usually sit playing chess (and keeping a keen eye on the goings-on in the street) on the slice of pavement in between the public house and the boarding house on stools and a table they have dragged out there. But now, they have moved indoors because it is storming a tantrum.

Mr Stone and Mr Brown are enthusiastic proponents of Divya's cooking.

'I didn't know what I was missing, sticking to my meat and two veg all my life. I thought I was being adventurous when I added pepper to food, and daring when I opted for mustard,' Mr Stone loves to say.

For Mr Brown, like with the other displaced sailors, Divya's food conjures up the flavours of home. Africa. He had arrived on English soil as a sailor absconding the brutality on board the ship where he'd worked for a time. Even now, his eyes took on a hollow, glassy sheen when he spoke of that time. 'I came here and never left. There was always work to be had on the docks and the factories. They were in need of men to help unload cargo, unpack crates and pack them again with different goods. So here I am. And I do enjoy beating Mr Stone at chess.'

'Not often,' Mr Stone interjected.

'Too often,' Mr Brown averred. His accent still carried the hum and rhythm of his homeland. The music of it chiming in every word. The longing. 'I will go back, perhaps, some day.' His voice deep and wistful, eyes haunted by yearning. 'The ships arriving from there, laden with sugar and rum, carrying the scent of home. I breathe in deeply of it.' He smiled but it was the saddest smile Divya had ever seen, and her eyes pricked with hot tears.

He had never married.

'I dreamed of having a family, a wife and a brood of children. But where would I find a wife here? And who would have me? What would I offer them? Ability to lift and move and pack and unpack crates and beat Mr Stone at chess?' He laughed, *boom*

boom boom, but it was oh so melancholy. Mr Brown had packed away his hopes like he did all the stuff he unloaded from the ships, his dreams of home like the thick, yellow fog that descended over the river overnight and washed away with dawn.

'Truth is, my darlin', I doubt I will recognise my home when, if, I get there. It has moved on without me. The sailors in the ships coming from there, they speak in the sing-song cadence of home but what they say, when they describe it, I do not recognise. I do not know the home they are from. I do not know the country they belong to. It has moved on without me.' His voice melancholy as the cry of a peacock that has lost its mate.

'We would take shelter in the public house when the weather was too blustery for our old bodies to cope with before you took charge of the kitchen here,' Mr Stone and Mr Brown tell Divya. 'Now, we come here, and also take all of our meals here. Now then,' they say, looking about the dining room, which is packed to bursting, not a chair or table free. 'This place is getting too crowded for comfort. We can't hear ourselves think, let alone speak. Isn't it time you set up a restaurant of your own?'

The idea takes root in Divya's head, a fantastic dream spawning wings.

What if I really could? Wouldn't that be wonderful? If there is war, I wouldn't be able to travel home for a while so I could do this instead, just until I can go home.

But how to go about it?

Stop spinning fantasies that can never become reality. What's got into you? her conscience chides.

Nevertheless, the dream dangles, juicily delectable as the first mango of the season, before her eyes and that night, she goes to sleep hugging it to herself.

32

Now Divya queues up for the best deals from the market vendors before they close up for the day. Smog is settling over the river, thick yellow, marbled with smoke.

Multi-hued flags of laundry strung in the tiny plots of land behind the tenements flap in the fresh and nippy breeze, which wafts an amalgam of scents: the salt and silt tang of the river clashing with the sugar and timber, grain and custard aromas from the factories beside the docks.

A steam hooter emits a God-almighty foghorn siren call, making the queuing women wince and a slumbering baby startle awake and start wailing. Six o'clock.

Sailors and factory shift workers walk past, some on the way home, others just starting, clutching the sandwiches wrapped in paper that their wives have packed for them.

The other women in the queue nod and smile at Divya as they rock babies in one arm while clutching their shopping baskets in the other, as they shout at their children to, 'Geroff the road this instant,' as they chinwag and complain about the cost of food going up.

'And 'ow are we supposed to feed the family? Shocking, so it is.'

'And the king and queen gallivanting in New York, so they are.'

'All right for some.'

'Ah, they're all right, our king and queen. Must maintain relations, don't they, if there be a war like they're saying.'

'Another war! I lost my brother and pa to the one before. I don't want to lose no more,' Mrs Boon spits.

'And wait till you 'ear this: my gel, instead of 'elping at home, is going on about joining the newly created Women's Auxiliary Air Force. Got ideas so she has, that one.' A hint of pride gilding Mrs Ross's voice at her daughter's stubbornness, even as she complains.

'Women's Land Army has been re-formed, they're saying,' one of the other women says.

'Preparing for war, they is. Mark me words, there'll be an announcement soon.'

Just what Mr Devine says each time he visits, Divya thinks, her stomach dipping. Even with her wages being increased now that they seem to be feeding the whole street and more besides at the lodging house, she still won't have saved enough for her passage home with a little left to tide her over for the first few weeks in India until the end of the year at least. And it appears by all accounts that war is imminent. That means her return home to India will have to be postponed...

And what will war entail for someone like her who is not of England but stopping here until she can earn the means to go home?

Will she be able to continue at the lodging house? She loves it there but it will all change with war, will it not? Charity says people will still need a place to stay and the lodging house will still be in business, but Divya can't help but worry.

* * *

The women who've already done their shopping and made headway with supper have settled themselves on the street in chairs that they have dragged out of their homes. They sit beside their polished half-circles, nattering away while ostensibly getting on with their chores. As per usual, there's not much in the way of good weather, a glower of clouds damning the sky, straggly rays of valiant sun struggling through. But the ladies take scant notice, cheerily gossiping away amongst themselves, calling down the street when another of their posse hefts a chair out to join them. Their flowery pinnies are dotted with flour, and scarves hold their hair in place; the frisky breeze, redolent with late-spring scents, smoke and grilled meat and ripening fruit, inciting wayward curls that have managed to escape the stricture of their scarves into a merry dance.

They keep a beady eye on their offspring playing on the street as they knit or darn or shell peas into their capacious aproned laps, yelling at them to, 'Leave the 'opscotch aside and get out of the bloomin' way of Mr Crosby's 'orses. Can't you 'ear them coming a-clattering down the street, eh?'

The children give up on hopscotch and start a game of hide-and-seek, nipping up and down the alleyways, playing peekaboo amongst the washing drying on lines to more hue and cry from their mothers, 'Git your grubby hands off them clothes or you'll be off to the wash house to do the laundry right this minute.'

One of the children comes running up to his mother. He is covered from head to toe in mud, only his teeth shining happy yellow from his splattered face.

'Look Ma, what I git from mudlarking on the Thames.'

'Apart from a clip on your ear, eh, 'arry,' his mother cries, making good her threat.

''Ow, what was that for?' the lad protests, jumping away.

'Lookit the mud an' soot on you,' his mother sighs, shaking her head.

Raucous cheers and chatter, smoke and hops and pungent vinegar drift from the brewery down the road where men are celebrating the end of the week, spending their wages less the housekeeping they've to give their wives – at least that is their intention. Whether it survives after a drink or two has warmed their bellies is another matter.

Some, emboldened by the ale they've consumed, exit the public house to slink surreptitiously to the Chinese gambling house down the street, hoping to escape matronly eyes spying on behalf of their wives, but here, they are bound to be disappointed.

'Don't think I don't see you, Charlie. Your wife will be expecting her housekeeping money to look after your nippers and another one on the way, sure as anything.'

'I'm only going to double the money, Mrs Kerridge,' Charlie says in a small voice.

'Ah so's you think. The foolish and misplaced confidence of youth, eh.' Mrs Kerridge shakes her head vigorously and goes back to her knitting.

Seagulls call mournfully, blots on the overcast sky.

A skirmish erupts among the children playing with marbles on a stoop nearby.

'You lot play nicely now or I'll take the marbles away,' their mother warns tiredly.

'But Ma...'

Their mother turns away, saying, tightly, 'I've to see to the bubba. No arguing or I'll cuff the lot of you.'

The sign of the rag merchant down the road clatters loudly in the breeze:

Bring your rags here.

The warm scent of toffee from the man, haunted eyes in a drawn face, who walks up and down hawking it from a basket slung across his neck makes Divya's stomach rumble hungrily. The toffee looks so enticing – she can imagine its heady caramel sweetness.

I must try and make it. It would be very popular served as part of the teatime snacks.

Indian shawls, African dolls, even dancing monkeys – everything and anything you can think of, and things you cannot imagine, arrive on the ships from all parts of the world and are hawked here in the market stalls.

Mrs Rosenbaum sweeps the street outside her shop meticulously although a burst of wind displaces the dirt she has just cleared, flinging it right back to her stoop.

The other women fight over the dregs of the produce at the market stalls but Divya doesn't mind waiting her turn in the queue – the vegetables she wants are not popular.

'And yet, you do delicious magic with them,' everyone who eats her food exclaims. 'These vegetables and herbs we haven't laid eyes on, let alone know how to use.'

The market traders like her as she buys the stuff that they can never usually get rid of.

But today...

'Ah, but you've competition, Miss Ram.'

'Competition?'

'Someone else bought all the coriander and mint and aubergine and okra off me.'

'What? Who?'

'A lascar. He's recently been promoted, he says, and is cooking for his fellows with whom he voyaged here as thanks for their hard work. A meal like they would have at home.'

It is the same story with the other traders from whom she buys her produce. 'The lascar got here first.'

She is disappointed and upset. 'But I am your regular customer.'

'He paid the amount we asked,' the market stall vendors say. 'He didn't even haggle!' They sound pleasantly surprised at this last, for the women on West India Dock Road (including Divya, a quick learner), will not rest until they get the best possible bargains and the vendors, although they try and put up a fight, are helpless in the face of this concentrated assault.

'Where is this man?' Divya asks.

'Don't know where he is stopping, gel.'

Ah well, she thinks, looking sadly at her empty basket. She will have to come up with something from the tins Charity has stocked for emergencies. And tomorrow, she will get here earlier, before this man, whoever he is.

As if the vendors have heard her dejected thoughts, one of them calls, 'Over here, gel.'

She turns, hopeful that this vendor will have some vegetables for her, and finds herself looking into familiar dancing eyes, smiling from a face that is at once known and (this stuns her with a jolt of surprise) missed.

Yet, she cannot place him for a moment even as her heart sings with recognition.

'Ma'am,' he says, smiling. 'Fancy seeing you here.'

Ma'am. Only one person has called her that and meant it. And it comes to her then, who this is. The lascar from on board the ship, when Divya was travelling to this country on the other side of the world to all that was familiar and known, who was so kind and respectful to her.

Raghu.

33

'How are you doing, ma'am?' Raghu asks, his eyes twinkling. 'What brings you to West India Dock Road?'

'I...' Divya takes a breath, still coming to terms with this miracle of seeing Raghu so unexpectedly, the lascar who was so kind to her on the voyage here when she was out of her depth. She had assumed he was still on his travels, circumnavigating the world while working on board ships. 'I am staying at the Paddy O'Kelly Boarding and Lodging House.'

'Ah.' His eyes shine with understanding. 'Your employers fired you when they no longer needed your services.'

'I always knew I would be let go when the boys had settled with a new nanny...' Even as she chats to Raghu about this, experiencing a pang of missing for James and Hugh, she marvels at how easy it is to talk to him, tell him what has happened to her since they saw each other last in the first few minutes of meeting him, knowing instinctively that he will understand.

And sure enough... 'Ah, but they didn't pay for your passage back.'

He gets it without her having to tell him.

'Yes.'

His eyes pools of empathy, care shining out of them. And suddenly, she recalls what he had tried to tell her on the ship as they were parting ways: 'I have heard...' and then he had stopped, not wanting to worry her, perhaps. Instead, he had insisted on giving her a means of contacting him. 'Just in case,' he had said, not specifying what that eventuality might be.

She says, 'You thought this might happen, which is why you repeatedly told me where I might find you if I needed help...'

'Yes, it happens more often than not. We lascars see so many ayahs destitute and abandoned here in an unfamiliar country not knowing the language or customs.' His eyes sad, voice frustrated. Then, smiling gently at her, 'But you are looking well. I am glad I bumped into you, although of course I wish your employers had honoured their promise and you hadn't had to stop here at all. I don't think I'm wrong in thinking that your stay in the lodging house here on West India Dock Road had not factored into your plans when you were making the journey over. I hope you are all right?'

Divya is just about to reply when one of the vendors calls, 'Ah, so you've met the man who's bought all the produce you wanted.'

And now, Divya's eyes land on the basket Raghu is holding, bulging with the gently wilting coriander and mint, ginger and garlic and chillies, aubergine and okra that she usually buys.

The street is quiet it seems, poised for a showdown. All eyes upon them.

Even Mrs Rosenbaum, who usually minds her own business, is watching curiously, now she's given up on trying to rid her stoop of every last speck of dirt. Her husband who is sitting beside her on the chairs they have dragged out, like the rest of the street, peers over the top of the newspaper he has open before him.

Men standing against the crumbling, soot-stained pub wall, smoking and setting the world to rights, cry, 'Ha, lascar mate, you're in trouble.'

'This here Miss Ram makes the best curry in the whole of the East End, in my opinion, and you've stolen her produce,' says Mr Stone, who plays chess with Mr Brown outside the pub all day long.

'I was not aware it was her produce,' Raghu says, clearing his throat nervously.

'We did try to tell you, mate, but you said you needed it to cook for your men and you would pay whatever we charged for it, no haggling,' one of the market vendors hollers.

'I have been promoted to head lascar.' Raghu's face glowing as he says this. 'And on the passage over, my fellow lascars worked really hard and I want to treat them. I like cooking and after the dry and bland food we've had to endure on board the ship, I wanted my fellow lascars and myself to have a proper home cooked meal of the kind we grew up eating.' Raghu's voice is soft but carries in the unnatural silence that has descended upon the street.

The children have stopped playing, the matrons have ceased gossiping – why would they when there is fresh gossip brewing right here on their street – and everyone is watching avidly. Even the dock cranes and the dockside factories appear to be quiet for once – perhaps they too are rubbernecking on the drama. The scent of hulled berries and boiling sugar from the jam-processing plant mingles with the zesty cinnamon and cardamom and ginger aroma wafting from the spice mills and the sulphurous stink of the tannery.

'But you undercut Miss Ram,' cries Mr Brown. 'We won't have curry now.'

'You will, Mr Brown don't you worry,' Divya says, 'I am not, how do you say it, a one-trick pony. I can make curries with no vegetables.'

'Hear, hear,' the whole street cheers.

'So can I,' declares Raghu, eyes twinkling at Divya. 'And I bet you, mine are better.'

'Ooh, he's a feisty one,' Mrs Kerridge breathes.

'And not bad-looking either,' Mrs Boon sighs dreamily.

Emboldened by the reception he's getting, Raghu sets down a challenge.

Turning to Mr Stone, he says, 'You say Miss Ram's curries are the best in the East End.'

'That's right, young man.' Mr Stone nods.

'But you haven't tasted mine,' Raghu says.

Gasps echo up and down the street, 'oohs' and, 'aahs' and, 'What do you say, Miss Ram?'

What *will* she say?

The door to the lodging house opens and Fergus, Connor and Paddy tumble out, followed by Charity, who's wiping wet hands upon her apron. She would have been cleaning the privy or the sink but must have hurried outside when the boys told her about the commotion on the street involving, 'Our very own Miss Ram'.

She looks at Divya and raises an eyebrow.

And at the sight of her friend – this woman who has given Divya shelter and a job and an identity as a chef – Divya finds her voice.

She clears her throat and the street falls silent, the smoggy, yellow air thick with anticipation. 'I say...' she looks at Raghu and smiles with a courage she doesn't feel, 'that you are so confident because you haven't tasted *my* curries.'

And once again, the street erupts in cheer. 'I say, Miss Ram! Hear hear!'

'I tell you what,' says Mr Stone, setting down the knight in his hand decisively upon the chess board. 'Why don't you both make your curries and I will be the judge of whose is better?'

'Why only you?' Mrs Kerridge grumbles. 'That's not fair, that is.'

'But I'm the one who said Miss Ram's curries are the best in the East End,' says Mr Stone. 'A statement this young'un challenged.'

'Well, if that's the case,' Divya says, 'then I will buy half the produce off you for what you bought it for,' she tells Raghu.

'All right.'

And thus it is decided.

'We will cook for the street,' Divya says and once again, everyone erupts in cheer. 'You invite your lascars so they can have the meal you promised – but I have a feeling they'll like my food better,' she says boldly.

'Is that so?' Raghu twinkles at her.

'What about us?' cry the market stallholders.

'You are invited too.' Divya smiles.

'Here, you can have our remaining produce for half price. Divide it between you.' They beam.

'Tomorrow evening here at 6 p.m.,' Mr Stone announces. 'We will have a street party and curry tasting and announce the winner.'

'Ale at half price all tomorrow evening to wash down the curry,' the publican, Mr Barney, declares, red head, cheeks and beard dangling from the open window of his pub.

Cheers all round.

'A street party, hooray!' the children scream. 'Will there be balloons?'

'What about ices?'

'And bunting?'

'Now hark here, you sproglets,' cackles toothless Mrs Neville, the children of the street flinching discreetly away from her. (The children of West India Dock Road are convinced she's a witch, who brews potions in a cauldron in her tenement. 'It smells something terrible – like a rat died in there. Perhaps it did, perhaps she needs it for her potion. And not only that, it bubbles vomit-green and frothy,' Paddy told Divya, his eyes wide and afraid, his voice earnest. 'I've watched her make it through the window myself, so I have. She was mumbling spells, I swear.' His voice breathy with terrified intrigue.)

'I tell you what there will be,' Mrs Neville shakes a bony finger at her fearful audience, even as she guffaws loudly. 'There will be curry and plenty of it.'

34

The day of the curry fest, as the residents of West India Dock Road are calling it, dawns to frantic activity in the lodging house.

Charity's brothers are helping, or getting underfoot is more like it. The lodgers have gathered to offer to taste and see if the curries are up to the highest standard.

The previous evening, once the curry competition was declared, smoke and excitement had rippled up and down the street, colouring the nippy air briny blue. The doyennes had stopped sunning themselves on the street, and shouting at their children while keeping a beady eye on the goings on. They had even given up keeping tabs on whose spouse was sneaking off to the Chinese gambling dens in the ever hopeful but ever dashed promise of doubling their money. They had stopped spying on the errant husband of one of their own, slinking to the pub to wash the housekeeping money down the watering hole and tumbling, not always in a straight line out of the pub, trying (and failing) under the watchful eyes of the street to walk steadily home. Instead, they had snapped to attention.

They had fixed their unwavering gazes upon Mr Stone and

Mr Brown, and Mr Rosenbaum, who watched them play chess but never joined in, grunting and tutting in disgust whenever he thought one of them had made a silly move.

'You play then,' Mr Stone would grumble, moving his roll up from one toothless gum to the other.

'No, no, I will beat you black and blue and there will be war to rival the last one. No more war; we want peace, I say,' Mr Rosenbaum declared.

'Ah, so you won't play for the sake of peace, eh,' Mr Brown cried. 'I say you're afraid that I will beat you.'

'Never,' Mr Rosenbaum blustered. 'I'm afraid that I will beat the both of you and then...'

'I will beat you,' Mr Stone averred. 'For I am the champion.'

'Rubbish,' Mr Brown boomed. 'I won the last three games in a row and have won twice as many games as you have since we started playing against each other.'

'Stuff and nonsense. Now you listen here...'

The evening of Divya's standoff against Raghu and subsequent curry challenge, the matrons of the street bravely waded into the fracas.

Mrs Rosenbaum, pulling her scarf down over her ears, looked fearfully at the gathered women, from her perch in front of her clean(ish) stoop across the street.

'That's enough,' Mrs Neville barked – quite loudly given that she was toothless.

The men – and not only Mr Stone, Mr Brown and Mr Rosenbaum, but all the males in the street, including the young ones, stopped and stared at her, quaking a little in their patched-up boots.

'Now then listen here, you lot: if we are having a curry competition, we need tasters,' Mrs Kerridge, not to be outdone by Mrs Neville, said.

At that, Mr Stone stood up as straight as he could – even so, he only came up to Mrs Kerridge's formidable bosom, as he was slightly hunchbacked and not very tall to begin with. Nevertheless, he said, trying to look anywhere but at Mrs Kerridge's magnificent breasts, heaving as they were with righteous emotion, but it was a losing battle as they were right in his eyeline. 'As you might recall, I was the one who issued the challenge, so I will be the judge.'

'Why are you squinting? 'Ave you got something in your eye?' Mrs Kerridge asked and Mr Stone blushed as red as the publican's hair.

'It has to be someone who knows curry,' Mrs Kerridge declared stoutly, Mrs Neville and the other matrons nodding assent.

And the men, defeated by this feminine onslaught, gave in of course.

'It will, without question, have to be Munnoo,' Mrs Neville quacked and once again, everyone nodded agreement. For Munnoo was the only person they knew who knew curry, had grown up with it, besides Divya and now, Raghu, of course.

Munnoo had arrived in England from India with his English Lord, as he was fond of telling anyone who would listen, at the turn of the century, as a young boy of fifteen. 'Nobody else could shave my master quite as well as myself so when he decided to move back home, he brought me along.'

When his master had died, a few years ago, Munnoo was left with nothing but a posh accent and an instruction in how to look after English gentry. But nobody else wanted him. He had ended up at the docks, hoping for a passage home although, as he said, he didn't know India any more.

Munnoo spoke like an upper-class Englishman and had 'high and mighty ways', reckoned the street, even though he was as dark as sin. He was now a permanent fixture at West India Docks. He had lived for a time at the Strangers' Home for Asiatics, Africans and South Sea Islanders and once it closed, he lodged where he could, doing odd jobs at the docks to pay for his lodging, day on day. He had stayed at Charity's once or twice when she had a room free.

'I let him pay what he can,' Charity sighed. 'When he can't afford the other places, he comes here. It is a step down in the world for him, you see.'

Since Munnoo was considered posh by everyone in the street, and by virtue of also being Indian, he was asked by Mr Stone and Mr Brown and Mrs Kerridge to judge the competition.

'And as to the rest,' said Mr Stone, always fair (which was why, he liked to say, he had risen up the ranks in his factory to head foreman back in the day), despite the fact that he had been ousted from being judge, 'let's have one representative from each community living on the West India Dock Road, one of each of us, Irish, Chinese, Jewish, African and English, to also taste the food and judge it, although Munnoo's decision will be final, what do you say?'

'Hear, hear,' everyone cheered.

'And I will oversee the competition,' said Mr Stone officiously, 'make sure nobody is cheating, mind.'

'Cheating,' snorted Mrs Boon. 'We're all respectable here on the West India Dock Road, so we are.'

It was decided that Mr and Mrs Rosenbaum would be the Jewish representatives: 'Make sure to have something kosher, mind.'

Mrs Kerridge: English.

Mrs Murphy (by virtue of being the oldest Irishwoman in the street, beating Mrs Neville by a whisker) would represent the Irish contingent.

Mr Lee from the gambling house although to all intents and purposes, he ran a small Chinese grocery – the legal front – from where Divya regularly bought spices, would represent the Chinese coterie.

Mr Brown would represent the African community.

Mr Brown, Munnoo and the other displaced here at West India Dock Road longed for 'home' even knowing it was just a concept, rife with yearning, that the countries they had hailed from had moved on in their absence, becoming unrecognisable, no longer the nostalgia-tinted abodes from their memories, populating their dreams. Divya's food, they told her often, brought this home, that existed only in their heads, to them, and for this Divya was pleased and thankful.

I will not allow too long to pass before I head home, war or not, Divya promised herself. Forever longing, forever unsatisfied, forever displaced, forever unbelonging. Like Mr Brown, like Munnoo, missing home but knowing that if they did go back, they would be outsiders there too.

I will not, several years on, when I am old and grey, regret things I didn't do, dreams I didn't realise.

35

Now it is morning and the lodgers have gathered to taste the dishes Divya is frantically preparing, the kitchen steamy and redolent with a clash of spicy and sweet scents, caramelised sugar and sizzling onions, crushed mint and shredded ginger, cardamom and cinnamon stewing in milk, the zest of roasting spices: chilli, cumin, coriander, pepper causing sneezing fits. The lodgers' contribution, they say, is 'in an advisory capacity, but vital, mind': to sample the food to see if it will pass muster with the judges.

'They will be very strict, mind,' says Billy Beynon, who likes to pontificate. ('Loves the sound of his own voice a little too much, does our Billy,' his friends tease fondly.)

Now, Billy declares, 'Your food needs to be liked by several different people with varied tastes. For example, Mr and Mrs Rosenbaum, apart from being kosher, like bland food. Mr Lee likes spicy but a different kind of spice to Indian. Same with Mr Brown although I have it on good authority that he'll eat anything, if he's hungry enough.' Billy's mates nod assent. 'And he will, of course, choose you. That's one vote guaranteed.'

'But he mustn't. It's supposed to be impartial and above board,' Paddy, a stickler for rules (although he's not above bending some every so often), cries.

'Oh Mr Brown says he's impartial, but he has a soft spot for Miss Ram and will choose her, definitely.' Billy says, undeterred by young Paddy.

'But how? Mr Stone says the judges will not know whose dish is which,' Paddy protests.

Yet again, he is ignored.

'Now Mrs Kerridge is a different kettle of fish altogether: 'ard as nails that one and very difficult to please. Then there's Mrs Murphy. Now she is the outlier. All depends on her mood, whether she's feeling Irish or English or something else altogether. Munnoo – he will be difficult to please as well; he can be very critical. It is going to be tough, Miss Ram, even for you. And I say this even knowing your curries have ousted my all-time favourite of pie and mash and parsley liquor to top favourite spot. And that was tough as there is nothing I crave on a Friday night quite as much. Or should I say, I used to until you came along and converted me to your delicious curries. My growing belly agrees,' Billy says, rubbing his stomach proudly.

'Growing! Two bubbas could fit in there,' his friends joke.

'Ach enough already,' Billy cries.

'Thank you, Mr Beynon,' Divya says.

'You do your best, gel. It will be more than enough.' Mr Quinn nods gently. 'He won't know what hit him, this lascar.'

'Ah but those lascars are good, you know. I've seen them concoct great feasts with very few ingredients,' Isaiah, who has a gambling habit and has lived with lascars, four to a tiny room meant for one, says. 'They come up with delicious dishes using the most basic ingredients.'

The other lodgers turn on him, 'Watch it. Whose side are you on?'

'I'm only telling Miss Ram here what she has to contend with,' he says.

'I will beat him,' Divya says, with a greater conviction that she feels. She's not happy with the vegetable curry – it doesn't have the nutty flavour she was going for. And the dhal is too spicy for Western palates. And the kheer... Oh God, what has she let herself in for?

Don't panic. Just cook. You've made these dishes so many times before. You can do this.

She takes a breath and turns to Charity's brothers, who are hovering beside her, ostensibly to help, but in actual fact getting in her way. 'Try my pilau rice, please, boys.'

'It looks beautiful. How did you make it multi-coloured? It is like a rainbow feast for the eyes,' says Connor O'Kelly.

And Divya's anxiety disappears in the wake of this boy's heart-felt compliment. She is overwhelmed. It means the world coming from, of all people, especially this child. For Connor rarely speaks and when he does, it is only if he deems it too important to go without.

'Thank you, Connor,' she says. Then, 'May I?'

He nods and she ruffles his hair as thanks. He shrugs but she can see him hiding his smile behind his arm. He doesn't like to be hugged but he does allow ruffling of his hair when he is in the mood for it.

'Miss Ram's cooking has made a poet of you, has it?' ribs Charity.

He smiles some more, turning away to hide it.

'Why is it called pillow rice?' Paddy asks.

'Not pillow, silly,' Fergus mocks. 'Pelove.'

'Pillow, pelove, what's the difference?' Paddy is petulant, lower lip pushed out in a pout.

'Let's see how it tastes, then.' Fergus is eager.

'Only a smidgeon each, mind; it needs to feed not only the whole street, but the entire East End, judging from the commotion out there,' Charity cautions.

'Yes, word of the competition has spread,' Benjamin Juma says in his deep voice. 'Everyone and their friend are planning to come and it appears they're already here. The publican is happy – he's been mobbed by customers since dawn!'

And it is true. The street is raucous and merry and has been since daybreak, and getting louder and jollier by the minute.

'Us on this street need no excuse for a party, mind,' Mrs Kerridge clucks.

The women have been busy since 6 a.m. polishing and scrubbing the half-moon outside their front doors to a shine, dragging chairs and tables outside even as their men have marched to the docks promising to be back early and with hollow stomachs hungry and growling for the feast awaiting.

The children of the street have been colouring triangles of paper and weaving them onto cord and now it is strung up and down the street waving cheerily – handmade bunting.

The residents of East India Dock Road and other adjoining streets have been collecting to ask, ''Ere, what's all the fuss about?'

And when they're told, officiously, about the competition by the matrons of West India Dock Road, they've brought their own chairs and tables, positioning them wherever they can find a space.

A hawker, taking advantage of the crowd, has set up a stall selling ices, much to the delight of the children, who have resisted going to school until their mothers have given them clips to their ears and sent them on their way.

A vendor is frying chestnuts at the other end of the road from the man selling ices.

The men too old to work have been collecting at the public house since daybreak and it is doing brisk business although it's not gone eleven yet.

'Irish tea and coffee,' Mr Brown and Mr Stone wink, two sheets to the wind already. 'And as a special treat, seasoned with brick dust.' They sigh at the construction work going on two doors down which means there's dirt raining down and the clamour of machinery in addition to all the other noises of the street, the dust adding a red tinge to the ever-present, thick, yellow smog.

'I don't know what that will do to your taste buds, seeing as you're one of the judges, Mr Brown, and to your ability to referee and make sure everything is above board, Mr Stone,' Divya sighs as she runs across to Mr Lee's for some last-minute herbs and sundries and catches the men clinking mugs, the dark liquid inside sluggish and wafting a suspiciously vinegary scent. The chess set lying abandoned as the men laugh as if Divya had cracked the world's funniest joke.

'This special tea,' Mr Brown declares, his words slurring ever so slightly, rendering his musical accent even more pronounced, 'will only sharpen my taste buds.'

At that, Mr Lee harrumphs and rolls his eyes, rivalling even Mrs Kerridge, whose eye roll, Divya has always thought up until now, was second to none. She now has a worthy adversary in Mr Lee, Divya decides.

He hands the groceries over to Divya and winks at her, saying, with a wide grin, 'I pick you.'

'No, Mr Lee, you judge fairly,' Divya says firmly.

'Yes, I judge fairly. I pick you,' Mr Lee beams.

Divya smiles and shakes her head. She crosses the street to the lodging house and even though she is busy and has a hundred things to do before the competition starts, she is blown away enough to stand still for a moment, transfixed.

The bunting made by the children before school sings in glorious colour above her, flapping in kaleidoscopic abandon in the frisky breeze, startling the seagulls into squawking in alarm.

The cobbles in front of doors up and down the street are shined to a polish. Similarly, the windows of the street gleam and glow, not a speck on them.

Tables have been set up in neat lines and pinned with newspapers in lieu of tablecloths that rustle in the wind, the headlines, *War Imminent, Hitler Ignoring Peace Treaty,* for now of no consequence, doom and gloom relegated briefly aside to flutter in the nippy sea and salt perfumed breeze carrying the mouth-watering scent of roasted chestnuts from the man who has set up at one end of the street. The vendor selling ices is at the other, waiting for the school children who will cajole their parents into parting with their pennies.

Women sun themselves, even as they knit and darn and gossip, looking askance at Divya. 'Don't you have cooking to do?'

'I'm going.' She laughs even as raucous laughter and snatches of song drift from the pub on a pungent, smoke-infused draught.

'They're getting lively in there.' Mrs Kerridge nods in the direction of the pub, shaking her head and sucking her teeth.

And Divya, despite the list of things she has yet to do resounding in her head, feels a warm sense of contentment and wellbeing sneak in. She loves cooking and now, here, all these people have gathered to taste it. An excuse for a feast. Celebrating her food. Cheering for her. She throws her head to the heavens, glower of clouds visible through the imperfectly cut and coloured, yet delightful handmade bunting, and just as she does, a golden ray of sun pierces through the overcast grey awning of sky overlaid with saffron smog and gilds her face.

Thank you, Ma, Baba. I know you are watching and this is your way of giving me your blessing.

'Divya, where have you got to? Something's only going to go and burn any minute now,' Charity calls and Divya scarpers, the women's laughter and, 'We warned you so,' following her.

36

'Ready, ma'am?' Raghu asks, grinning from ear to ear.

He appears unruffled and completely at ease, while Divya is hyperventilating with the stress of getting everything ready, presentable and perfect.

'Call me Divya, please,' she manages, glad that her voice is steady and not showing her nerves. Why is she worried? It is, at the end of the day, a bit of fun, an excuse for a street party, for East Enders to escape their woes, poverty and the threat of home-lessness – those living in tenements are constantly worrying about the rent which the crooked landlords keep hiking, while they do nothing to fix the privy door that's falling off or the walls that have damp and mould, or the rooftop that's inaccessible, or the myriad other complaints lodged by the tenants – and now, the looming, inevitable spectre of war.

'As if we didn't have enough to worry about, trying to get by day to day without enemy warships and whatnot trying to kill us too,' Mrs Boon lamented when she saw the latest grim headline.

This cooking challenge might be an excuse for merriment, but Divya can't help being anxious all the same. She has found her place here at West India Dock Road, an identity as a cook whose food is much adored and who has won over even the most resistant of English, Irish, Chinese and African palates. And now she is also discovering a new side to her personality – that she is very competitive. She *wants* to win this. She doesn't want to let the street down, as all day long, in fact since the competition was declared yesterday, people have been coming by to wish her luck and offer help and tell her that they know she is going to win.

Jack Devine, having heard the news, popped by this morning to wish her luck, 'Although you don't need it, of course.' Eyes shining with conviction. 'Since I tasted your food, I haven't looked back, and me a die-hard meat and two veg man. This lascar might be a good cook, but Divya, nobody can beat your cooking.'

Jack had started calling her Divya when she insisted that she would only address him by his first name if he called her by hers.

'That's fair,' he'd smiled, green eyes crinkling. 'I like your name. Divya. But I am pronouncing it wrong,' he had said. 'Not like how you say it. Please, could you say your name again? I want to get it right.'

And he had practised until he did, albeit with a slight English lilt to it, which she very much liked.

'What does it mean?' he asked.

Nobody had asked her that and she was touched. 'It means divine light. Which is what my parents said I brought them when I was born. They wanted many children but my mother had several miscarriages. I was the only one who survived, you see.' Her eyes clouded at the mention of her parents.

Jack, ever observant, noticed.

'They're...' She swallowed, bitter bile, as she tried to answer the question in his eyes. 'They died,' she said and tasted sorrow, heavy and wet upon her tongue.

'I'm sorry.' She could see that he meant it. 'I lost my mother very young, as I've told you, and it is hard. Living with a gap that nobody else can fill.'

'That's exactly it,' she said softly. 'They died and I had to fend for myself. Which is why I got the job as an ayah,' she added.

'Ah. I see. Well I for one am glad that you did, for I've had the privilege to meet you and taste your amazing food. You've brought your divine light to West India Dock Road,' Jack twinkled at her.

'Ah, you say the nicest things.' She was overwhelmed.

'I do.' Then, looking at her, 'But in your case, I also absolutely mean them.'

Once again, she was touched. 'Thank you,' she said, a hand on her heart. His kindness meant the world.

He smiled, reading what she couldn't say but was trying to convey.

'Sadly, I have to go to work, but I will be back at 6 p.m. cheering you on, and helping celebrate your win,' he said, smiling widely and was gone.

Everything that could possibly go wrong has done so. The salt pot overturned just as Divya was going to season the vegetable curry. Thankfully, it didn't tip over into the curry – now that would have been a disaster.

'Bad luck. Throw some over your shoulder, quick,' Charity cried.

'I thought you were Catholic and didn't hold by all this...'

'I can be religious and yet still hedge my bets. Go on, Divya, sprinkle some of the salt over your left shoulder.'

'Ow,' cried Paddy, who had just entered the kitchen. 'Miss Ram, why are you chucking salt at me?'

The dhal had a little too much spice, and Charity, who tasted it, turned quite alarmingly red, giving them all a fright, while Fergus, who also had a spoonful, suffered a coughing fit. Divya has managed to fix it by cooking another batch with very little spice and mixing the two but she is not happy with it all the same.

And the rice, she worries, is slightly overcooked, and...

She is jolted out of her musings and into the here and now by Raghu's voice. 'Panicking yet, ma'am?'

'Never,' she manages. 'Us opponents need to be on equal footing, so please call me Divya.'

'All right, um... Divya.' Is that a blush colouring Raghu's countenance deeper brown? 'My fellow lascars are bringing over the food I've prepared. Hope you are hungry.'

'It's not me you have to impress but the judges,' Divya says archly. She might be worried but that's her secret. No one, least of all her competitor, must get wind of it. And so, she adds, 'I hope *you* are hungry for you will not be able to resist my food.'

Raghu laughs and it brings to mind temple bells ringing in glorious celebration.

'So you are Divya's contender.' Charity eyes Raghu, hand on hip.

'Yes, ma'am. I am Raghu, the lascar who is going to win today.'

'Ha! You're confident, I'll give you that. But it is misplaced. I'm Charity.' Charity sniffs. 'I don't hold with Ma'am, especially from someone as young as you.'

He laughs again. 'If you'll permit my saying so, you're young yourself, perhaps even younger than me.'

Now it is Charity who laughs. Then, 'You think you're worthy of our Divya then?'

As always, when Charity says 'our Divya' so casually, it warms Divya's heart, displacing her nerves briefly.

'I'm not asking for her hand,' Raghu grins.

'Cheeky so and so.' Charity mock-swats at him even as Divya blushes. 'I meant your food.'

'Well have a taste, go on. I'm confident I'll win.'

'I don't think you stand a chance, not against our Divya,' Charity maintains staunchly.

'Well, the judges will say otherwise once they've sampled my food,' Raghu points to the judges, standing eagerly (Mr Brown needing to be propped up by Mr Stone, both of them as hunched as the other), waiting to set the competition in motion.

Children of the street and their friends, having rushed home from school instead of dallying as they usually do, skip and jump from foot to foot, dancing too close to the covered dishes which the lodgers have arranged on tables for Divya.

Don't topple them, Divya thinks, crossing her fingers behind her back, even as she admires Raghu's nonchalant confidence. *What if his cooking really is better? Don't think that way. You are good. You will win.*

The air smells of toasting chestnuts, spices and anticipation.

'We're hungry,' children cry.

'No you're not; you've had two ices, not to mention the chestnuts,' their mothers retort stoutly.

'Wait until the tasting is done and the winner is announced and then you can have the food.'

It's been decided that the curries will be sold at half a crown a heaped plateful, thus covering the cost of the ingredients and hopefully also making a profit.

Raghu's lascar friends have finished setting up and now, Mr Stone props Mr Brown against Mr Lee who almost doubles over from having to hold up a man twice his size.

Mr Stone clears his throat and claps sharply.

Women stop nattering and hailing each other across the street, trading gossip and one-upmanship, sarcastic remarks not very expertly couched as compliments which their opponents can instantly see through and try to better, delivering sharper putdowns with saccharine smiles.

Mothers call their children to heel and the ices vendor and the chestnut vendor stop shouting their wares – not that they need to, for they've both had queues forming since daybreak. The hubbub in the public house dies down and conversations up and down the street quieten to murmurs before stopping altogether, until only a baby's plaintive wail is all that can be heard above the cranking of the dock cranes and the whirling and clattering of machinery, churning dust into the ever-present sooty smog.

Mr Stone waits patiently until even the baby's wail quietens to shuddering sobs and then he says, softly enough, but with solemn authority, and in the sudden, anticipatory silence, it reverberates up and down the street: 'Let the competition begin.'

37

And now Divya's nerves ambush her in full force. No matter how much she tells herself that it's just fun after all, she feels jittery with anxiety as she watches the judges taste the offerings, the kosher dishes placed in front of Mr and Mrs Rosenbaum, the crowd whispering agog beside her.

Quite a mob has collected, word having spread and people living in all the streets around the docks seem to have gathered to see what the fuss is about, with more appearing by the minute.

Divya is glad now that she cooked a lot, although that presented a challenge in itself as she had to ensure that taste was not sacrificed when spicing and flavouring such large quantities.

She and Raghu had agreed to make pilau rice, naan, vegetable curry, dhal, raita. And for dessert: kheer, rich and milky rice pudding studded with raisins and cashew nuts.

Mr Stone the adjudicator has taken his duties seriously and made sure the dishes are placed in identical, unmarked containers in front of the judges.

'How I pick you if I not know which yours?' Mr Lee had asked Divya, looking puzzled.

'That's cheating, that is,' tutted Mrs Kerridge. 'I told you not to pick 'im.' She turned on Mr Stone. ''E's not trustworthy, seeing as 'ow 'e runs a gambl—'

'She give me custom; I pick her,' Mr Lee maintained stoutly. 'But which one yours, Miss Ram?'

'Just pick the one you like the taste of, Mr Lee.' Divya smiled.

'Ah, you've fans, I see,' a warm chocolate voice whispered in her ear, raising goosebumps. 'New ones each time I visit.'

Jack Devine. 'Hello Jack,' Divya said. His name stuck in her throat for it felt frivolous to address him by his first name. For Jack was a big man, an important man. His father had started a roofing business that had done very well and now he ran a thriving and ever-expanding property business along with his son.

But Jack was so down-to-earth, he had not let his wealth or position define him, and most importantly, he hadn't turned his back on where he came from. He still kept in touch with everyone from his childhood, when he had been as poor as the next person and he never rubbed his wealth in anyone's face.

'I will win fair and square, just you wait and see,' she said, forcing a conviction she didn't feel into her voice. For she had to admit, Raghu's dishes looked good and smelled inviting. And besides, he seemed so very confident of winning.

'I have no doubt at all of that, for I have tasted your curry and have yet to find one more delicious,' Jack said, smiling warmly at her, so she blushed, fiddling with her apron.

As she turned away, Divya noted that Mrs O'Riley, taking advantage of nearly the whole population of the East End turning up in their street, had set up a stall selling Irish stew, soda bread and porter cake over by the chestnut seller, with her enterprising lad hawking, 'Treasures from the Thames,' which he'd strong-armed from the mudlarking boys.

Mrs Porter, not to be outdone, was at the other end of the street, selling pie and mash with pound cake and lashings of custard beside the man with ices.

A steady queue had formed at both women's stalls.

Each woman looking across at the other and harrumphing or cheering whenever her queue was shorter or longer than the other's respectively.

Now, taking a deep breath, Divya waits as the judges, to a bated breath and hush from the crowd – even the babies have stopped wailing and complaining it seems – sample the dishes. Their faces do not give anything away as they taste the food. Mr Brown is swaying on his feet while Mr Lee holds him up with one hand and helps himself with the other. Munnoo's face is scrunched in concentration as he bites and chews, nodding gravely once he's finished with each dish, and beckoning Mr Stone over.

Mr Stone circulates among the judges, keeping score on his notebook – a self-taught chess master and factory worker (head foreman) of several years' experience, he is very methodical and has columns for each dish with scores by each judge.

There is immense quiet – it seems even the Thames' usual swell and surge is on pause. No boats' booms or ships' foghorns sunder the tense silence. Even the seagulls, usually squawking like nobody's business, are peaceful. And the building work two doors down is on pause it appears, most likely because the workers are taking a break to be here, at the curry tasting.

The judges taste and nod and consider, looking very solemn, none of the joy they usually display when they sample Divya's dishes in evidence. The whole street is watching and they have to maintain a certain gravitas, which is why their faces look so grim, isn't it? Nothing to do with the food and that, perhaps for the first time, it has not lived up to their expectations – which are no doubt sky-high because of all the build-up.

No, don't think this way, Divya's practical self berates.

But she can't help it. *Oh Ma, Baba, what have I let myself in for?*

Beside her, Jack, as if picking up on her nerves, winks at her kindly, whispering, 'It's absolutely no contest. You've won hands down.'

Mr Stone confers with the judges, his glasses sliding self-importantly down his nose.

When the judges have set down their cutlery and Mr Stone has walked up and down the row of judges twice, he clears his throat.

Once again, there's absolute silence among the crowd.

'The judges have sampled the dishes and made their decision,' he says, looking at Divya and Raghu in turn, his face completely expressionless, no tell at all. 'I will add up the scores now.' And here his face relaxes into a small smile directed at Divya and Raghu. 'May the best curry win.'

'Hear, hear,' hollers the crowd. And now, the seagulls join in, making up noisily for their earlier quiet, calling loudly and joyfully, echoing the street's rousing cry.

Divya looks across at Raghu, who meets her gaze with a nervous one of his own – his confident manner of before no longer in evidence. He nods at Divya, his lips lifting in a smile that looks anxious, exactly how Divya is feeling.

Mr Stone looks up from his notebook, his face stern.

'It was a very close call,' he says. 'The judges liked both the samples immensely. The judging was fair, and while all the judges had a say, Munnoo had the deciding vote. In the event it was not needed as the judges were unanimous in their verdict.'

Beside Divya, Charity is biting her nails to the quick. Her

brothers have their gazes fixed on Mr Stone. Paddy is looking seriously worried.

'Come on, tell us the winner,' someone gathered in front of the public house behind Mr Stone heckles, startling Mr Stone into nearly dropping his notebook.

Mr Stone turns to give the heckler the eye but Mrs Kerridge gets there first. 'You keep your opinions to yourself, Jimmy sonny, or I will have a word with your wife about one or two things she ought to know.'

'Sorry, Mrs Kerridge.' The heckler's voice is very subdued.

'As I was saying,' Mr Stone says, 'the judges liked both samples...'

'We are hungry and would like to taste the curry before it gets cold. Get a move on,' Mrs Nolan calls.

'We don't need him to say it. It's our Raghu who is the winner,' one of the lascar crew cries. 'Nobody makes dhal as tasty as his.'

'Miss Ram cooks the tastiest curry in the whole of London, perhaps all of England,' Fergus declares staunchly.

'As I was saying.' Mr Stone clears his throat and tries again. 'The judges liked both samples immensely. However one sample was the clear winner – the judges rated the pilau rice, naan, raita, vegetable curry and the kheer from this sample more. All the judges except chief judge Munnoo and Mr Lee preferred the dhal from the other sample.'

'I'm confused; has he told us who won yet?' Mrs Neville asks loudly.

'I'm getting to it,' Mr Stone bites.

'Do it quickly then. This is why women are better for the job. They get to the point sooner,' Mrs Neville snaps. 'Vera would have finished the announcement ten minutes ago and we'd all be eating by now.'

Mrs Kerridge beams at Mrs Neville, her smile more than a

little surprised. 'Never in all our years of living side by side in this street have you put in a good word for me, Gracie. Wonders will never cease,' she says, shaking her head, her eyes moist with emotion.

'We women must come together, hen, what with the war an' all,' Mrs Neville clucks. 'The men will be gone and it will be just us again running the country.'

'Ah don't be bringing the war into it now; we'll be here forever. Get on with it, will ya,' Mrs Boon grumbles.

'And the winner is...' Mr Stone pushes his glasses up his nose and looks at Divya and Raghu in turn. 'Curry Sample Two. Every judge liked Curry Sample Two over Sample One, except as I was saying the dhal...'

'And who the blazes cooked Curry Sample Two?' Mrs Neville shrieks, sounding very much like a witch just then, her screech making several children start crying while others inch closer to their mothers, the toddlers climbing onto their mothers' laps or hiding behind their skirts and looking fearfully at Mrs Neville from this safe refuge.

Mr Stone opens his mouth. 'The cook of Curry Sample Two, and therefore the winner of the competition is...'

38

The crowd inches closer to Mr Stone, the better to hear, even as Divya closes her eyes and keeps her fingers crossed.

'...Miss Divya Ram,' Mr Stone announces, beaming at Divya, whose eyes fly open when she hears her name.

She is aware of an overwhelming relief replacing her nerves, so much so that her legs threaten to give way and she leans rather heavily against Charity, beside her.

The street resounds with applause and cheer, missing Mr Stone's pronouncement of, 'Miss Ram received forty-five out of fifty points, winning over Mr Raghu Kumar in all sections, where the judges liked her dishes better, except the dhal where he gained half a point over her. Mr Raghu Kumar wasn't far behind though, earning forty out of fifty points.'

'See, I told you,' Charity throws her arms around Divya in a hug, while Jack's chocolate voice brushes her ear.

'Well done. It was always going to be you.' His gaze twinkling warmly at her.

'Now that's decided, can we have our curry?' Mrs Neville hobbles over with her plate and her half crown.

Charity's brothers dance happily around Divya. 'Miss Ram, what did we tell you? You won, you won!'

'See, I vote you even though I didn't know,' Mr Lee beams. 'Good instinct, me.'

'The public house is still open for business; get your ales here, at half-price all evening,' the publican calls.

He puts rousing Irish jigs on the gramophone which waft down the street, mingling with the spicy curry aromas.

Young couples, still in their overalls and hairnets, having arrived straight from work, not wanting to miss the curry competition, start dancing. Girls laugh in their beaux' arms, heads thrown up to the soot and smog sky, their skirts ballooning around them.

Raghu comes over to Divya holding a plate heaped full of Divya's dishes. 'I spoke too soon, was too confident. Your curry definitely rivals mine. You are a worthy winner.' He smiles at Divya. And then, his eyes twinkling merrily, 'Although my dhal is better.'

'I will have to taste it and see,' she says, smiling.

He lays the plate down and holds out his hand.

'You won fair and square. Congratulations.'

She takes his hand and feels her heart shift. An electric tingle setting her body ablaze.

Does he feel the same?

He is smiling at her.

'I'm going to try your food now,' she says.

'Allow me to bring you some,' he says and then he's gone.

'Dance with me?' Jack holds out his hand. And when she hesitates, 'Please, Miss Ram, curry chef extraordinaire, may I have this dance?'

'I don't know how,' she says.

'I'll show you. It's easy. You just follow my lead,' Jack says, his warm eyes glowing, 'Trust me.'

She does and he is right. It is easy.

She is in Jack's arms, enjoying herself immensely now the tension of the day is past, twirling and laughing, when over Jack's shoulder, she sees Raghu return with a plate full of food. His face falls when he notices she is dancing.

He quickly rights his expression into a smile but it wavers at the corners.

She holds up a finger of the hand she has wrapped around Jack's shoulder. *Just one moment*, she gestures.

He nods.

He is watching her so he does not see the men advancing. A mob of white sailors carrying sticks and cudgels, with murder in their eyes.

Divya sees them. It chills her heart, makes it stutter.

Up and down the road, people are busy eating, chatting, laughing, drinking, dancing like she is doing.

Nobody has noticed the gang advancing towards Raghu and his crew of lascars, led by a man with a raised red mark under his left eye and stretching to his chin, his face set in a tremendous glower.

'Look out!' Divya calls, but it is too late.

'You black thieves, you take our jobs so we are left with nothing and now here you are, making merry,' the man with the red mark on his face yells as he and his fellows, with their fists and the sticks they brought with them, set upon Raghu and his friends.

'No,' Divya cries, shivering, even as Jack gently disentangles her from his arms – she had not realised that, in her fear, she was clutching him for dear life – and wades into the fray to try and fend off the sailors.

'Now look here... What's going on? What are you up to?' Mr Stone, Mrs Neville, Mrs Kerridge and others call, their voices distressed. 'What is the meaning of this? Stop right this minute, I say.'

To no avail.

Children cheer, not understanding that this isn't a show put on for their benefit.

The older children and their elders look on with terrified gazes.

Men tumble out of the pub, some to join the fight; others, like Jack, to try and maintain order, pull the mauling men away.

As it dawns on them that it is really a fight and not playacting, the children's cheers morph into tears. Babies wail and mothers try and fail to soothe them – the kids picking up on their mothers' fear and sobbing harder.

The plate Raghu had fetched for Divya flies through the air, landing face down on the shiny, scrubbed pavement, staining it turmeric yellow, bloody red.

The street party descending into mayhem and fisticuffs.

No...

No, no, no...

39

'No, no, no,' Divya cries, numb with horror as she watches the happy atmosphere disintegrate into anger and fear and loathing and fighting.

Just a few moments ago, as she had danced in Jack's arms and looked over at the street enjoying her curry, chatting, laughing, eating, dancing, all different skin colours mingling, she'd felt happy, content, a warmheartedness of belonging.

Now, as she hears the words flung, 'Black thieves, stealing our jobs,' she feels despair.

Pain on Raghu's behalf even as the men in the street, Jack and the publican and Mr Brown and Mr Stone attempt to pull the men off the Indian lascars.

No, they will never belong in England. People of her colour. They will always be marked as different, outsiders by their skin.

In India, white men are revered even though it is a country of brown people.

Here in a white country, white men are also revered and brown people and black people, anyone who is different, is 'other', no matter how much they might pretend otherwise.

In the end, it is Jack whose intervention brings a halt to the brawl.

'Enough,' he yells as he wades into the mayhem. He holds the men at bay. 'Enough, off you go.'

Afterwards, Charity will tell her how he used to be part of a street gang in the wild days of his mis-spent youth and still commands respect for it, even though he has cleaned up and smartened up and is on the right side of the law now.

That is afterwards...

But now...

The sailors who set upon the lascars leave, but not before issuing threats of what they will do to the lascars if they keep taking their jobs.

Jack follows them, saying, 'Just to make sure they don't stir up more trouble. I will say my goodbyes now.' Looking at Divya, 'Your food was delicious, a clear winner. Thank you. And you're not a bad dancer either.'

To which she manages a small, shaky smile in return.

Divya and Charity and some of the other women go to the lascars and gently help them up while others tut as they begin setting order, shooing the children. 'Go play now, the party's over. If you stay here, you must help us clear up.'

The ices vendor packs up and so does the chestnut hawker.

Mrs Porter and Mrs O'Riley take their wares – not much left – home, having made a nice profit, surreptitiously counting the coins in the purses tucked into their bosoms, each convinced she made more than the other.

The bunting stays, waving madly in the wind, which has picked up.

The tables and chairs are scrubbed and taken indoors.

The women throw pails of water onto the cobbles and wash down the street.

The men retire into the pub to discuss what happened over a pint or two of ale.

Fergus, Connor and Paddy help the lodgers lug the leftover curry into the lodging-house kitchens.

The wounded lascars are carried into the lodging house too.

Raghu is in a bad way and, once Divya has put the curries away, she sits beside him.

'How are you?' As soon as the words exit her mouth, she wants to take them back. What a stupid question – of course he's not all right.

He opens a swollen eye, the other sealed shut, and manages a bloody-toothed smile. 'I'm all right, ma'am.'

She feels hot tears sting her eyes. She blinks them back. She can't cry when he is being so brave.

'Divya, please,' she says, swallowing past the lump in her throat. And, 'I tasted your curry.' She had, when she was putting the food away, although it was seasoned with her tears, because he had wanted her to. 'I think it's wonderful.'

Now he manages a proper smile even as he winces from the pain. 'Thank you.'

40

Divya spends the night sitting beside Raghu, keeping vigil as he is feverish and in pain, she knows, for he was involuntarily moaning in his restless and delirious slumber, and she is worried.

The other lascars had escaped with small wounds which were tended to and then they returned to their lodgings. But Raghu had fallen into a fevered faint and the lodgers, themselves veterans of many brawls, advised that it was best he spent the night at the lodging house.

'Sadly, this is all too common, Miss Ram. The white sailors don't like us. They think we take their jobs. But we are paid so much less than them. They complain about this. Say this is why the ship captains pick us. As if it's our choice. The regulatory bodies keep announcing that lascars and sailors from the colonies shouldn't be employed, that they should employ more white sailors, but the captains find their way around the law and employ us. And we, well, we too have to make ends meet. If we are offered a job, we take it.' Mr Benjamin Juma shrugged sadly, the other lodgers nodding agreement while looking at Raghu, lying in the front room on the settee, comatose with fever. 'But we don't want to be here, given the choice. We are looking for ships bound home. They don't realise this. They think we are stealing their jobs. Their grievance should be with the ship captains and not us. But it is easier for them to take out their anger on us.' Mr Juma sighed deeply, the other lodgers joining in. 'They have turned on Raghu because he has been promoted to head lascar recently.'

'Yes.' Divya recalled how his eyes had sparkled with pride and joy when he told her.

'The other lascars say he is a worthy leader and that's something. That he works very hard, and is not afraid to do the most demanding and the most menial jobs. That's how he rose up the ranks: by doing the jobs even other lascars shy away from. They say he deserves to be promoted for working so hard, cleaning toilets and the like.'

Those eyes that had shone when Raghu told her of the promotion were now bruised and swollen shut and he was moaning feverishly.

'He doesn't deserve their ire,' Mr Juma said, all the lodgers nodding, their eyes haunted with ghosts of brawls past, hurt and pain and violence and rage that had found the wrong target. 'But who's to tell them? When they talk with their fists and not their mouths? They see our colour; they don't see *us*. They don't realise that we think, feel the same as them. That we have families back home, loved ones. Lives we want to go back to.' Mr Juma said, his eyes and the other lodgers' shining with longing and sorrow. 'They don't realise that we are exactly like them, all striving to work, live, get by. We don't want to steal their jobs. We want to go home.' There was pain and yearning in that one word. *Home.*

All these displaced men who haunted West India Dock Road and other streets by the docks, trying to earn enough for their passage home.

Divya prepares a medicinal potion with herbs, like her mother used to when Divya was ill – she doesn't have all the herbs she needs here but she makes do.

She applies the potion to Raghu's wounds. She puts cold compresses on his forehead in a bid to bring down his fever. She keeps vigil through the night.

He tosses and turns in his sleep.

'Ma,' he cries. 'Ma.'

She soothes him, her own eyes stinging. But he will not relax until she reaches out, takes his hand in her own. It is burning hot. She gently squeezes it.

'Ma,' he says softly and finally he sleeps, keeping tight hold of her hand, as if it is his anchor, tethering him to this world.

When he is fast asleep, conscious that a single woman shouldn't be holding a man's hand even though he thinks, in his feverish delirium, that Divya is his mother, even though she is far away from home and there's nobody to police her, she gently retrieves her hand.

As dawn breaks over the sky, his fever drops. He sleeps peacefully instead of tossing and turning restlessly.

As light inveigles into the room, buttery gold, she sees that the swelling on his wounds has reduced somewhat, although there are great big bruises where he has been beaten and kicked.

He opens one of his eyes fully and the other, swollen one a fraction. Blinks. Trying to make sense of where he is. Who she is.

Then he smiles. 'I thought an angel was tending to me,' he says. 'And it is true.'

She blushes. 'You thought I was your mother at some point.'

'Did I?' he asks and his bruised eyes shimmer with great melancholy.

'Is she... at home?' Divya asks.

'No. She... she died. While I was on one of these voyages. I started working as a lascar to provide for her. She was ill, you see, and we couldn't afford a doctor. Being a lascar paid more than any job I could get at home,' he says, each word steeped in pain.

Divya nods, tears stinging. She understands only too well.

'But that meant I had to go away from her. My father died when I was a baby. It was always only my ma and myself. Then she fell ill.'

He takes a breath.

'If it's painful, you don't have to...' she begins, tasting the sea in her mouth.

'I want to,' he says. 'The villagers promised to look after her. I sent my wages back but I had to travel away from her to be able to afford a doctor for her.'

'I understand,' she says.

'I know you do,' he sighs. 'She died anyway.' His voice is a funeral hymn. His eyes shine with tears.

'I'm sorry,' she says. She understands his pain only too well. This man, he speaks to her on a deeper level. There is a connection here. Perhaps it's because they've been through similar experiences. Both orphans. Both at sea in an alien world.

'You are a good listener. Sorry for burdening you,' he says.

'It's not a burden,' she says. It really is not and she wants him to know that and so, 'I understand,' she adds. 'My parents. I lost them too. Flash flood. Both at once.'

And now, her voice breaks.

Raghu extends a hand, but drops it before he touches her. He knows that culturally, a single woman is not supposed to touch a man. Even what Divya has just done, sitting vigil beside Raghu through the night, if it was back in the village, would have ruined her reputation, meaning she would never be able to get married.

'I'm sorry,' he says instead, offering solace through words and with his eyes that exude empathy.

She can only nod for she is choked up.

'You've been here all night?' he asks.

She nods. 'I couldn't leave you in this state.'

'Thank you,' he says. 'I'm sorry. I've caused trouble.'

'It wasn't you who caused trouble,' she says firmly. 'And in any case, I don't have to cook breakfast this morning as there's all the leftover food.'

He smiles. 'You really liked my curry?' he asks.

'Stop fishing for compliments. I already told you once that I did.'

He chuckles and it is a beautiful sound.

'Where did you learn to cook like that?' she asks.

And now his eyes cloud over again, becoming haunted.

'My ma. A man should be handy around the house, she always said, causing shock and scandal in our village. But I'm so glad she taught me. Cooking relaxes me. No matter how hard a day I've had, when I cook, I feel better. The times cooking together with my ma make up some of my happiest memories. And now she's gone, cooking her recipes has, in a way, brought her back to me. When I cook, I hear her voice. When I taste the recipes she taught me, it feels like I am speaking to her. Communing with her even though she's gone.'

The tears Divya has been holding back overflow and spill onto her cheeks. 'It's the same for me too,' she says. For he has put into words exactly what she feels when she cooks.

And this time, he reaches across and he holds her hand.

His touch is comfort, even as it causes her whole body to tingle.

41

'The country is gearing up for war,' Jack says.

It is a fortnight since the curry competition and subsequent fracas and Jack is visiting the lodging house. Divya has just served him his favourite lamb biryani with raita and roti with dhal which he is eating with gusto, talking to Divya, Charity and the other lodgers in the dining room adjoining the kitchen in between mouthfuls.

'Another war,' Charity sighs, her eyes sorrowful and face crimped in a frown, thinking of her father, ruined by the previous war, no doubt.

'We will show that Hitler what's what,' Fergus says and his brothers nod solemnly.

'Off with you lot,' Charity says. 'Go and play, won't you, instead of getting underfoot. And don't let Da hear no word of war, mind. He's traumatised enough from his time in the last.'

'I will be fighting this time and we will bring victory,' Fergus says bravely.

'No talk of that. You're too young,' Charity cries. 'Now off with you.'

'I will be fourteen soon: school leavers' age,' Fergus says, face set in a stubborn scowl.

'A few months to go yet, after which you can apprentice with—'

'I will sign up. Didn't you say, Mr Devine, that conscription has been introduced?' Fergus persists.

'For older men, lad. You're young yet,' Jack says gently.

'Not for long,' Fergus protests.

'Off with you,' Charity says again, swatting her tea towel at him.

Once they're gone, Charity sits at the table and drops her head into her hands. 'Another war?' She sighs deeply.

'Without a doubt,' Jack says. 'The Women's Land Army has been re-formed. The Women's Royal Naval Service re-established.' Jack counts off on his fingers, setting his cutlery down. 'The Women's Auxiliary Air Force has been created...'

'You can join up, Charity,' Fergus calls from the hallway.

'Off you go, Fergus, mind your own,' Charity yells in her no-nonsense voice.

'We will all have to do our bit,' Jack is saying.

'I'll have to consider what to do with the boys.' Charity sighs. 'Send them to the country perhaps. With us being near the docks, we will be the first under fire...'

'Ah, we won't let it get to that, don't you worry.' Jack smiles at Charity. 'After the last war, we're more prepared. Your Fergus is not wrong. We will show the Jerries what's what.'

'Hear that, Charity?' Fergus calls, and his brothers giggle.

'You must hand it to the boy, he's nothing if not persistent.' Jack laughs and Charity can't help but crack a smile.

'This is delicious.' Jack smiles at Divya, wiping the straggly remnants of dhal on his plate with his last slice of roti and popping it into his mouth, eyes closed in an expression of bliss.

'See, those of us who have eaten your food knew without a doubt that you would win the competition. Although your competitor's food was good, his cooking didn't stand a chance against yours,' Jack says.

At the thought of the competition and what happened after, how it began as a festival and ended in mayhem, Divya's face falls.

Jack notices. 'Things are all right now, aren't they?' he asks.

'Raghu says so, but then he and his fellow lascars who are looking for work try to stay out of the way of the white sailors who are also looking for work so their paths don't cross. But it's hard, he says, as there are only so many docks and only so many jobs for sailors. And it is not the Indian lascars' fault that they are paid less than their white fellows and thus get first preference on any jobs going...'

Raghu had left the morning after the competition and subsequent riot, thanking Charity profusely for her kindness in letting him stay and insisting on paying for it.

He visits Divya often for chats and exchange of recipes.

The wounds on his face have healed but there are faint scars and Divya thinks they must be elsewhere on his body too from the kicking and beating he received. But she also understands that, more than the physical impressions of violence, it is the emotional bruises branded into his soul that are harder to explain away.

'Raghu is very grateful to you for your help that day,' Divya says to Jack.

'You are on a first-name basis with him, I see,' Jack says and although he is smiling, there is a tightness to his words, a narrowing of his eyes.

'Ah, but I am on a first-name basis with you too.' Divya smiles easily.

'What did I tell you, he's keen on you,' Charity mouths from behind Jack.

Divya rolls her eyes. What would a man like Jack want with her? He is a successful businessman, jointly running a property business with his father, now that he's on the straight and narrow after dabbling in crime during his youth. She likes him. He is streetwise with that edge to him but kind-hearted and fair, seeing people for who they are, not discriminating between rich and poor, black and white. But she doesn't dare even think of anything more. They are too different, with completely contrasting upbringings and cultures. After promises reneged on by the Ellises, and the racism she has endured, Divya is wary and refuses to consider anything except her goal, which is to earn enough money for a passage home where everyone is like her. Not the white Sahibs who govern India of course. But there is a clear demarcation. She, like every Indian, knows her place, second to the white ruler – they have been conditioned to it after years of colonial rule although now they are fighting back with the Free India movement led by Gandhi. In any case, at the end of the day, in India, she would be with *her* people.

Who also shunned you because of bad luck.

But when she goes back hopefully and starts again somewhere else, in another village or town, she could start with a clean slate.

It hurts when she thinks of leaving Charity and her brothers and other friends she has made: Jack, Raghu, Mr Stone, Mr Brown, Mr Lee, Mrs Kerridge and others on West India Dock Road.

But she needs to find her place. Find herself. This is a limbo and she must not let herself forget it.

'Here Jack is again,' Charity would say, whenever Jack visited, raising an eyebrow archly at Divya. 'We never had him visit us this often before you arrived.'

'That's because he likes my food,' Divya always countered.

'He likes *you*, silly mare.' Charity shook her head in exasperation. 'Can't you see it?'

'He's a friend.' Divya was defensive.

'He's *my* friend.' Charity smiled gently. 'We have a jokey relationship. But you and him...'

'That's exactly what I have with him too,' Divya cut in. 'And I am grateful for his friendship.'

'But the way he looks at you, that's different. Don't you feel anything for him?'

'For one, I don't have the time, and secondly, I have more important concerns than romance on my mind.'

'I see you dodged my question expertly.' Charity smiled.

'No, I...' Divya blushed.

'So, you have more important concerns than romance on your mind. Like what, for instance?'

Like going home, Divya thought. But she didn't, couldn't say it out loud. She knew Charity liked having her, that if it was up to Charity, Divya would stay on in the lodging house for the foreseeable. In fact, she had said as much, several times. 'The attic room is yours for as long as you want it. You are family now, Divya.'

It touched Divya and tears sparked in her eyes every time Charity said it, for she could see Charity meant it.

Family. It meant the world to an orphan who had no one and nothing to her name and she knew Charity knew this, even though Divya couldn't put it into words as her mouth had flooded with salt and emotion.

'Thank you,' she said instead, giving her friend a hug, breathing in her rose and apple and soap scent.

And so, when Charity asked what bigger concerns she had

than romance, Divya didn't want to sound ungrateful by saying that she wanted to go home.

Aren't you happy here? Charity would have asked.

And Divya was. Happier than she had been since she lost her parents.

But... although being with Charity and the boys felt like home and here she had a purpose, it was not *her* home. She needed to find herself and her place in the world. And for that she had to be somewhere – India – where, despite allegations of bad luck, she still belonged without question, blending in seamlessly, her presence not pointed at and queried, her skin not branding her, making her stand out, marking her as different, other.

'What about you?' Divya parried, turning the question on Charity. 'Aren't you interested in finding someone?'

'Not yet.' Charity sighed, her arms full of the bed linen that she was sorting. 'I have Mammy and Da and the boys to look out for, and this lodging house to run.' Divya's friend smiled but her eyes shone with anxiety and her forehead furrowed with the burden of her concerns and Divya was sorry she'd asked. Charity had so much to worry about, such responsibility upon her tender shoulders, which hunched and buckled beneath their weight, that she had neither time nor energy for anything else. Divya felt humbled and ashamed. She might have her own concerns but nothing compared to what her friend was carrying, what Charity had to deal with day upon day.

Divya squeezed her friend's hand as they sorted the pile of laundry side by side.

'Who do you think of when you go to bed, last thing?' Charity, never one to give up, piped up with another question, when an answer to her previous one was not forthcoming. 'If it's Jack, then he's more than just a friend.'

'Ah, don't.' Divya swatted at Charity with the pillowcase she was folding. 'I'm so tired by the time I get to bed that I fall asleep not thinking of anything at all.'

This was a lie. Recently, she had been thinking of Raghu last thing before sleep claimed her. His soulful eyes when he told her of losing his mother while he was on a voyage. How his eyes had sparkled with unshed tears. How he told her that cooking was a way of communing with his mother. The feelings he aroused when he touched her.

But this too she pushed away. It was impractical. He was a lascar and had a nomadic life. He could not feature in her plans to go back to India and find her place, her tribe. Make a home for herself, a life in the land where her parents had brought her up, where they had lived and died. Her real home.

Now, Jack says, 'What are your plans, Divya?'

Has he read her mind? Divya wonders. Jack is perceptive, kind; perhaps, true to his name, he's divined what she wants to do.

Charity is perceptive too, but she will not countenance Divya leaving even though Divya had shared her intentions when she first came here. And Divya must admit the thought of leaving Charity and her brothers who bring so much joy and lightness and *life*, hurts. But Divya must do it as she needs to find herself, who she is, independent of others.

'I think you must start a restaurant,' Jack says, jolting Divya from her musings. 'I can see you as a proprietress of your own establishment.'

'Hey,' Charity complains. 'I'm very happy having Divya here, thanks. Don't you go putting ideas into her head.'

'Britain needs to be fed, especially if there is to be a war. And curries lend themselves well to rationing, for that will surely follow. Especially your recipes, Divya, which make the most of whatever you are able to procure from the vendors at the end of the day at a discounted rate. And if nothing is available, you still somehow make do.' Jack smiling warmly at Divya.

'Don't,' Charity cries. 'I don't want to think of war and rationing.'

'You have to, Charity,' Jack says gently. 'War is coming as surely as my name is Jack. You must account for and make provisions for it. The basement can act as an air raid shelter and—'

'Stop, Jack. I will deal with it when it comes.'

'No point burying your head in the sand.'

Divya listens to their banter with one ear, while in her head imagining herself running a restaurant, everyone enjoying her food. Someone else, she can't recall who, had mentioned it. It sounds wonderful. Being her own boss. Making magic with food. Watching people eat and come back for more to Divya's own place.

Perhaps that's what she'll do when she goes back home...

'In fact, Divya,' Jack says, bringing her back down to earth from her daydreaming clouds. 'I know just the place.'

'What?' both women exclaim at once.

'The building opposite which used to be Mr Ming's place. He upped and moved to Limehouse, Divya, just before you came here, claiming Mr Lee stole all his clientele.'

'He and Mr Lee almost came to blows.' Charity sighs.

'Well, the building has come on the market finally and my da has put in an offer. It would be perfect for your restaurant, Divya...'

'Jack,' Charity says sharply. 'Stop constructing castles in the air.'

'I'm not. Hear me out. I've given it some thought, pondering this idea that came to my head as soon as I heard that Da was planning to buy Mr Ming's place. It's across the street, two paces away if that. The lodgers and you and the boys could go there for your meals like you do here, same as always.' Jack takes a breath, eyes shining. 'It would free up your dining room and kitchen, Charity. You could have a smaller kitchen just for your da and mammy's meals and the other rooms could be converted. You could take in more lodgers or keep it for your own use as the basement would be an air raid shelter.'

Charity is looking at Jack as if he has grown two heads and Divya is sure her own expression mirrors her friend's.

'And as for you, Divya, there's room upstairs for living quarters and downstairs could be the restaurant.'

'You've thought it all out,' Divya whispers.

'Well, you are so talented. It would be a waste not to put it to good use. I could lease the premises to you and help you with the conversion.'

'Jesus, Mary and Joseph, you are serious,' Charity exclaims.

'As I've ever been. Look, my girl, your friend can't stay in your attic forever. She needs her own place,' Jack says.

He is so perceptive and thoughtful, Divya muses again. And on the heels of that thought, *I wanted my own place in India. But this does sound wonderful.* She is carried away on the wings of the dream Jack has painted. Perhaps she can go to India later and try her hand at this now? In any case, the ships will be requisitioned for the army if there is war, which is why Raghu and his fellow lascars are angling desperately for work on ships bound to India before it starts.

Divya still doesn't have enough money for her passage home with a little left over to tide her until she gets a job, and won't earn what she needs before the war starts, if it is as imminent as Jack seems to believe. So she would have to wait until war ended anyway. And Jack is right; even during the war, people still need to eat. The nation needs to be fed. And like Jack pointed out, Indian food will lend itself well to rationing. She has cooked curries with just mustard seeds and squashed tomatoes and a couple of spices. If eaten with slightly stale roti, or rice, it makes a delicious and filling meal. And if she uses the money she has saved until now for the restaurant, once it takes off, she can start saving again and when the war ends, hopefully she'll have made enough for a passage home...

Enough. Stop right now.

It will most likely never happen. For there is the question of money...

'How much would it cost?' she asks, thinking of the coins she's collected and saved, starting with the money she'd found in the coconut-shell scoop after her parents died.

This is a pipe dream, her conscience warns, *all dependent on whether you have enough.*

Jack smiles. 'Now we're talking. Since you're onboard with the idea, I will discuss it with my father and come back to you.'

'Thank you,' Divya says. *Don't imagine or dwell or plan or concoct fantasies until you hear back from Jack.*

'Anything for you, Divya.' Jack beams, green eyes twinkling.

'What did I tell you?' Charity says when Jack has left. 'He's keen on you. Mind, you could do worse. And that plan of his...' She turns to Divya, face glowing. 'Now that I've started to think about it, why, it doesn't sound half bad. Imagine, your own restaurant, Divya!'

And Divya, despite the caution of her conscience, does, savouring the dream on her lips, jalebi sweet.

42

True to his word, Jack is back within the week with a forecast of how much Divya needs to pay to lease the premises opposite.

He has also drawn up plans of how much it will cost to renovate and costs involved in getting the restaurant up and running. 'But,' he says, 'you can take a loan for that – I will help with it. First step of course is to see if you can afford to rent the place.'

If she can do so, does she want to gamble all of her savings on this instead of going home?

Yes, her heart tells her. *Yes, yes, yes.*

She will go home after the war but she really wants to try her hand at this first.

Divya counts her savings, her whole being thrilling with anticipation. *Please, let it be enough.*

She has been afraid to dream. But she didn't realise just how much she wanted this to work until she realises that she just falls short.

Hot tears stinging her eyes. A salty lump in her throat as she tells Jack, 'I'm sorry, I don't have enough.'

The end of a fantasy she did not even know she wanted desperately to come true until the idea was floated.

'How much do you have?' Jack asks gently.

She tells him.

'Ah, I can make up the rest. I'll lend it to you and you can pay me back,' Jack says easily.

For a brief, golden moment, she is sorely, sorely tempted. Her dream within reach. But no. She can't. 'No, Jack, I can't let you do that. You're already doing enough.'

'Hmmm... but you really want this, Divya? If you had the funds, would you go for it?'

'Yes.' She doesn't have to think about it. It wasn't an option she had seriously considered, thinking it out of her grasp, not for the likes of her. But now she wants it so much that she has to admit, a small, greedy part of her wishes, even now, to take Jack up on his offer.

Enough. It's not going to happen so don't dwell. Save the money for a passage home. Perhaps you can start a restaurant in India – that could be your fresh start in a new town.

'All right then, how about if we partner up?' Jack's words bring her back into the here and now. 'I will invest in your business for a share of the profit. I will draw up a contract so it's all above board and in writing. How is that?'

And once again, as always with this kind and thoughtful man, Divya is overwhelmed. Touched. And above all, elated. Her dream might still come true, once again thanks to Jack.

This amazing man whom she literally bumped into when she needed help the most, rescuing her from a tricky situation. And who has been helping and rescuing her ever since.

Serendipity. Or, and she believes this more, her parents' doing.

Thank you, Ma and Baba, she whispers in her head.

'Thank you, Jack,' she tells her friend. 'I cannot put into words how much this means.'

'Ah,' he says, smiling, 'I have an ulterior motive. I am a shrewd businessman and know this venture is going to be a success and will be making huge profits. And not only that, but I will also get to eat your wonderful food for free, I hope, given I will be a partner?' He grins cheekily at Divya.

And she can't help but grin back.

43

Jack sets things in motion immediately, making up the funds Divya needs to lease the property, drawing up a contract so he has a 10 per cent stake in the business, arranging for Divya to obtain a loan for the renovation of the property and initial running costs with him as guarantor.

When Raghu next comes round – he pops by whenever he's working in the area – Divya tells him of her plans. She is tentative for she still can't quite believe this is happening.

'That's wonderful, Divya.' He beams at her. 'One of our people, setting up a restaurant here. That's really something.' He is glowing with happiness – and is that pride? – on her behalf. 'Your parents would be so proud,' he says. 'You must be wishing they were here to share this with you.'

And seeing his reaction, hearing him put into words exactly what she has been feeling since this fantastic idea is set to become her reality, she starts, at long last, to believe it herself.

'Yes,' she says, tasting salt in her mouth and in his sparkling eyes she sees that he doesn't need her to say any more.

'We – my fellow lascars and I – can help you renovate the place,' Raghu offers.

'Thank you for the offer. But I don't want to put all of you out...'

'You won't be putting us out. Those of us working will come by to help after our shifts are done,' Raghu says earnestly.

'Well in that case, I would like to pay you for it. Jack has helped me make a forecast and I have set aside some funds for the renovation from the loan I took.' Which Jack had also helped her obtain. She has so much to thank him for.

'Oh, you are on a first-name basis with your landlord?' Raghu asks. His tone is casual but stiff, and Charity, who is coming in with a load of bedding she's just washed, raises an eyebrow.

'Landlord?' Divya laughs. 'I don't think of him that way, or even as a business partner, although he's both of those things. He's my friend.'

'Friend.' Again that tightness, a dark undertone to Raghu's voice, the enthusiasm and joy of earlier quite gone.

Charity looks at Divya, hands on hips.

Divya knows that she's in for a lecture and sure enough, the minute Raghu leaves, earlier than he usually would, refusing her offer of cardamom tea and snacks, which is unusual, like his manner, the stiffness never quite leaving for the duration of his stilted visit...

'He's sweet on you too, Divya. You better make up your mind, and soon,' Charity says.

'The only thing I'm sweet on, right now, is getting the restaurant up and running as soon as possible,' Divya says, savouring the words on her tongue even as she says them. *Her* restaurant!

'Well, you better make a decision one way or another or there will be trouble,' Charity says darkly as she folds the sheets. And then, archly, 'I know who I would choose.'

'Who?' Divya asks, although she knows.

'Jack, of course. He's the better bet. Solid, dependable and kind with it.' Charity takes a breath. 'And not forgetting his wealth, of course. He grew up here, as you know. When his father came into money, he took Jack out of our school and sent him to one of those fee-paying schools populated with the sons of the rich and famous from all over the world. He never fit in. He was teased something terrible which was, I think, one reason why he went so dangerously off the rails. He rebelled against his father, came back here, fell into crime. But what is impressive is that he managed to come clean and turn his life around. And through it all he never forgot his roots. His wealth has not gone to his head, unlike some, and he uses it for good, like helping you, for example, but that, I suspect, is because of deeper motives than altruism.' Charity winks at Divya.

'He helped me because he—'

Charity does not let Divya finish. 'He's a good one, is Jack. You never have to worry when with him. He'd take care of you instead of the other way round.'

'Are you implying that Raghu would not take care of me?' Divya asks. 'I'm just curious. At the moment, I'm not interested in anything except getting this restaurant up and running.'

'I'm saying that when it comes to Raghu, you are the stronger one in that relationship. He relies on you. And I get that it is very empowering, when someone looks up to you. Something you haven't had since your parents died and you had to leave your childhood village. But take it from me, Divya, love, it gets tiring, after a while, trying to be strong, not only for yourself but for someone else too. Sometimes, it's nice to be looked after.' Charity's eyes sparkle with earnest sincerity. 'Raghu looks up to you. Whereas Jack, he will look after you.'

44

The lodgers all pitch in to help Divya with the task of converting the residence opposite the lodging house, of which Divya is now proud tenant, into a restaurant. And as promised, so do Raghu and his friends, along with everyone in the street – excited and pleased for Divya, with the lascars doing most of the heavy lifting and fixing and arranging and renovating.

The two rooms upstairs are converted into living quarters for Divya.

The downstairs rooms are fashioned into seating areas for the restaurant.

Jack knows where to get the best deals for the utensils and sundries that Divya will be needing for the restaurant kitchen.

With everyone's help, the restaurant – what Divya thought was a fantastic idea, a dream she did not dare envisage – takes shape in a matter of weeks.

The unveiling of 'Divya's Curry House' is set for the first of August.

Jack suggested the name and everyone enthusiastically agreed that it was brilliant.

Even Raghu was full of praise – despite knowing it was Jack who had come up with the name. He and Jack have met in the course of setting up the restaurant and each man is stiff with the other. Raghu, usually friendly and open with everyone, is closed and monosyllabic with Jack and vice versa.

'Divya's Curry House – it's perfect.' Raghu beamed at Divya. 'I wish I'd thought of it,' he added ruefully.

Only Divya was not too keen.

Always observant, Jack noticed. 'What's the matter, Divya? Don't you like it?'

'It should be Divya and Jack's Curry House,' she said.

She saw Raghu's face fall, his lips tighten as he turned away. She noted that he had bunched his palms into fists. She wanted to explain not only to Raghu but to everyone. 'You are a partner.'

'I hold a small stake in the business. This is your venture through and through,' Jack said.

'This is a joint venture,' she said firmly.

'All right then, as a partner in this joint venture, I would like a say in the name of the place. Please can we call it Divya's Curry House? Divya and Jack's Curry House doesn't have quite the same ring to it.'

Divya laughed. 'You're a stubborn man.'

'He's a cheeky so and so, but in this case, I agree with Jack,' Charity said.

'All right, I give in. Divya's Curry House it is,' she said and couldn't help smiling as she looked at her friends. A restaurant bearing *her* name.

Ma, Baba, I hope you are watching.

As if he had heard her thoughts, she heard Raghu whisper in her ear, raising goosebumps, 'Your parents would be proud.'

She did not know when he had come back to her side, but she was glad.

She looked at him and nodded, eyes moist.

When she turned round, she caught Jack watching, his face crimped in a thoughtful frown.

PART VI

45

The opening day of Divya's Curry House dawns bright and sunny and cloudless, slices of bright gold sky visible between the smog that hovers over West India Dock Road, sooty yellow.

Like on the day of the cooking competition, there is a festive atmosphere in the street.

The children make bunting, the ices man sets up shop, as does the chestnut man at the opposite end of the street. The pub opens an hour early and is full within minutes, men spilling onto the street with their tankards of ale.

But unlike on the day of the cookery competition, this time, Raghu and Divya work in tandem, Charity's brothers as usual 'helping' but really getting underfoot.

Raghu is a great asset, and he and Divya work well together, concocting great big vats of pilau rice and lamb curry and biryani and dhal and rotis. They make African dishes with ingredients off ships just come in from the African colonies, following recipes Divya has sourced from the sailors missing home food. They make kosher food for the Jewish community and Chinese dishes to satisfy the Chinese residents of West India Dock Road. They start at dawn and by midday, when the restaurant is due to officially open, there's a queue snaking round all the way into East India Dock Road.

'The smells,' Mrs Kerridge, first in line, says as Divya throws open the doors of *her* restaurant, to a loud cheer, 'have been making my stomach growl louder than the Thames barges.'

Once everyone is inside and the scent of fresh paint and roasted spices and sizzling onions and caramelised sugar has been diluted with sweat and eagerness, Divya says, 'I'd like to say a few words.'

Everyone is chattering away, exclaiming with awe about how the place has been transformed. 'It looked so cramped when Mr Ming had all his stuff in every nook and cranny,' Mrs Neville crows. 'But now it appears so big. It can fit so many. Who would have thought?'

'You're not loud enough, Miss Ram,' Paddy says.

'This is how you do it,' Jack grins. He clinks his spoon against a glass. 'Miss Ram would like to say a few words.'

'Thank you,' Divya says, 'to all of you for helping me, supporting me, in all your different ways. You have made me feel so very welcome on West India Dock Road and now, you have made this impossible dream come true.'

'Hear hear,' they cheer.

'Thank *you*, my girl,' Mr Brown booms, 'for going to the trouble of recreating our childhood dishes for us. You have, haven't you?'

'Of course, Mr Brown. This might be a curry house but it does cater to different tastes.'

'Good, good. That's what I like to hear. Thank you kindly, darlin'.'

'There's also kosher food,' Divya adds.

'Thank you,' Mrs Rosenbaum says in her soft voice.

'And Chinese delicacies.'

'Miss Ram, you jewel.' Mr Lee beams.

'There will be specials every day from different parts of the world, and of course there will be curry,' Divya says.

Everyone laughs.

'Now, I'd like to say an extra special thanks to Jack – Mr Devine – who came up with the idea and not only leased me this place, but also put his own funds into making my dream a reality when my own came up short. Thank you.' She smiles at Jack, her voice thick with emotion. 'Without you, I wouldn't be standing here now, about to serve the inaugural meal in our joint venture of a restaurant.'

Jack nods, eyes sparkling.

'Thank you to Charity, Fergus, Connor and Paddy Junior – you are wonderful and I am so lucky and blessed to have you as friends.'

The room erupts in applause even as the boys cheer while Charity nods at Divya, her eyes moist.

'Thank you to Mr Raghu Kumar, who helped cook this meal you are about to eat.'

'Wonderful, so it's going to be truly the best curry as it has been cooked by the two best curry chefs in the East End and perhaps the whole of England,' Mr Stone exults.

Raghu, who has been heating up the dishes, pops his head out of the kitchen to grin and wave at the gathering, to thunderous applause.

'Thank you, once again to the lascars, the lodgers at Charity's boarding house and to you all for bringing this about, making this possible. I feel lucky and blessed in you.'

'Hear hear,' everyone cheers.

'What about me?' Munnoo interjects in his posh voice. 'I judged you the winner of the curry competition.' He has arrived wearing his suit, and both he and his suit appear very much the worse for wear. Divya is touched that he made the effort to come. Mr Juma had informed her, when Divya enquired after Munnoo and remarked that she hadn't seen him around lately, that he has been sorely ill.

'She included you when she thanked everyone,' Mrs Kerridge sniffs. 'And in any case, we all judged her the winner, or are you forgetting it?' She gives Munnoo one of her looks that could, Mr Stone has declared, 'Freeze the Thames even in the height of summer'.

'Thank you, Mr Munnoo,' Divya says.

'I'm Munnoo, my dear,' Munnoo says graciously, inclining his head towards Divya. 'No titles or salutations for me. I was a nameless orphan when my master, Lord Haslett-Harris, took me on. He gifted me my name, Munnoo, and that's what I go by.' This sorry tale at odds with Munnoo's diction, his posh vowels like the chime of polished crystal.

'Thank you, Munnoo,' Divya says, smiling at him. 'And now, everyone, please eat. On the house.'

The applause that follows is noisy enough to bring down the roof.

Raghu brings out the dishes with the help of Charity's brothers, to more cheer.

As the residents of West India Dock Road help themselves, Divya's hand snakes to her heart, which overflows with gratitude.

Jack comes to stand next to her, his face glowing. 'You did it, Divya.'

'*We* did it, Jack. As I said, I wouldn't be here without you.'

He opens his mouth but she gets there first. 'Go, eat. Please, you've earned it.'

'Aren't you coming?'

'I'm too full to eat,' she says.

He nods. He understands.

Across the room, Raghu, busy serving, looks up, meets her eye and nods, beaming.

And this moment, Divya thinks, is one of the happiest in her life, even counting the times when her parents were alive.

Afterwards, on full stomachs, the residents of West India Dock Road declare that it is truly the best food they have ever tasted, the displaced among them thanking Divya and Raghu personally, with tears in their eyes, for bringing a taste, a slice of home to this remote corner of the world they find themselves stranded in.

46

'Air-defence tests in action as thousands of planes take to the sky.' Mr Brown shakes open the newspaper, raining droplets from the morning's shower onto the table, and reads aloud from the headlines in his deep voice, his accent lending sinister music to the chilling words.

'War is inevitable,' Mr Stone sighs.

Divya's curry house is thriving.

She looks about the restaurant seating area at her customers – Mr Stone and Mr Brown are permanent fixtures. They've taken to playing chess in her restaurant rather than outside, on the cobbles in between the pub and the lodging house. And Divya must admit, it is wonderful company, their interesting conversation and good-natured sparring providing delightful background to her cooking.

In the mornings, once she's up and dressed and made a start on cooking breakfast, when she throws the doors open, Mr Brown and Mr Stone are ready and waiting to come in, chessboard tucked under Mr Stone's arm, newspaper from the boy who hawks it at the docks tucked under Mr Brown's, his other hand clutching the bag with chess pieces. They are soon followed by Charity, her brothers and the lodgers, who take all their meals at Divya's restaurant. Divya makes Charity's parents' meals as well, Charity finally giving in to Divya's repeated requests that she help in this way. They are creatures of routine, unlike their children, who eat everything and love to experiment, and are a joy to cook for.

Jack comes by most days to eat and to chat. 'See, what did I tell you.' He beams, taking in the packed dining area, customers eating and nattering happily. 'Never a dull moment – your restaurant is always busy.'

'*Our* restaurant,' she says, smiling.

Divya knows all of her regulars' favourites now, and they are grateful that she remembers and makes sure they are served what they like no matter how busy she is.

Raghu comes and gives her a hand whenever he's in between jobs.

'I love cooking with you. It rejuvenates me,' he says.

'I love cooking with you too,' she parries. And she does.

They work in tandem, somehow intuiting what the other is aiming to achieve with the recipe without it having to be spelled out. When they touch every once in a while, accidentally, while reaching for something, or passing an ingredient the other needs, Divya experiences that electric thrill that reverberates through her entire being. But she is too busy to dwell on it, even as her body angles towards him, wanting more.

He brings a different, fresh take to her recipes, enhancing them, avoiding them getting tired and boring.

They are chopping onions together and she is sniffing and rubbing away her onion-induced tears with the back of her hand, remembering her ma's voice in her head, her fond laughter, 'Bring an onion close to her and she starts to cry, my sensitive child. And yet she's a fantastic cook. How do you explain that?' Shaking her head but her eyes glowing with pride and affection as she beamed at Divya.

Raghu's words jog her from her reverie. 'I'm still unable to find a passage home,' he is saying.

When he says *passage home,* it makes her feel hollow to the base of her stomach.

Having Raghu visit is comfort. For Divya, his visits, being with him, provide the slice of home that the other immigrants derive from her cooking. Once he returns to India, she will never see him again. She will miss him.

'I don't know why I crave home so much. I have nothing binding me there now Ma is gone,' he says, his voice soft with melancholy and musing.

'Same as me,' she says.

'I suppose it's the fact that there, I will belong without question or resistance,' he says.

She's about to say, *You've put into words exactly how I feel.*

But he speaks first. 'Do you plan to go home at all, leave all this?' He points to the customers chatting amiably as they eat her food. 'You have something tangible here, Divya. You came here with nothing and you've created this.' His eyes sparkling with earnest pride. 'You bring joy to people through your food.'

'Yes,' she says. 'But...' And now, she says, 'You put into words exactly what I feel. That in India, I will belong without question.'

'You belong here,' he says with bright conviction.

And it warms her heart that he thinks so, even as the thought arrives in her head: *I belong more when you are here beside me.*

She shrugs it away firmly, tuning in to Raghu's next words, and immediately wishing she hadn't.

For he is saying, 'If I'm still here when war starts then I'll sign up.'

His bald statement igniting a fiery ache in her heart. The thought of him fighting a war, putting himself in the way of danger, making her hurt.

She looks at the scars on his face, similar ones she is sure are elsewhere on his body. Faded relics of the beating he received at the cookery competition.

What more scars will be wrought by war?

And why does the thought of him wounded and hurting hurt her so?

47

Raghu and Divya are working side by side cooking up spiced roast lamb with mustard-seasoned potatoes and devilled vegetables. They have been getting more experimentative every day. Some recipes are enthusiastically welcomed, others not so much. Based on their regulars' feedback, they adapt their recipes accordingly.

Divya muses that the reaction to this particular effort will be mixed. Since she started cooking, she's been surprised by people's reactions. Some, like Mr Stone and Mrs Nolan, who had never sampled a spice before she started eating Divya's food, love everything she makes and surprisingly, do not mind if she adapts stolid English fare and gives it her own spicy twist.

Others, who she would have thought more open to experimenting, like Mr Brown who has travelled the world on ships in his day, are quite fussy when it comes to food. They like what they like. When Divya prepares plantain to Mr Brown's specifications, he is grateful, but one day, when she deep-fried raw plantain coated in gram flour seasoned with cumin and mustard and chilli, he had refused to touch it. 'That's not how I eat it.'

When she made spiced porridge with peas and carrots, again he declined. 'That's not porridge.'

'No, it's not. It's what we would call upma in the village where I grew up. It's wholesome and nutritious.'

'I'm sure it is, my dear. But I don't want it.'

'Try some, it's delicious and ever so filling too,' Mr Stone urged, even as he helped himself to another bowlful.

But... 'No thanks. I like my porridge with milk and sugar, luvvie, if you don't mind.'

So now, as Divya bastes the lamb while Raghu gets on with the carrot cake and carrot halva they are serving for dessert, thinking how content she is, how happy cooking with him, she knows that there will be some who will not touch the lamb while others will tuck into it with gusto.

In any case, there's the usual fare too – biryani, and fried rice which she has made to suit Mr Lee's tastes. Wanton soup, again for Mr Lee. There's dhal and roti which are firm favourites. She has also made aloo parathas, Indian bread stuffed with spiced potato, which customers can eat with coriander and mint chutney. There are onion bhajis and samosas, which are again loved by most. There's also raita – yoghurt with cucumber and cumin seeds, and pilau rice which many pronounce as pelove rice.

'Because it's yellow but it has peas,' Divya had heard Paddy, who earns pocket money bringing food to the tables when they're busy (which is nearly all the time), explaining earnestly to one of the customers and she'd hid her smile behind the scarf she uses to tie her hair back away from her face when she's cooking.

For dessert, kheer is a firm favourite. Even Mr Brown will eat it as, 'It's basically rice pudding spiced with cinnamon and with the added advantage of nuts and raisins which I love.'

Why he will not apply the same logic to the other – savoury – dishes she prepares, Divya doesn't know, but both her and Mr

Stone's efforts to convince him are met with stubborn recalcitrance. Divya is hopeful he will come round one day. Even the kheer he only got a taste for after trying it at the cookery competition. He was too drunk to remember sampling the other dishes, 'Although I'm sure I voted for you, Miss Ram.' But he does remember the kheer which he insists on calling rice pudding. 'Just absolutely delicious.'

Divya also makes a good bread and butter pudding, she's been told, with her own twist of course (which is cinnamon and cardamom added to the custard). Her Indian sweets – jalebis (deep-fried tubes of syrupy nectar), gulab jamuns (milky dough balls doused in rose-water-infused sugar syrup) – are, like her experiments with twists on traditional recipes, hit and miss with the regulars.

'Too sweet for me,' says Mrs Kerridge of the jalebis and gulab jamuns but she is partial to the rasgullas. Mrs Boon on the other hand loves the jalebis but does not like the texture of either the gulab jamuns – 'too soft and slippery' – or the rasgullas – 'too coarse'.

Munnoo drops by when he can and enjoys Divya's food. 'These delicacies bring to mind the food prepared by the cook and his battalion of servants in my master's mansion in Bombay. Oh, those were the days.' But he is only able to eat very little of it. Divya worries about Munnoo – he doesn't look well at all and appears steadily weaker each time she sees him.

'I don't hold by doctors,' he says but Mr Juma tells her it is more that he can't afford to see one.

Of all the regulars, only Mr Stone will eat anything and everything Divya and Raghu prepare with happy gusto. 'If you don't like it, that's your loss. More for me.' He grins. 'My stomach has grown bigger than Hitler's army since Divya opened her restaurant.'

'Do you have to bring that blasted Hitler into it? We've come here for a bit of respite from all the doom and gloom,' clucks Mrs Neville.

'But you're the one who always brings up the war.' Mr Stone is perplexed.

'There you go again,' Mrs Neville sighs. 'Don't you get the message? Can't believe I used to be sweet on you once.'

'You did?' Mr Stone sits up higher in his chair, preening, the grains of rice in his moustache, and his belly straining against the table ruining the effect slightly.

'Not any more, mind,' Mrs Neville cackles so hard that toddlers cry while the youngsters hide under the tables and Mr Stone deflates, only to perk up when Divya brings her newest recipe – spiced egg bites – for him to try.

The regulars at Divya's restaurant might not all like the desserts she makes but they all unanimously enjoy her deep-fried gram flour coated banana dumplings served with cardamom and cinnamon infused custard.

Raghu's speciality is baking cakes with Indian twists – milk cake infused with cinnamon and rose essence, semolina cake with cashew nuts. Again, hit and miss – more hits than misses though, so they keep making them alongside more traditional sweets and biscuits: fruit scones and jam tarts (made with rose jam), mango fool, jam roly-poly, syllabub...

It is fun planning menus, experimenting with recipes, cooking for her customers, and even more so when Raghu is with her. And although Divya goes to bed tired to the bones, knowing she has to wake up early the next day to start all over again, it is happy tiredness, replete with fulfilment, contentment.

Now, as Divya and Raghu cook together, from the restaurant wafts the happy murmur of customers tucking into their starters even as they anticipate the mains.

'Smells lovely. I think we're going to like this new take on roast lamb that you're planning to serve us,' Mrs Kerridge calls, loud enough for Divya to hear.

'You will, Mrs Kerridge,' Divya calls back.

Mrs Kerridge is one of her most enthusiastic customers, and, given that she would stick to her meat and two veg before she tried Divya's curries, one of the most accepting of new tastes. It is really rather wonderful, Divya thinks.

She looks up to see Raghu smiling at her.

'It is lovely to hear you humming as you cook,' he says and his expression, the way he is looking at her, eyes shining, his voice soft with… What is that she sees on his face? It makes her heart jump even as her body tingles as if he has touched her.

The sound of the restaurant door opening intrudes into her musing.

Usually, she doesn't hold with omens but now, just as the door opens, Divya's knife drops, cutting her hand.

She gasps sharply.

'Are you all right?' Raghu asks.

She waves him away, finding a cloth and holding it to the cut. 'I'm fine. You get on with the cake.'

Accidents such as these are commonplace in the kitchen. Timing is everything when attempting roasts and baking cakes. Raghu knows this just as well as she does.

From outside, Divya is aware of a sudden lull in the pleasant conversation.

Always aware of undercurrents, Divya shivers.

Raghu continues to cook, unconcerned, unaware of the shift in mood.

'I've heard he's hanging in here, the darkie. Where is he?' a brash voice calls.

And now Raghu stops mixing the cake, looks up at Divya,

eyes wide and worried and then towards the door leading from the kitchen to the restaurant dining hall.

'Now then, young man!' they hear Mr Stone interject, warning in his voice.

Divya sees Raghu wince and rub at the scars on his face, unaware, she is sure, that he is doing it. 'Raghu, go out the back door,' Divya says urgently, still in the process of holding a cloth to her hand, the wound bleeding through it. The knife must have cut deeper than she thought.

Raghu looks at her and she sees the panic he is bravely trying to hide and it lances her right in the heart.

And that is when Divya understands, with sudden and blinding clarity, what Charity is always trying to tell her.

With Jack, Divya feels looked after, cared for. He is always there for her when she needs something and even when not. He is dependable, kind. Her rock.

But Raghu – she gets him. Worries for him. Hurts when he hurts. Experiences his anxiety and wants to ease it. He has had a similar upbringing to hers, has been through several of the same trials. He arouses intense feeling deep within her. He touches her heart and his touch ignites fiery heat in her entire being.

'No, Divya, I am not a coward.' Raghu's voice shakes slightly, giving a lie to his brave words. He sets down the mixing spoon, takes off his apron, hangs it up, each movement precise and to Divya, unbearably poignant.

As if he has heard Raghu, from outside, in a mocking voice, the sailor who had set upon Raghu at the cookery competition – for it is he, both Divya and Raghu recognised his voice instantly – sneers, 'Hiding, is he?'

'Raghu, you don't have to,' Divya says urgently.

'I'm sorry to have brought trouble here, Divya, truly. You don't deserve it.' His eyes huge and shiny with the fear he tries to but can't quite conceal.

She wants to hold him to her, not let him go, somehow with her sheer will to protect him from the man outside. The scars on his face are all she can see, suddenly, vivid and glaring reminders of his last encounter with the man.

'You don't deserve it either,' she says, feeling faint from blood loss and worry on Raghu's behalf.

'That cut,' Raghu says as he passes her on his way out, his eyes bright with concern for her, edging out the fear briefly, 'you need it seen to.'

He smells of onions and chilli and that ginger musk scent that's uniquely him. She wants to hold him, stop him. Her eyes sting with tears.

She opens her mouth to stop him but he's at the door which leads into the restaurant now, opening it.

'Ah there he is, the darkie, he and his kind stealing our jobs from right under our noses,' the sailor drawls. The raised red birthmark bisecting his left cheek from beneath his eye to his chin confirms Divya's suspicion that he is the leader of the gang who had set upon Raghu and the other lascars at the curry competition. He and his five mates crowd the restaurant dining room, faces clenched in identical snarls.

'Can we please take this outside?' Raghu says calmly.

How can he sound so unruffled when Divya knows he is scared? Divya herself is shivering and can't seem to stop even as she throws her arms around herself.

The sailor and his crew stand there, in her restaurant, their faces flushed with anger, everyone having stopped eating, their food going cold, to watch them.

Mr Stone and Mr Brown pausing in their chess playing – they eschewed the starters and are waiting for the roast. Spiced for Mr

Stone, normal and without frills, which Divya has also prepared, for Mr Brown.

They will be waiting a long time, Divya thinks and wonders why she's worrying about something as inconsequential as this, now.

Divya knows how afraid Raghu must be yet he bravely walks right past the men, making for the front door.

It causes her heart to hurt even more than it is doing – he does not want trouble in her restaurant.

'Hey, where do you think you are going?' the sailor with the birthmark, the leader of the gang, asks.

But Raghu ignores him and keeps on walking.

'I am talking to you,' the sailor says.

Raghu does not falter.

'You snatch the jobs meant for us, over and over. We've not had a decent day's work since you and your mates arrived at the docks.' The sailor is getting more and more het up, his fellows growling. 'We've had to queue for hours to get half a day's casual work, if that.'

Divya wants Jack to be here. He would know how to try and defuse this situation that's brewing, the restaurant thrumming with tension and barely contained anger that is surely going to end in violence. He would do it in a jocular way, without ruffling feathers. She has never wished for Jack's particular brand of charm as much as she does now.

But he's not due to come today. He's working.

Now that she thinks about it, it occurs to Divya that Jack only comes when Raghu is not due to help Divya in the kitchen. Is he avoiding coming when Raghu is around or has it just worked out that way?

Raghu is now out the front door and walking away.

'Now look here.' Mr Brown bravely stands up to the sailor and his mob.

'You shut up, soot face.'

Mr Brown's face is impassive but his eyes flash. 'Son...'

'I'm not your son. I would die before I was related in any way to you, darkie.'

And now Mr Stone stands up. 'That's enough, young man.'

The sailor ignores Mr Stone summarily and storms out, his fellows following.

Everyone stands and rushes to the windows, Divya included, her heart beating frantically within the confines of her panicked chest, the wound on her finger gushing with blood so the cloth is now bright red.

Raghu is walking steadily.

He's past the pub when the sailor and his mates catch up with him.

Divya knows what's coming and yet she flinches even as she cries out.

Raghu crumples at the first blow, falls to the ground even as the patrons from the pub and the publican come running outside to pull the sailor and his friends off Raghu, who is still on the ground, bleeding where his head hit the pavement.

'No,' Divya calls, her bruised hand upon her wounded heart.

'You're bleeding, Miss Ram,' she hears as if from afar.

Then blackness descends and with it blessed oblivion from war and aggression, both international and personal.

48

It is Mr Stone who first smells the smoke.

'Something's burning,' he calls. 'Miss Ram, have you left something unattended on the stove?'

'No,' Divya says coming out of the kitchen, wiping her hands on her apron – she was scrubbing potatoes at the sink. 'I checked.'

It is mid-afternoon, two weeks after the sailor and his gang attacked Raghu, and the restaurant is empty save for Mr Stone and Mr Brown, ensconced at their chosen spot by the dining-hall window, best placed to see all the goings on, even as they play chess.

Charity, her brothers, the lodgers and other regulars and guests have had their lunch and left to do their chores. They will be back for tea and snacks in another hour or so, for which Divya is planning to prepare puri bhaji and potato vadas to serve with tea along with fruit scones and cucumber sandwiches.

'It smells smoky, as if something's on fire,' Mr Stone says, his voice bright with anxiety.

'Oh dear, look outside,' Mr Brown cries. 'Have we been

bombed? Has the war started?' Befuddlement and fear colouring his usually even voice the dark blue of nightmares.

'They would have announced it, surely.' Mr Stone's voice stumbles as he looks worriedly at Divya and Mr Brown in turn.

Clouds of sooty, navy smog billowing and ballooning, making night of day.

Divya, Mr Stone and Mr Brown rush outdoors, only to be swamped by the swarming smoke and the burning-hot brand of fire.

Everyone else up and down the street is doing the same, coughing as they inhale fiery smoke, eyes watering as they look at each other in confused anxiety.

'What's going on?' The puzzled words coughed out in between gasps. 'The public house, look. Oh dear, it is on fire.'

They stand paralysed and watch in stunned horror at the men spilling out of the public house, coughing into their hands, faces sooty, eyes running, whether from smoke or shock, it's hard to tell.

Fire engines keen into the street and some firemen rush inside while others use hoses and buckets of water to put out the fire, which is still raging, orange flames cavorting merrily, angling towards the sky.

More people are collecting on the street, coughing and pointing, identical shocked gazes, red, smarting eyes, even as firemen carry out wounded men from the burning building.

At long last, the flames are under control, the air scented with devastation, burning saffron blue, and charred to a smoky crisp.

'Is everyone out?' someone calls.

The street waits with bated breath which turns to agonised upset as firemen come out of the building bearing covered stretchers.

Stunned horror on every face in the street.

Divya's hand covering her mouth to hold the scream inside.

Mr Stone swaying and Mr Brown, his face ashen, gently sitting him down on the restaurant stoop.

Divya rushing into the restaurant kitchen and bringing glasses of water liberally doused with sugar – good for shock – and drinking one herself, her hands, her whole body trembling.

'Someone died,' Mr Stone whispers, putting into words what Divya and no doubt also Mr Brown are thinking.

'That sailor with the birthmark and his friends, haven't they taken to frequenting the public house since they tried to beat up your lascar friend?' Mr Stone says, adding softly, 'I didn't see him among the men coming out of the public house or carried out by the firemen just now, although I did see one of two of his thuggish mates among the wounded.'

Divya's mouth is dry with fear of a completely different kind, her heart seized with dread.

Since the sailor and his friends came to Divya's restaurant and threatened Raghu and beat him up, her friend has not been back. She supposes it is because he does not want to cause any more upset at her premises. She recalls his eyes, wide with fear and upset, as he said, 'I'm sorry to have brought trouble here. You don't deserve it.'

He had walked so bravely past the mob mocking him and kept on walking, straight backed, once outside the restaurant, until he fell when they hit him.

Mr Barney, the publican and others in the very public house that is now a smoking ruin had pulled the sailor and his fellows off Raghu, calmed them down, taken them into the public house, plied them with alcohol and let them rant.

Divya's customers who'd all left their food to watch what happened through the restaurant windows, later told her that

Raghu, once the sailor and his mates decamped to the pub, had stood up, dusted himself down, and walked away.

'Nobody helped him?' she whispered, shocked.

'No, he walked away on his own.' They looked up at the ceiling, down at their plates, anywhere but at her.

'But he was bleeding,' she cried.

'Not much,' they assured her.

She understood why nobody had helped Raghu. They did not want to fall foul of the sailor and his gang.

If she had not fainted right away from fear and blood loss, she would have gone to Raghu's aid. Charity, Divya was sure, would have done so too, but she was busy with a new lodger, who wanted the attic room, the very one that Divya had occupied for so long, so she missed it all.

When she came to from her faint, Divya went to the spot where Raghu had fallen. There was still the faint maroon stain of his blood on the cobbles.

It made Divya sob. Charity, who had shown the lodger into the room, and, when she came back downstairs, heard all the hullabaloo, came out and led her away gently. 'Come now, he's not dead, you know.'

'It's just...' Divya cried. 'He's all alone in the world. I feel...'

'He's not all alone,' Charity said, smiling tenderly at her. 'He has you.'

'But I... I wasn't there when he needed me. I was busy fainting like a coward while he walked away on his own after he'd been hurt.'

'He's all right, Divya. You care for him. That's more than can be said of many.'

'I should have helped him.'

'His fellow lascars will look after him.'

'He'll think that I too, like the others, did not help him because I'm afraid of the sailor.'

'He knows you. He'll think no such thing.'

'Do you think I... should go and check how he is?'

'No, it wouldn't look seemly for a young woman to visit the all-male lodging house that he shares with the other lascars.'

'But...'

'Also, he might not want you to see him like that, at his most vulnerable.'

'You think he is vulnerable?' Divya was assaulted by fresh worry.

Charity smiled. 'You've got it bad, haven't you?'

'I...'

'Divya, love, he wants you to let him be, believe me. No man wants a woman to see him when he's been beaten by someone else.'

'How did you get so wise?'

'I've always been wise. You just refuse to acknowledge that side of me.'

And for the first time since the sailor and his gang entered her restaurant while she and Raghu were cooking together, Divya smiled.

A few days on, there was still no sign of Raghu, although the sailor and his friends had been coming to the public house every day, souring Divya's joy and comfort in West India Dock Road and her place there, proprietor of the Curry House.

She had found clumps of frothy spittle in front of her door, the cobblestones of which she proudly polished each morning and evening, and a dark smear tarnishing the sign proudly stating that this was *Divya's Curry House.*

Raghu had carefully painted that sign and hung it up when they were preparing to open the restaurant. It hurt Divya, an actual physical cramping of her stomach, to recall his look of concentration as he meticulously worked on the sign, how he had climbed up the ladder which his fellow lascars were holding in place and proudly hung it up. His face shining with joy as he called for her, 'Divya, what do you think?'

She was overwhelmed, looking at the sign proclaiming in bold, red letters that this was *her* curry house, her hands creeping up to her heart, touched and overcome. He had met her gaze and his was shining too, even as he smiled, conveying, without words, *So proud of you.*

Since then, he had said it often. 'You are amazing, Divya. You came here, destitute, a brown-skinned woman in a white man's land who was left to fend for herself and you have turned yourself around.'

To which she always replied, 'It wouldn't have been possible without Jack's help, Charity's, yours, that of the people on this street.'

And he countered with, 'Don't sell yourself short. You have overcome every setback to arrive here. Your own curry house. It is an impressive achievement.'

When she saw the brown stain obliterating the sign – Raghu's handiwork – it hurt. She had got Charity's brothers to hold the ladder and climbed up to rub the smear off herself although Fergus had volunteered to do it.

But she was adamant *she* would. For she had an idea of what it would be and she did not want Fergus – sweet, idealistic Fergus – to encounter it.

And sure enough, it was what she was suspecting. Faeces. And not from the seagulls either. Human excrement. Someone had climbed up here and applied it and she could guess who.

Recoiling from the foetid reek, she had scrubbed and scrubbed until the sign was clean and the letters Raghu had carefully painted on bled red tears, so they didn't sparkle as brightly scarlet as before, their light dimmed, dulled by what they had been subjected to.

The next morning, when she woke, there it was again, a dark-brown splodge besmirching the sign, and more globules of spittle on her stoop and on the cobbles in front of her door.

Again, she cleaned up and again the next day, once more they appeared.

She stayed awake in a bid to catch them at it. And heard them through her window, late at night, after the public house shut shop, as they came and, laughing raucously, flung it on. 'Brown as dirt, as their colouring. Brown as the curry they eat. Stinking like it too.'

When it came right down to it, she wasn't brave enough to confront them, cowering in her bed, sheet pulled up over her head as she heard them laugh and fling insults along with the excrement and spittle outside. And she was too ashamed – although she shouldn't be, she knew, she wasn't the one doing this – to ask for anyone's help, except Charity's brothers to hold the ladder so she could clean the sign, or tell anyone, even Jack, who would have talked to them, and one word from him would have stopped it.

Instead every day she scrubbed it off, the paint bleeding more each time, red tears becoming pink and then dirty yellow. The sign dulled more every day, her heart hurting as she imagined Raghu's face, even as she told herself that the faded signage added character.

But it did nothing to soothe the turmoil in her heart.

Usually, after long days cooking and seeing to her clientele, as soon as Divya's head hit the pillow, she would fall almost instantly into a deep and dreamless sleep. But these past few days, since the sailor and his gang had entered her restaurant threatening Raghu, her sleep was harangued by nightmares – on those nights when she did manage to sleep, that is. And then, there were the sailors outside her window in the dead of night, keeping her awake and making her feel ashamed that she was too afraid to confront them.

But then three days later, it stopped.

That night, she was surprised to hear a familiar voice interrupting the sailors' drunken merriment at her expense.

Jack. Her kind friend.

She heard him intercept them as they came, in the night after the public house shut, to vandalise her sign.

'So lads, this is how you get your highs now, is it: by stooping so low as to befoul, in the cowardly darkness, a lone woman's honest establishment?'

'Honest? She harbours men who steal our jobs. And in any case, this establishment brings down the tone of this street. It reeks. It is horrible, smelly food.'

'Don't eat it then. Plenty will say otherwise. Here's a suggestion: why don't you go and do something useful instead of hounding a defenceless woman, lads?' And, still pleasant, 'If I see you here again, or if I hear this establishment has been vandalised, well, then stricter measures will need to be taken, you understand?'

Jack's voice was friendly and conversational, but with threat implicit.

And yet...

'She's cowardly coming running to you,' they blustered. 'Who are you to her anyhow? Why are you associating with darkies when there are plenty of our kind?'

'Ah, lads, but she didn't come to me. I have my ways of finding out everything that goes on around here.' His voice now radiating warning, tight and hard, all friendliness quite gone. 'And who I associate with is my business. If I hear you talk like that again...'

'We're going,' they said.

'Do. And I will ignore what you said this once.'

That night, for the first time since the sailor and his mob had set upon Raghu outside her restaurant, Divya slept through the night.

She woke up refreshed and when she wandered outside to wash her stoop, there was no sour spittle maligning it. And the sign, while faded and worn from all of her scrubbing in days past, was untainted by smears.

Jack came in that morning for breakfast. 'I had a bit of time before starting work and thought I'd avail myself of your wonderful cooking, Divya.' He smiled easily at her. 'How are you? How has everything been? Restaurant doing okay?'

'Yes,' she said just as easily, setting tea, Indian style, spiced with cinnamon and cardamom and ginger, which he loved, before him. An omelette, this too with an Indian twist, plenty of chopped onion and grated ginger, cumin seeds and coriander leaves, which he had grown to love, with toast from bread she'd baked that morning.

'This is good,' he said, tucking in. Then, gently, 'Why didn't you tell me the sailors were vandalising the place? If Paddy had not mentioned it, I wouldn't know. I've been here once or twice since it started. Yet, you kept mum.'

'I wanted to solve my problems myself.'

'Come now, Divya, we're friends. I'd like to help.'

Her throat clogged with tears at his tenderness, his gentle chiding. 'I know. Thank you.'

He waved her thanks away. 'Promise me you'll send the boys with word if there's any more trouble?'

'I will.' Then, looking at her apron which she was twisting into knots, 'But Jack, what they said last night...'

'You heard?' His gaze sharp.

She nodded.

'I hoped you'd be asleep,' he said softly.

'Jack, I'm sure it's not just those sailors. Others too must think that way about me... They may not say it out loud, but they will whisper it. They will think it.'

'So?' he challenged. 'Plenty of people will say plenty of things. They don't like the Irish, the blacks, anyone different. They cannot see past colour, identity, to humanity. That's *their* problem.' He took a breath and looked up at her, eyes glowing with sincerity. 'Listen, Divya, their opinion doesn't matter to me and it shouldn't to you either. I don't give two hoots for it. For me, what matters is the opinion of those whom I care for. And you,' looking into her eyes, 'are one of them. Promise me that if there is trouble again, you will come to me.'

'I promise,' she said, but she did not meet his eye. 'You are so good to me.'

'You are good to me too. This breakfast has set me up for the day.' He smiled.

The days passed. The sailors kept coming to the public house.

And yet, or perhaps *because* of them, because he knew they were there and because he did not want to get Divya in trouble and for her restaurant to suffer repercussions, Raghu stayed away. She missed him sorely, missed cooking alongside him and their chats while doing so.

Jack came every day and Divya was grateful for it, not least because it deterred the sailors and they stayed in the public house, across the road.

'They are so noisy and bawdy with it,' Mr Stone complained.

Divya wondered if they were being purposely loud, so that

she would hear and know they were there, watching, waiting, and then chided herself for it. *You are being paranoid.*

'Their language!' sighed Mr Brown. 'Unfit for civilised ears.'

'Honestly Miss Ram, we are grateful for your curry house. If we were playing chess on the street outside the public house like we did before you opened this restaurant, their language and their raucousness would put us off our game.'

'Who is winning?' she asked, more to distract herself from her worries than anything else – despite Jack's reassurances and his calming presence each morning, she seemed to be permanently on tenterhooks.

'Oh, I am,' said Mr Stone.

'But I am,' cried Mr Brown.

'Overall, I am the clear winner,' protested Mr Stone.

'You might think so but you would be misinformed,' declared Mr Brown grandly.

Divya laughed dutifully but her heart was not in it.

When she had a spare moment, she confided in Charity. 'Raghu has not been back since that day and I am worried.'

'He will come and see you when he's good and ready.' Charity took Divya's hand and smiled fondly at her. 'If he's staying away, it's because he wants you to stay away too, to concentrate on your restaurant.'

And so she does. And the days pass but they seem a little emptier, a little lackadaisical even though she cooks more than ever, and she is just as busy.

At night, her dreams are of him. That look in his eyes. Bravely walking out of her restaurant so that there wouldn't be trouble inside.

Falling as the sailor hit him.

His vulnerable back.

Those shining eyes.

When she wakes, it is to a pillow wet with tears and prayers: *please let him be all right.*

And now, fire in their street.

The firemen bearing covered stretchers, which can only mean one thing...

'Two of the sailors dead. The gang leader, the one with the birthmark on his face, who beat up that lascar, Miss Ram's opponent, after the cookery competition, and his right-hand man.' Then with fearful glances at Divya, soft whispers trying and failing to be discreet, words that cause ice to form in her heart. 'They say the fire was not an accident.'

'Oh?'

'Word is he was seen just before the fire.'

'Who?'

'Keep up. That lascar. Miss Ram's cookery competition opponent as was. Rumour has it they are now very close.'

'Who?'

'*Miss Ram and the lascar.* He's always hanging about at the curry house, cooking with Miss Ram in the kitchen.'

And their voices dropping further, but Divya hears them all the same, her heart seizing. 'They say the fire was the lascar's revenge.'

49

'A treaty of non-aggression has been signed between Molotov and Ribbentrop.' Mr Brown sighs.

'What does that mean?' Divya asks.

'It means war is certain, my girl,' Mr Stone says gently.

'Why? I don't understand,' Divya says, sitting down beside Mr Stone and Mr Brown.

Charity, her brothers and the lodgers have had their breakfast and left to get on with their day. They will return for lunch – Charity, her brothers and those lodgers who are nearby and able to get to the restaurant. For the others, who are working further away, Divya usually packs a lunch – if they ask for it, that is, although since the fire at the public house, they don't. And she sends Charity back with lunch for her parents, like she did with breakfast.

Now it is the lull between breakfast and lunch.

Even so, several of the matrons of West India Dock Road would, usually, have dropped in for a cuppa and a chinwag alongside an Indian sweet or a slice of cake. 'Having elevenses early,' Mrs Boon would joke.

'And resting my feet a tad,' Mrs Kerridge would grumble.

'I would need to rest my feet too, if I had to carry that body,' Mrs O'Riley, thin as a bean, although she ate more than all the rest put together, would snigger meanly.

'Hollow legs,' Mrs Ross would sigh enviously as she watched Mrs O'Riley reach for her third piece of cake. 'I wish I had that problem.'

'And in any case,' Mrs O'Riley would hold forth on the subject of Mrs Kerridge needing to rest her feet, 'she doesn't lift a finger around the house. There's cobwebs thick enough to catch an elephant in there, so I've heard. And the sheets dusty as hell and never changed.'

Mrs Kerridge and Mrs O'Riley have a long-standing war that started when Mrs Kerridge stole the boy Mrs O'Riley was step-ping out with several decades ago. All of this explained to Divya by Mrs Devlin, only too happy to talk about the women in the street to a listening ear, seeing as she'd lost her sons and husband to the first war and was lonely as anything.

But in recent days, since the fire at the pub and subsequent deaths, the residents of West India Dock Road and surrounds have stopped coming to Divya's.

In fact, it's not unusual these days to have just Mr Stone, Mr Brown, Mr Lee and Charity's lot at the restaurant, which usually would be humming with people, all the seats full nearly all of the time.

Jack comes every day and has started bringing 'friends' along. Divya's friends – Charity, Mr Stone, Mr Brown, Mr Lee and Jack – treat her like she's fragile, delicate, breakable, and are extra gentle with her. Charity keeps giving Divya hugs and asking if she's all right while others on the street ignore her. Only Charity's brothers behave just the same towards Divya as always, and for this she is grateful.

Mrs Kerridge, Mrs Neville and the other matrons, who would usually gather to natter in Divya's restaurant, have returned to sitting outside their front doors on chairs they've fetched from their homes, ostensibly doing their chores, but heads together gossiping, more like. When they see Divya, instead of hailing her cheerily, they turn away.

The market vendors don't give her bargains any more. Or save the veggies for her like they had been doing.

'We don't like doing business with pals of the darkie who killed our boys,' she's heard them say within earshot of her. 'He took their jobs. But that not enough for him, was it?' Spitting vehemently, 'He had to take their lives too.'

Mr Lee is kind and loyal as always. 'That lascar your friend, so I believe he no do what they say.'

Some of the lodgers, who were always friendly to Divya, now give her downright ominous looks when they come round to have their meals. She can see that they don't want to but due to the arrangement between Charity and Divya, they have no choice and their expressions show her that they're not happy about it.

'A treaty of non-aggression signed between Germany and the Soviet Socialist Republics,' Mr Brown says now. 'Molotov is the Soviet foreign minister and Ribbentrop is the German foreign minister.'

'So how does this spell war?' Divya asks.

'Previously, the Soviets wanted to sign this treaty with Britain and France. Now they have signed it with Germany. That means two big powers are allies. This will make Hitler confident enough to attack. He was waiting for just something like this.'

'Ah,' Divya says, one hand going to her heart.

She looks about the empty restaurant and her heart hurts.

War is imminent but war has already been declared in West

India Dock Road and she knows which side she's on. The bad side, the side deemed guilty by association.

'Who is it who saw Raghu by the public house the day of the fire?' she had asked, when she heard the rumour. She might have sounded hysterical. A bit loud. Maybe even aggressive.

'No need to get so bolshy,' Mrs Kerridge had huffed.

'We heard that he was there, acting furtive,' Mrs Nolan was cagey.

Charity had laid a warning hand on Divya's shoulder.

Divya, in a calmer tone, had asked again. 'But who is it who saw Raghu?'

Nobody knew.

All they were certain of was that *someone* had seen him hanging about the public house and acting in a suspicious way. And as was the way with these things, rumour had become fact. Crystallised, as it passed from mouth to mouth, into truth.

'It is vicious gossip most likely spread by the sailors who were part of the gang,' Divya had cried to Charity.

And Charity, always gentle and wise, had said, 'You don't know that. Mind you don't say this to the wrong person, my love. You'll be doing what you're accusing them of and spreading rumours.'

'Do *you* believe Raghu had anything to do with it?' Divya had asked and again, she couldn't help her voice from rising, getting angry, defensive.

'I don't know,' Charity said.

And even though Charity was being fair, it hurt Divya. She felt she could not even trust her friend to take her side. Even though she knew that she was being unfair to Charity. But she had wanted Charity to say, immediately and without a second thought, 'No.' To sound outraged to even consider it.

So Charity's reply was a disappointment.

'Nothing has been proved,' Charity was saying. 'The fact is that two lives have been lost, and the publican is lying gravely ill in hospital, and the public house is damaged. That's not good.'

You're blaming Raghu, perhaps, in your heart of hearts, Divya thought and once the thought was there, she couldn't get rid of it.

And so, she didn't ask any of her few remaining friends what they thought for fear they would make her feel the same. But she looked at Mr Stone and even Mr Brown, and of course Jack, and wondered if perhaps they too, in their hearts, couldn't quite stop themselves doubting Raghu.

Only Mr Lee was unequivocal. 'He friend of you. So he no do it.'

And Divya almost wept with relief. She could have kissed Mr Lee.

Mr and Mrs Rosenbaum stayed out of it. In any case they, alongside the other Jewish residents of the street, had their own worries, with war looming, having already had to contend with slurs and worse.

'Raghu is not at fault. He wouldn't do this,' Divya declared loudly to the street. The women sitting outside their front doors turned away from her, sniffing loudly.

Mrs Kerridge, spokesperson for the street, huffing vehemently, 'You don't know this.'

'And you don't know he's guilty either,' Divya cried.

'He was seen at the public house around the time of the fire,' Mrs Neville snapped.

'I know him and I *know* that he is not capable of arson,' Divya insisted.

'Someone saw him behaving suspiciously near the public house,' the women insisted stubbornly. 'Next thing you know, there's a fire and two of the men who had disagreements with your lascar friend are dead. And poor Mr Barney the publican is fighting for his life in hospital.'

'These black people are known to use underhand methods to get their revenge,' someone behind Divya yelled loudly and angrily. 'Where is he? Why is he hiding? And why does this girl have to defend him? Shows guilt in my book.'

When Divya turned around to see who had spoken, everyone was otherwise occupied, busy with whatever task they were pretending to do, a convenient cover for gossip and hearsay.

In any case, what Divya learnt from the whole process was that however much she might think herself part of the community, when push came to shove, she was an outsider.

And in tense situations, the street would band to defend people of their own colour, blame the outsider, label them guilty.

'You've all eaten the food he has cooked,' Divya cried, trying to appeal to the street about Raghu's innocence one last time.

'If someone is a good cook, that doesn't mean they cannot commit crimes. In fact, the lascar would know exactly how to start a fire, given he's used to doing it while cooking. Look at Mrs Oswald, who lived at number twenty-two. She was the best cook around here. Her cakes were to die for. She killed her husband with her rolling pin when she had had enough of his bossing. Hung at the gallows, she did.'

So in the eyes of the residents of West India Dock Road, these same people who had accepted her and helped her set up the curry house and eaten her food and Raghu's with happy gusto and praised it to the heavens, Divya was guilty of being in cahoots with a murderer.

'Never liked the food anyway. Just pretended to. Can never get rid of the smell. Sticks to my clothes and, what's more, upsets my stomach something terrible, it does.' Mrs Neville having the last word, the other matrons nodding assent.

50

Jack bursts into the restaurant, brandishing a newspaper, Charity's brothers at his heels. 'Have you seen this?'

'What is it, son?' Mr Stone asks, pausing in the act of moving his knight to capture Mr Brown's rook.

'War will be declared in the coming weeks,' Paddy announces self-importantly. 'And both Jack and Fergus will sign up.'

'You bet I will,' Fergus agrees.

'Not Fergus, not yet,' Jack says to Paddy. And to Fergus, gently, 'You're not old enough, son.' And, looking at Divya, Mr Stone and Mr Brown in turn, 'Listen to this.' He reads aloud, 'Parliament is recalled several weeks early, Army reservists are called up and Civil Defence workers placed on alert.'

'Ah, not looking good, is it?' Mr Stone shakes his head.

'War within the week, mark my words.' Mr Brown sighs.

'I already said just that.' Paddy is indignant. Then, to Divya, 'I'm hungry. What have you cooked today, Miss Ram?'

And Divya, who has been feeling panicked, her stomach swooping with nerves and upset, could kiss the boy. Feeding people, her favourite thing to do, to try and not think of what war on an international level will mean. For her and for the restaurant, especially in light of the ongoing war on the street against Raghu, and Divya by association. What it will mean for England, India. For the world.

51

Rat-a-tat-tat.

It is a soft enough knock on the back door of the kitchen which opens onto the alleyway but in the dead of night, it is loud as an explosion.

Divya is terrified, cowering in her bed under the sheets, hoping the knocking will stop.

But it doesn't.

Should she go downstairs, open the front door and run across to Charity's, begging for help? But her whole body is seized by panicked paralysis and she cannot do anything at all except hide under the sheets in a cowardly manner.

Rat-a-tat-tat.

Going on and on, more urgent by the minute.

Go away.

But they do not.

She can't take it.

Her entire body shaking, she shrugs off the sheets and goes downstairs on jellied legs, holding onto the banister for dear life.

Once downstairs, she looks towards the kitchen door, where the knocking continues, softly persistent.

She's still tempted to ignore it, run to the front door, fling it open and run across to Charity's.

But Charity sleeps downstairs and Divya knocking at the front door will likely disturb the whole house – Charity, her ailing parents, her brothers *and* the lodgers who all suffer long, hectic days and need their night's rest to rejuvenate and face the next day.

She needs Jack. But he doesn't live around here, and is too far away to go running to for help, not least in the middle of the night.

And in any case, you are an adult. You should face your troubles yourself instead of relying on someone else – Jack, Charity – to sort them for you.

But… what if it is the sailors' mob, intent on revenge?

No, it isn't them. This soft but insistent knocking isn't their style. They would be loud, raucous, demanding attention and causing mayhem.

Perhaps I am underestimating them. Perhaps this is exactly what they would do to get round Jack.

Enough dithering, her inner voice shouts. *Go and face whoever it is bravely. For they are not going to stop until you do.*

She stands at the door opening out of the kitchen onto the alleyway from where the knocking is coming, on and on, and asks, in a voice that trembles like it has been set upon by an earthquake, 'Who is it?'

'Divya, it's me.'

She gasps, a hand going to her heart. She wasn't expecting to hear this.

A familiar, much longed for, much missed voice.

Raghu.

'I'm sorry for scaring you. I thought of throwing pebbles at your window but it faces the street and I couldn't risk anyone else seeing me. And in any case, my aim is rubbish. It would have hit someone else's window and what a disaster that would be.'

Her heart sings even as it leaps with exultant joy.

Raghu is here!

In the flesh.

At long last.

She flings open the door, not caring that it's past midnight. Not heeding the advice of the elders in the village where she grew up, so often repeated that it is branded into her conscience, their voices screaming caution in her head: 'For a woman, her reputation is most important. Don't ruin it by letting a man into your house in the dead of night.'

Not caring that in this street someone is always awake, minding other people's business.

Even though this is the door to the alleyway, some of the tenements look down upon it.

Someone will no doubt see Raghu entering her restaurant in the middle of the night and jump to conclusions. And she will be even more of a pariah than before, willingly allowing entry into her home, the man they have branded a murderer in addition to an arsonist.

But she's too relieved to care.

'Are you all right?' she asks, hungrily drinking him in.

Seeing that he really isn't.

Haunted eyes.

He's lost weight. He's so thin, a puff of wind would carry him away.

The scars wrought by the first beating he received standing out prominently on his gaunt and sunken face.

'I'm sorry for barging in on you like this,' he says.

'I'm glad you did,' she says fiercely.

'I scared you,' he says.

'I...'

'I'm sorry, Divya.' He rubs his face wearily, eyes shining. 'So sorry for everything. I tried to talk myself out of coming to see you but I... I wanted to tell you in person.'

'I'm glad you came,' she repeats firmly. She wants to touch him, assure herself he's real. She wants to hold him close and not let go. She's missed him so much.

'I'm going to be hanged,' he says.

'Stop being dramatic.' She laughs. 'Have you eaten? I can make some rice and dhal quickly...'

'Divya,' he interrupts. 'I mean it.'

And the way he says it, urgent yet defeated, gets through to her, making her heart, which was joyously dancing in her chest, even as it worried for him, looking so shockingly underfed, seize in stunned shock. 'What are you saying?'

'One of the sailor's gang has come forward as a witness.' He sighs.

'To what?' she whispers even though she knows.

'They claim they saw me start the fire.'

'Oh.' She clasps her heart which is beating so hard with panic and fear for him that it is threatening to burst out of her rib cage.

'I have been in hiding but it is only a matter of time before I'm caught.'

He doesn't say, *And sent to the gallows* but the threat of it is there, harsh and unfathomable, between them.

And on the heels of it, another thought. He has been in hiding and yet he has risked being captured to come here, meet with her.

Oh Raghu.

'But you didn't start the fire,' is all she can say.

'I didn't.' He appears relieved that she believes him.

It hurts Divya that he even considered that she wouldn't know, instinctively, that he didn't do it.

'I haven't doubted you for a second,' she says. 'And neither has Mr Lee.'

And now he smiles. A wan smile but one all the same, the shadows under his eyes shifting, the hollows in his cheeks displaced briefly.

It lights up her heart even as it aches desperately. For it is so meagre the number of people who believe in him without question. Apart from herself and Mr Lee, a mere two people, nobody else, not even Charity or Jack, she suspects, has staunchly believed in Raghu's innocence. And now she understands why he was worried she would doubt him. He must have had the same experience, even among fellow lascars. She has been hurt when people she considered her friends have not believed in Raghu. But how much worse must he feel when his own friends turn against him, don't quite trust him?

She is thinking all this because she cannot process what he said: that a witness has come forward, that, if he is caught, he will be hanged... *No. No, no, no.*

'I know you,' she says, looking right at him. 'And I know you would never hurt anyone, even if *they* hurt *you.*'

His eyes shine with jewels of tears.

'I am sorry,' he says again.

'Why?'

'For bringing trouble to your door.'

'Not your fault.'

'But because of associating with me...'

'I have never regretted it for one second,' she cuts in stoutly. Which is the truth. Even though, in spite of Jack's best efforts to garner customers from among his acquaintances, the restaurant is currently operating at a loss, and Divya is lying awake night after night worrying about Raghu with one exhale and Jack the next. Jack, who will surely be secretly castigating himself for investing in Divya's business. For how is she going to pay him back for his share in the business when she will not even be able to afford the rent for the coming month? The vegetable and meat vendors don't give her discounts any more; in fact, they've hiked their prices. However kind and understanding Jack is, if she can't pay the rent and the business goes under, which is likely where it is heading, he will be answerable to his father, as they run the properties together. It breaks her heart for Jack has been so kind to her, but not as much as her heart is breaking now, for this man who stands before her who, if caught, is going to be tried and hanged for a crime he did not commit...

No, no, no.

'Can't you try and escape?' she asks, her voice desperate.

'I thought of that,' he says, eyes shining. 'But Divya, I... I'm a stranger in this country. I haven't been further than the East End. I stand out because of my colouring. I don't know anyone except for my fellow lascars and men who've employed me before in the factories around the docks. And even many of my own lascar mates don't believe me. I will not be taken on in any of the ships, not now the police are circling the docks searching for me, a coloured man wanted for a crime where white men's lives were lost.'

Divya feels desperation claw at her belly. How to help Raghu?

'You could stay here—' she begins but Raghu does not let her finish.

'No. *No.* As it is, I've already caused enough—'

'Don't say it. You have not,' she says fiercely.

He flashes a small smile. 'We'll agree to disagree.' And then, 'In any case, I refuse to bring the police to your door.'

And then it comes to her. Jack. He has always been there for Divya. But would he help Raghu? When there is a witness who says they saw Raghu start the fire?

Nevertheless, she says, 'I could go to Jack, ask him to help.'

Raghu's face hardens. 'No,' he says. 'The man who says he saw me... the so-called witness... your Mr Devine knows him. They were part of the same gang during Mr Devine's criminal days.'

Divya's heart shatters all over again.

'There must be something we can do,' she says.

Raghu smiles softly at her, his eyes glowing in the shadowy light of her kitchen, 'Thank you for saying "we". For being on my side.'

'Of course. I... I care for you. I will always be on your side.'

He smiles again, his eyes shimmering. Then, 'You have done something special here, with this restaurant, Divya.' And, the smile leaving his face, his voice melancholy, 'I... I've ruined it for you.'

'You haven't—'

'I rue the day I crossed paths with you here.'

'I don't,' she says, tears smarting her eyes.

'Without me, you would have thrived.'

'Without you, I wouldn't have started this venture at all. Winning that competition is what started all this.' She waves her hand around the restaurant, the faint scent of spices lingering in the air.

'No, Divya, your cooking had already impressed everyone here. You would have done this one day sooner rather than later. And now I...' He swallows, eyes sparkling with remorse. Then, 'But listen, whatever happens, promise me, please Divya that you will continue with this venture however hard it gets.'

How, she thinks, *if I have no customers? How will I pay the rent? How will I cook when groceries are so dear?*

But she smiles brightly, nods. 'Yes.'

'It is your passion, your love for cooking and feeding people, your flair and your talent that has created this restaurant, kept it going.'

It breaks her heart afresh that while he is in such a fix, possibly staring death in the face, if he is caught, he is still worrying about her, lauding her capabilities.

'You were left to your own devices in an unfamiliar country and yet, despite all setbacks, you started this and made it a success. I am so proud of you. I only wish—'

And now, she interjects, her mouth tasting of brine, salty, bitter, 'No, don't say you shouldn't have crossed paths with me. I am glad I met you. You enrich my life.'

His eyes shine with tears. He takes her hands in his. And she feels the familiar jolt of connection she always experiences when he touches her, her entire being responding, coming alive.

Does this mean a part of her will die when he... if he...?

No, it won't happen. Don't think that way.

And then, 'I love you, Divya,' he says, putting into words what she hasn't been able to but feels with all her heart, finally recognising, acknowledging that that is what it is. Love. 'You have filled the yawning gap in my heart occasioned when I lost Ma,' he is saying. 'You are my family. I don't deserve you, your friendship, your fierce loyalty but I'm grateful for it.'

She cannot speak, her mouth thick with emotion, tears choking her throat.

'I wasn't going to tell you, burden you with this knowledge. I just came to say goodbye. But...' And now, the tears he's holding back fall upon his gaunt, scarred cheeks.

He withdraws his hands from hers.

She grabs them back. And looking into his tear-sequinned eyes, she finally locates the words she wants to say in her emotion-clogged mouth, 'I'm glad you came to see me. I'm glad you told me how you feel.'

She looks at him, this man she loves, tears trembling on his eyelashes, making them sparkle like jewels.

'I have missed you. You complete me. It is exactly as you said: you fill that yawning chasm left behind after my parents died. You are *my* family. I love you too.'

'I did not dare hope that might be so, Divya,' he whispers even as more tears join the ones creating tracks upon his sunken cheeks. And then, 'I'm sorry. You will lose me soon.'

'No. You're going to be fine,' she says brightly, hoping that by just the strength of her belief, he truly will be so. 'You won't be caught. And even if, worst case, you *are*... nothing will happen to you for they will realise that you are innocent.'

'How? When a man has come forward as a witness?'

'You are innocent.'

'You and I know that. But it's our word against theirs.' The hopelessness in his voice breaks her. 'I wish it was different. He... that sailor who died...'

'The one with the birthmark on his cheek?'

'Yes. He hated me and not just because I won jobs meant for him. He had a personal vendetta against me.' Raghu takes a breath and when he speaks, his gaze is far away, looking into the past. 'We were on a voyage together and there was this white Memsahib. A countess. He was assigned to her as a valet but she... she dismissed him and asked for me.'

'Ah.' Now the sailor's dogged picking on Raghu makes sense.

'Divya...'

Her name on his lips. A poem of lament.

'You deserve better than me.'

He tries to retrieve his hands but she keeps hold of them, leans forward, bridges the gap between them, and, disregarding the loudly vocal voices of the village matrons in her head screaming warnings at her about her reputation that will surely now be destroyed forever, she kisses him.

And for the first time since her parents died, her heart feels replete.

But then... he pulls away.

Don't, she wants to cry. Her heart, which beats with love for him, hurting.

But he's going. 'Goodbye, Divya. Forget me. Live your life, please.'

She stands there long after the door closes behind him with a gentle but firm click leaving her distraught.

Wanting.

Worrying.

Missing.

52

When Mr Stone and Mr Brown come into the restaurant the following morning, they are in a subdued mood.

She is too. She did not sleep after Raghu left. Upset. Devastated. Anxious. Replaying their conversation – and the kiss – over and over. Wondering where he went. Agonising that she should have insisted he stay with her, in relative safety.

She opens the door to her restaurant, the women scrubbing the half-circles in front of their houses turning away from her, wondering for how much longer she can do so. How many more days before it folds, this business she is so proud of, that she loves? Why is she even thinking of that when the man she loves and who loves her is in hiding from the police, bound for the gallows if he is caught? Her heart bleeds. It keens even as it longs for him.

Mr Stone and Mr Brown mumble good day but won't meet her eye.

She wonders why briefly, before putting it down to the looming threat of war playing on their minds.

She is subdued herself and not inclined to smile or make small talk and so is grateful for their quiet nods.

Nevertheless, she asks, 'Everything all right with you both?'

'Yes,' they say simultaneously. 'Why?' they ask, still looking anywhere but at her.

It appears they're hiding something. They look like little boys caught out in mischief by their mother.

Usually, she would have teased it out of them. But today, she doesn't have it in her.

She sets their breakfasts in front of them. Chai and porridge upma for Mr Stone. Black coffee and porridge with milk, and plantain cooked the way he likes it for Mr Brown – although she won't be able to make plantain for him for much longer, for the market vendors have hiked the price of plantain exorbitantly, knowing she's the only one who buys it, so she can't pull them up on quoting different prices for different customers. They are willing to do this even though, if she doesn't buy it, they will not sell it, thus making a loss. This is how much they and the residents of West India Dock Road have turned against her.

Mr Stone and Mr Brown tuck into their food silently. Again unusual as normally, they would be grumbling and complaining about the impending war, reading the headlines out loud and worrying about what was coming and placing bets about how soon. They would banter about who was leading at chess and whose wins were higher.

It is only when Charity, her brothers and the lodgers come in that Divya believes the reason Mr Stone and Mr Brown have been so cagey is nothing to do with the war and everything to do with her. For Charity too, her warm, open friend, uncharacteristically will not meet Divya's eye.

'What is it, Charity?' Divya is moved to ask, her heart sinking.

And now Charity looks at her and her gaze is bright with

something Divya can't quite read. Charity takes Divya's hands in both of hers, like Raghu had done the previous night, and says, softly, 'We need to talk, my love, after breakfast.'

Does she know of Raghu visiting Divya during the night? Has the news spread already?

The lodgers give her the death glare, even more angry and taciturn and sullen with her than they have been before.

They know.

Even the boys are quiet, subdued, not meeting her eye.

'What's the matter, eh?' she asks the brothers gently.

'Nothing,' Fergus mumbles, while Connor as usual is silent, both of the boys looking at everything but her.

'Charity said not to tell you, that she will,' Paddy pipes up.

'Paddy!' Fergus admonishes.

'Charity?' Divya tries again, her heart beating so loudly, she is sure they can all hear it.

'After breakfast,' Charity says evenly.

'What, tell her that someone saw the good-for-nothing lascar who's always hanging around her start the fire? That he has been arrested?' one of the lodgers barks.

Divya blanches, her hand clutching her heart, which wails for Raghu. His gaze when he said goodbye soft and shining with love.

When did he get caught? He had left hers after midnight.

Perhaps the police were lying in wait for him. He had been hiding and had risked getting caught to come see her. It was the wrong thing to do.

Does this mean he will be hanged?

No, no, no.

She is tempted to leave the restaurant and her customers, to run to Jack for help. But... Raghu's words echoing in her head: 'The man who says he saw me... the so-called witness... your Mr

Devine knows him. They were part of the same gang during Mr Devine's criminal days.'

Why would Jack help rescue a man he believes to be a murderer?

'Divya, you've gone quite pale. Here, sit down.' Charity pulls out one of the chairs nearest Divya and leads her to it.

'Seamus, I'd like a word later. I wanted to tell her and not like this.' Charity turns to the lodger who spoke just now, even as she passes Divya a glass of water.

Seamus has the grace to blush and shovel his food in his mouth, concentrating on eating as quickly as possible.

Divya drinks up and then stands up to her full height, which isn't much. 'He didn't do it,' she says, tears stinging her eyes.

Charity sighs and shakes her head.

Fergus and Paddy say, both at once, 'But someone saw him, Miss Ram.'

Connor nods assent. Even the boys believe Raghu did it.

'You know him, boys; do you think he would hurt someone?'

'You don't understand, Miss Ram. A man actually saw him start the fire,' Paddy says.

'Miss Ram, he may not have meant to hurt anyone,' Fergus says kindly. 'He might have just been meaning to give them a scare. But the fire got out of control, perhaps.'

She shakes her head. 'He didn't do it,' she says again.

Mr Brown sucks his teeth and Mr Stone looks sadly at her. 'Your loyalty is admirable my girl,' he says.

The lodgers stand up as one and walk out, shaking their heads, their palms bunched into fists, even as Charity calls after them, 'Where are you going? You haven't finished.'

'We don't want to eat the food that a murderer's friend has cooked,' they toss over their shoulders. 'Who knows, maybe she's poisoned it.'

'Don't you dare...' Charity cries, but they've already left before she can finish, slamming the door hard behind them.

Divya slumps back into her chair. She is defeated. Her heart bleeding, eyes wet. Everyone believes Raghu did it. He will die at the gallows just because one man had a vendetta against him for doing his job well and being chosen over him. And this man, fuelled by a desire for revenge, convinced his fellows that Raghu was stealing their jobs.

Raghu will be hanged because someone lied to implicate him, and everyone believes the liar over the lascar and the Indian woman who maintains his innocence.

He will be hanged.

53

The door has barely shut behind the lodgers, the entire building reverberating with the force of their angry exit, when Jack bursts in. He looks from one to the other, taking in their identical sombre expressions. Divya has wiped her eyes with her apron. She refuses to allow the sorrow choking her and moistening her eyes access, not here, in front of her friends, for she doesn't want their pity. She wants instead for them to believe her, which they will not do.

'I take it you've heard about the Coventry bombing by the IRA,' Jack says.

'What?'

Everyone starts talking at once.

'You haven't heard? I thought that's why you all looked so upset,' Jack says. 'What's the matter?'

'You tell us what's happened, son,' Mr Stone says.

Jack doesn't need more prompting. 'An Irish Republican Army bomb exploded in Coventry, killing five and injuring seventy. And not only that: in London too, police found two similar bombs – thankfully before they could go off and cause havoc – and arrested four terrorists.'

'Oh no, this is not good.' Mr Brown shakes his head.

'Will the English be angry and turn on us because we are Irish?' Fergus asks, both him and Connor looking worried.

'Mr Devine won't let anything happen to us,' Paddy declares stoutly and Jack smiles and ruffles his hair.

'Too right, I won't,' he says.

While the boys and Mr Stone and Mr Brown are plying Jack with questions, Divya goes to the kitchen to collect herself. She is worried for Charity and the boys and the other Irish living on this street but she can't help her worry about Raghu taking precedence.

Charity and the boys are part of a community that will band together, with Jack and others supporting them, if there is trouble. But for Raghu, there is no one but Divya – she doesn't know if Mr Lee will support him now there is a witness who claims to have seen him start the fire: given the reactions of the others, most likely not. Her heart is wrung inside out. Raghu is going to die. She can't let him. She can't. There must be *something* she can do.

Charity comes to find Divya, which is so kind of her and so quintessentially Charity. Caring about and looking out for Divya even though her brothers are worried about the bombings and how it will affect them.

'How are you doing?' Charity asks.

What to tell her? How to make her understand that even in a room full of people she considers her friends, Divya feels lonely, alone, for they do not believe her. Instead, they look at her sadly, thinking of her as deluded for maintaining that the man they all knew, someone gentle and kind, who cooked for them and whom they had welcomed, is innocent of the charge against him.

Instead, she turns the question back on Charity. 'How are *you*? Will this bombing and terrorist attacks have repercussions on you?'

Charity had confided in Divya that the last time something like this happened, there had been clashes between the Irish and the English. 'It was a scary time,' she'd said, eyes wide with remembered fear and upset. 'There were even incidents at the boys' school. I was afraid to let them out of my sight.'

Now, Charity says, 'There's going to be war soon, so this will be forgotten, I hope. Especially given nothing happened in London and the police got to the bombs in time.'

Divya sees that Charity is keeping her fingers crossed behind her back. And her broken heart goes out to her.

'I'm sure it will,' she says, squeezing Charity's hand.

Charity sighs deeply. Then, 'Now tell me, my love, how are you?'

'He didn't do it, Charity.'

Charity sighs again. 'Someone saw him, Divya.'

'They lied.'

'You are loyal and that's—'

'Charity, he didn't do it. I promise.' She doesn't want to confide even in Charity that Raghu was here mere hours ago. If her friend doesn't believe that he's innocent, she will be worried that Divya was with him, alone, the previous night.

'Promise me one thing,' Charity says, eyes large and worried.

'What is it?' Divya asks.

'Promise me you won't tell anyone else that Raghu is innocent.'

'But—'

'Keep your head down, Divya. Tempers are high. Two men lost their lives. The publican is in hospital, unconscious. His business was affected, the pub was burned. People are angry.'

'But Charity, Raghu is innocent and he will die for something he did not do. How is killing an innocent man the answer?' Divya's voice breaks.

Her friend puts her arms around Divya and holds her while she sobs. But it is no comfort.

54

When Divya has composed herself and comes back out into the restaurant dining hall with Jack's breakfast, he looks at her kindly. 'I heard about your friend. I'm sorry.'

'He didn't do it,' she repeats, woodenly. Knowing that Jack too, like the others, will not believe her. Especially given he's acquainted with the witness who claims they saw Raghu start the fire.

But...

'I know,' Jack says.

She looks at him, surprised.

'That man who said he saw him, Jim, he will say he ate the moon and he will do it convincingly. He came out of his mother's womb lying. I know the lad. He's doing this out of misplaced loyalty to his dead fellows.'

'So our Divya is right?' Mr Stone and Mr Brown cry in unison.

'Yes, I believe so,' Jack says.

He believes me.

Divya feels relief surge through her along with affection for her friend, this man who has helped her every step of the way since she serendipitously bumped into him. He is now standing by Raghu, whom he barely knows, taking her side just when she feels the most alone.

And not only that, if Jack believes in Raghu's innocence, then he will do something about it, Divya knows this much. Her devastated heart perks up, hope rising from the ashes of her despair, even as she thinks, *Oh, why didn't I go to him sooner, like I wanted to? Why didn't I believe in him, trust him, trust that he would, like always, be there for me and, by extension, my friend?*

'Someone should talk to this Jim,' Mr Stone is saying. 'This is not right, condemning a man to the gallows for something he may not have done.'

Divya notes Mr Stone's choice of words: *may not have done.* He is still not convinced of Raghu's innocence.

'Already so much devastation has been caused.' Mr Stone sighs. 'Two men have lost their lives. Another is in hospital fighting for his life.'

'Three wrongs will not make a right,' Mr Brown says.

'I will be heading to find Jim right after I've had my breakfast,' Jack says. 'I wanted to check if you were all okay first.'

Divya is so moved that she goes to Jack and gives him a hug.

He smiles, his eyes soft and glowing with emotion.

'Thank you,' she says. 'He didn't do it.'

'I know, Divya. You're a good judge of character. You've chosen to be my friend, haven't you?'

And he smiles gently at her.

55

Divya thanks Jack again as he leaves after breakfast to find Jim.

'Thank you for believing in Raghu's innocence. For trying to help him.'

'I care for you, Divya,' Jack says softly, the warm tenderness in his gaze as it sparkles at her leaving no doubt as to what he means. It almost exactly mirrors how Raghu had looked at her the previous night. 'I'm doing it for you.'

Mr Stone and Mr Brown pretend to be absorbed in their game but their pieces are suspiciously still and Divya would bet they are listening to every word.

'And I know that you care for him. However much I'd like it to be otherwise.' Jack sighs.

She looks at him and his eyes shine with emotion.

'But I wouldn't want his death on my conscience. I know Jim is lying out of misplaced loyalty. I will try my best to get your Raghu free for you.'

He sounds so sad when he says, *your Raghu*.

'You are my friend,' she says.

'I will have to be happy with that.' He nods, sighing again and brushing a hand roughly across his eyes. Then, in his usual tone, bright and brisk, 'I'll be right back and hopefully with good news.'

'Thank you.'

'You don't have to thank me, Divya.'

'I do.'

But he is gone.

Mr Stone clears his throat.

Divya turns from her scrutiny of Jack's rigid back, his loping strides as he walks past her window and out of her sight.

'He's a good man,' Mr Stone says and his voice is croaky.

Mr Brown sniffs. 'That 'e is.'

Divya nods and wipes her eyes with her apron. 'I'm lucky in him.'

'That you are.'

And Mr Stone, cheekily, adds, 'Can't we convince you to change your mind, Miss Ram?'

'I'd choose him if I was younger and of a different persuasion,' Mr Brown declares, causing Mr Stone to snort in surprise.

* * *

Afterwards, Divya returns to the kitchen, leaving Mr Stone and Mr Brown to their game.

She needs to cook, to take her mind off what is happening, worrying about whether Jack has managed to find Jim, and if he has, whether he'll be able to make him tell the truth, free Raghu.

There will, once again, be only Charity and the boys and those lodgers who are working nearby and able to get to the restaurant, Mr Stone and Mr Brown and perhaps Jack if he's back in time for lunch.

Please, she prays, *Please let Jack be able to convince the sailor Jim to tell the truth.*

Usually, when she is worried or upset, or when she needs solace, cooking provides it. It centres her.

But not today. Now, it causes more worry to spawn. As there isn't enough fresh produce to concoct a decent meal, what with the vendors refusing to serve her, calling insults and hiking up the prices when they see her – which is only going to get worse, she predicts, now that Raghu has been arrested, if the lodgers' reaction is anything to go by.

And there her mind goes again, dwelling on and agonising about Raghu's fate.

Don't think about that. Jack is sorting it.

She is so grateful for Jack. He is always there for her, whatever the circumstance.

His admission just now... Charity is right. He does care for her, in *that* way.

But she isn't right for him and he will soon see it. He deserves better. She will only drag him down. If he is with her, people will treat him differently. They will make fun of him, if not to his face, then behind his back. She doesn't want that for Jack.

Let me be the judge of that, he would say, she knows. *I will deal with it if it happens.*

But she would rather not put him in such a position at all.

In the end, after dithering about what to cook, she settles on chilli, ginger and garlic seasoned beans and cumin rice, potatoes fried in mustard oil, the last straggling dregs of vegetables coated in gram flour and deep-fried – they are wilted but when cooked this way, it doesn't matter, they taste great.

She makes parathas stuffed with the last of the cauliflower which she has spiced and mashed, and for dessert, she prepares coffee cake and cardamom-infused banana bread.

'Something smells nice,' Mr Stone calls from the dining hall.

'I can hear his stomach growling louder than a tiger,' Mr Brown cries.

'He wouldn't know a tiger growling if it appeared in front of him,' Mr Stone counters.

'I would,' Mr Brown calls. 'It would sound exactly like Mr Stone's stomach. The aromas are putting him off the game – he's no longer a worthy opponent.'

'How dare you,' Mr Stone cries. 'I'll show you who's a worthy opponent.'

Their banter quietens as they concentrate on their game and Divya focuses on cooking.

As she cooks, to take her mind away from worrying about Raghu as much as anything, she thinks of future steps – she will try and keep her restaurant going for as long as she possibly can. It is what she'd pledged to Raghu the previous night. 'Promise me,' he'd said, his eyes bright with care. There she goes, thinking of him, agonising about him. With effort, once again, she reins in her wandering mind. She has enough money saved up for two weeks' rent. That will keep her going until mid-September. For groceries, she could go to Mr Lee. He will serve her, she knows, and fairly too. However, most of the veggies and other sundries that he stocks – save the few she uses for preparing the dishes he likes, which he has instructed her on how to use – are not ones that she is familiar with. In any case, she has no choice but to adapt – she'll ask Mr Lee's advice on how best to use them.

And in between all this, there is, always, the sinister threat of war and the additional worry of how that will affect things, people, produce, way of life.

Whatever happens, if, come mid-September, she is not earning money, the restaurant will have to close. The thought is a stab in her heart but... *Needs must*, her conscience reminds.

She knows Jack would give her credit and advise her to carry on with the restaurant, even when it is running at a loss, but she will refuse, standing her ground, for she will not have the means to pay him back for his initial investment.

But she is determined to repay him – for that, she would have to get a job. Perhaps Charity would keep her on like before? But where would Divya stay? The attic room is occupied now. And even if that was taken care of, the boarding house's kitchen is now even smaller than it was before – Charity has converted the dining room and part of the kitchen into more rooms to let. Practical as it brings in more money.

Divya will have to find a way to cook for all the lodgers in that tiny kitchen somehow – that is, if Charity will keep her on.

She is lucky to have Charity, her brothers, Jack, Mr Stone, Mr Brown and Mr Lee. She is *lucky*. She's had the opportunity to run her own business. She has good friends. She will count the positives from now on instead of dwelling on…

An almighty, resounding crash from the dining area jars her from her musings, followed by the tinkle of shattering glass.

56

Divya drops her knife and runs into the dining area to find Mr Stone and Mr Brown cowering.

The window has been smashed, cracks radiating from it.

Hot tears sting Divya's eyes and she tastes chilli-hot ire on her tongue, even as her heart catches in fear and upset.

'Someone threw a brick.' Mr Stone's voice shakes.

They are packing up their chess set with trembling fingers.

'Are you both all right?' Divya's voice is none too steady as she takes in the damage. A hole in the window, ushering in a draught and noise, the usual sounds of conversation and busyness from the street, and through which she can see the burnt bricks of the public house opposite, the faint scent of smoke and ruin hovering in the smoggy air.

In one corner stands a huddle of the women of the street, watching her, turning away when her shocked gaze attempts to meet theirs.

Broken glass littering the room, twinkling silver bright. And in the midst of it all, the offending brick, scarred by smoke. The vandal has used one of the pub's fire-damaged bricks to convey his violent message.

Thank goodness Mr Stone and Mr Brown were sitting beside the other window. But even so, some shards of glass have found their way near them.

'We're fine, my dear, just about,' Mr Brown says, standing up, holding out a hand to assist Mr Stone, who is trembling all over.

'You're not hurt?' Divya asks, just to make sure.

'No,' Mr Brown says.

Mr Stone takes out his handkerchief and wipes his forehead. It takes a few tries as his hands are shaking.

'Just taken by surprise, is all. The glass missed us, don't you worry, love,' Mr Brown says, as he tucks the chess set under his arm, draping the other around his distressed friend.

'Where are you going?' Divya swallows, tasting bile and upset.

'It's dangerous to be here, love.' Mr Brown sighs.

'But...'

'It will all die down, soon, we 'ope,' Mr Brown says, and he and Mr Stone do look sorry. 'But until then, we're better off playing our game somewhere else.'

'Please, at least wait until I sweep up the glass...'

'Sorry, my dear. It's... We are...' Mr Brown swallows. Then, 'It was scary.' He admits. 'We'd like to leave now.'

She watches them walk out of her restaurant, her broken heart splintering even further, much like her window, two scared old men, one white, one black, arms linked, gingerly navigating the floor so as to avoid stepping on shrapnel. One with a chess set tucked under his arm. The other clutching the bag with the chess pieces as if for dear life. Good friends who've seen each other through so much.

And suddenly, her fear and upset is replaced by a great hot rush of anger.

She's had *enough*.

She strides to the door, not caring if she's stepping on glass, and holds it open for Mr Stone and Mr Brown.

The women have dispersed from their rubbernecking gaggle and are now sitting in front of their houses sunning themselves.

They look at Mr Stone and Mr Brown leaving the restaurant.

'About time,' they sniff. 'Finally, you've seen sense.'

'It's not right,' Mr Brown says. 'The girl has done nothing wrong. She doesn't deserve this.'

'She was harbouring a killer,' Mrs Kerridge says.

'You don't know that,' Mr Stone cautions. 'In fact, Mr Devine is...'

'Why is that lascar in prison then?' Mrs Neville asks.

That is it. Divya will not take any more. She comes to stand next to Mr Stone and Mr Brown and faces the women, who turn away from her, suddenly busy with shelling peas, with their darning.

The public house opposite is now an eyesore, stained black with soot. The faint scent of charred smoke and burnt flesh in the air.

Divya shivers.

She looks at her restaurant. The (once cherry red, now faded yellow) sign has been besmirched again.

The window is shattered. Tears sting her eyes.

'Did any of you see who did that? Threw a brick at my window?' she asks.

They don't reply. Ignoring her. Concentrating on their chores. She has become a pariah with these same women who had welcomed her, included her in their fold.

'Mr Brown and Mr Stone here could have got hurt,' Divya says.

'Does she mean like the two men who died opposite?' Mrs Kerridge calls to the other women, her voice laced with venom.

'Solving violence with violence will not achieve anything. It will not bring those men back. Or cure the publican,' Divya says, loud enough for the whole street to hear. 'If it makes you feel better, you can hound me, smash my windows, throw faeces at my sign. But it will not bring them back. It will only cause more hurt. I did not hurt those sailors. I did not even know them. And Raghu did not hurt them either.'

'He has been imprisoned for it,' Mrs Kerridge huffs but her voice is subdued with none of the venom of before. 'Someone saw him do it.'

'Raghu did not hurt those sailors,' Divya says again. 'He did not cause the fire. And when it is proved so, you will feel bad for doing all this.'

Her voice, which has been clear until now, shakes at the last, trembling like a leaf in a squall.

She takes a deep breath and goes into her empty restaurant.

She shuts the door, leans against it and crumples down to the floor, her legs giving way as everything catches up with her, and she is finally ambushed by the tears she has been holding back.

57

By the time Charity, the boys and the lodgers come for their midday meal, accompanied by a sheepish-looking but visibly restored Mr Stone and Mr Brown, Divya has pulled herself together, having given herself a stern talking to. She has cleaned up the glass and has tried to patch up the hole in the window with one of her scarves. She is brisk and businesslike as she serves their food.

Charity and the boys try their best to sound normal and upbeat but the general mood is one of subdued caution, what with the bombing in Coventry and the apprehending of IRA terrorists in London, the looming war, and the conflict happening right here on the street.

But there is one piece of good news.

'Mr Barney, the publican, is showing signs of getting better,' Charity tells Divya. 'You know he's been unconscious since the fire. Well, he opened his eyes this morning and was trying to speak. "He never stops talking and I get fed up at times, you know," his wife cried, wiping her eyes when she relayed the news to us,' Charity says. '"But was I glad he was trying to talk again. I will never shoo him off, ask him to go trouble his regulars with his chattering again." That's what his wife said.'

Divya smiles, her cheeks hurting with the effort. For it feels like she has not smiled for years.

After they've eaten, the lodgers come up to her as one. 'Thank you, Miss Ram. Your food was delicious, as ever. We are sorry. You were right, what you said outside.'

'You heard?'

'You know this street,' Charity laughs. 'Within seconds of your saying it, it was up and down the docks and beyond.'

And Divya smiles again.

'We are sorry we blamed you,' the lodgers say, 'when it is not your fault. You did not hurt anyone.'

'I did not,' Divya says. 'And neither has Raghu.'

At that, the men's expressions tighten.

Charity sighs.

'It is the truth,' Divya maintains, looking at her friend.

'*Your* truth,' Charity says gently.

'*The* truth,' Divya persists, stubbornly.

Seamus, the spokesperson for the lodgers, says, 'We will fix the window for you. And clean the sign too. Nobody will do anything like that again, we'll make sure of it.'

'Thank you,' Divya says.

* * *

The lodgers are true to their word. As dusk falls, mellow grey with a nippy bite, they repair her window and clean the sign, the children who have been playing hopscotch on the road watching avidly, alongside the neighbourhood women, who can't help putting their oar in and pointing out to the lodgers what they are doing wrong and how they should go about correcting it, much to the lodgers' barely suppressed irritation.

It is evening and Jack is still not back.

He had promised to find Jim and convince him to tell the truth and to update Divya as soon as possible.

Does this mean that he hasn't been able to find Jim? Or that he *has* but hasn't been able to convince him to come clean and admit that he lied, that Raghu was nowhere near the public house?

Divya sits inside the restaurant, watching the lodgers fix her window under the keen eye of the neighbourhood matrons, and she talks to her parents in her head, her version of prayer. *Please, Ma, Baba, let Raghu be freed. Please let him live.*

58

Divya opens her restaurant the next morning and it is as if it was never vandalised. The window is fixed, and the sign squeaky clean thanks to the lodgers.

She had treated them to kheer and lemon cake as thanks, Mr Lee handing out shots of his potent baiju, a very strong liquor.

They had sat in the restaurant drinking and eating long into the night and Divya was glad of the company and the noise. She did not want to be alone with her thoughts. But inevitably, the lodgers, Charity and her brothers – the younger two had been allowed to stay up just this once – decamped to the lodging house and Mr Stone, Mr Brown and Mr Lee stumbled home on unsteady legs and she was alone with her fears.

Charity, kind and thoughtful as always, had said, 'Do you want to come back to ours tonight? We're full but you can share with me – I can make up a bed.'

'Thank you, Charity, but I'll be fine here,' Divya said. She did not want to inconvenience Charity and she also didn't want to make a habit of relying on her friend.

She was an adult; she needed to behave like one.

But once everyone left, her bravado shrivelled into nothing as all the fears she was holding at bay came rushing back, swamping her. She thought of how the previous night, Raghu had been here, telling her he loved her, his gaze soft and tender. She relived their all too brief kiss and wondered if she would ever get to see him, touch him, kiss him again. She agonised about where he was now, how he was feeling, what was going through his mind. She recalled his gaze as he said goodbye, the despair in it.

She did not sleep.

Divya gets up to face a new dawn with worry sitting heavy on her chest, wondering why she hasn't heard from Jack and whether it is bad news that is keeping him.

Why else hasn't he come?

If it was good news, she would hear, surely?

Feeling groggy and a bit lightheaded, she opens up the restaurant and there, on her doorstep is Jack.

He is not smiling. He looks tired, lines wrought onto his face, circles under his eyes.

It is bad news.

'Come in. I'll make you chai,' she says.

'Just the ticket,' he says.

Neither of them speaking their mind. Divya not asking what she wants to and he not relaying what he has come to say.

Mr Stone and Mr Brown follow on Jack's heels, Mr Brown with the chess set tucked under his arm, Mr Stone carrying the bag with the pieces, both looking the worse for wear. With the window repaired, they're back at their usual spot beside the other window.

'A bit of a late one last night, was it?' Jack asks.

'Ah,' Mr Stone cries, 'that Mr Lee's Chinese liquor is potent, I tell you.'

'Nothing Divya's breakfast can't fix,' Jack says.

'You can say that again,' Mr Stone smiles.

'You look like you didn't have an early one either, son,' Mr Brown says, assessing Jack.

'No, I didn't,' Jack runs a hand down his face wearily. And, 'Ah thanks Divya. Just what I need,' he says as Divya sets spiced potatoes, a chilli omelette and chai with liberal amounts of cinnamon and ginger in front of him.

She waits until he's eaten, serving Mr Stone and Mr Brown.

Once he's pushed his plate away, however, she pulls out a chair and sits next to him. 'You didn't find Jim?'

If he had, he would have told her, she knows.

'No, I didn't. I'm sorry. I looked in all his usual haunts. Was out during the day and much of the night searching for him. But he's laying low.'

She nods, feeling desperate, devastated, hopeless. Seeing Raghu's face, eyes bright with unshed tears of longing and despair as he said goodbye. He will hang for no fault of his.

'I'm sorry. I will keep trying,' Jack says.

'Thank you,' Divya says, trying to convey her gratitude through her gaze. It is all she has. It is not enough.

59

After Jack leaves, she goes through the motions, thinking of Raghu. How he had kissed her, conveying everything he felt, all that was unsaid, all his love with it, knowing that was all they had.

He will die in a strange country on the other side of the world to his mother. He will be hanged for a crime he didn't commit.

She buys vegetables and groceries from Mr Lee.

'I sorry for you friend,' he says. 'He cook well.'

'Yes, he does,' she says.

'Not good as you. But that no crime.'

Her eyes fill up. Mr Lee is trying to placate her by trying to crack a rare joke.

'Thank you, Mr Lee. For believing in him when no one else does.'

'They see colour of skin and think you guilty. It wrong.' He shakes his head. 'They should see heart.' He bangs his chest.

'Yes.'

'No pay for grocery today,' he says as she roots around in her purse for change.

'No, Mr Lee, please let me—'

'No, I please. My shop, my rule.'

And now she cannot stop the tears from overflowing, over-whelmed by his kindness, and he comes around the counter and awkwardly pats her back.

Afterwards, 'Thank you, Mr Lee,' she says, wiping her eyes. 'Sorry about this.'

'No, you cry anytime. My pleasure.'

She smiles wetly and he beams.

* * *

Divya gets back from Mr Lee's to find that a miracle has taken place.

Mrs Kerridge is in the restaurant, chatting to Mr Stone and Mr Brown.

She looks up when Divya comes in. Holds Divya's eye. Her face red when she says, 'I owe you an apology. You were right, what you said yesterday. I should know better, me a mother of three. You've not hurt anyone. I'm sorry for hurting you.'

Mr Brown and Mr Stone are looking at Divya anxiously, wondering what she will do.

For a brief, mean moment, Divya is tempted to turn away, like Mrs Kerridge and the other women of the street have been doing to her these last few days.

But, like Mr Brown said, two wrongs do not make a right. And she appreciates how hard this must be for Mrs Kerridge, who famously, she has heard from various different sources, never accepts that she is wrong even when she is in the wrong.

And so, she nods, accepting the older woman's apology.

Mr Stone and Mr Brown grin happily and go back to their game.

Divya notes that Mrs Kerridge is waiting expectantly, her gaze upon the nearly empty plate of snacks – vegetable pakoras and potato-stuffed bondas and sponge cake – that Divya placed beside Mr Stone and Mr Brown to sustain them while she was doing the shopping.

Taking her cue from that, Divya says, 'What can I get you?'

'Now we're talking.' Mrs Kerridge smiles. 'I have missed your food.'

'Not too smelly for you then?' Divya can't resist the jab.

Mr Stone and Mr Brown look up with identical worried expressions.

Mrs Kerridge colours. 'No,' she says.

'Would you like the same as Mr Stone and Mr Brown, with a cup of spiced tea?'

'The bondas are to die for,' Mr Stone says, grinning cheekily. 'I wouldn't mind a couple more and another slice of that cake. It's heavenly, Miss Ram, your best yet.'

And with a pang, Divya thinks of Raghu, who would bake such wonderful cakes so effortlessly.

Enough. There's nothing to gain from worrying.

'That would be good.' Mrs Kerridge smiles, pulling up a chair beside Mr Stone and Mr Brown.

* * *

Throughout the day, more people trickle in, the residents of West India Dock Road gracing her establishment again, now Mrs Kerridge has taken the lead.

Divya's Curry House is heaving.

Back to what it was.

No, who is she fooling?

For before, she wouldn't be subject to sheepish grins when

she is looking and hard assessing glances when they think she's not.

Before, they wouldn't be whispering about Raghu when she was in the kitchen.

Before, Raghu would, more often than not, be cooking beside her.

Now he's headed for the gallows.

She has to ask Paddy to taste her dishes to check the seasoning – to her, they're all much too salty.

60

Late evening and the matrons of West India Dock Road are all in the curry house instead of on the street.

Through the shiny-as-mirrors windows – thanks to the lodgers at Charity's who, in addition to fixing the broken window, also gave all of them a polish – they can still keep up their hawk-eyed surveillance of the goings on in the street.

'We can keep a beady eye on the children while enjoying a cup of spiced tea – what do you put in it, Miss Ram? It is so creamy and thick, more like pudding,' Mrs Ross exults.

'I do love this sponge. It's so very moist,' Mrs O'Riley says and the other ladies nod assent, even Mrs Kerridge, who is Mrs O'Riley's sworn enemy.

'I like the cashew biscuits – perfect dunked in the tea,' says Mrs Boon.

'Ooh, you're right you are. These are moreish, Miss Ram,' Mrs O'Riley is saying, when Charity bursts in, breathless and panting.

'Have you heard?'

'Have we heard what?' Everyone looks up.

'What is it, girl? You seem all in a tizz,' Mr Stone queries.

Charity looks up at Divya, who is wringing her tea towel anxiously, trying to read her friend.

Charity does not look devastated – so that means Raghu is all right. Well, as much as he can be in prison. Even if Charity might think Raghu was guilty, Divya knows that her friend would be upset on Divya's behalf if anything happened to him.

'Well, you know I said the publican was waking up and wanted to talk?'

'Yes.'

'His wife sent word and there was nobody on the street so her boy came into the lodging house.'

'Ah,' the matrons sigh ruefully, regretting, no doubt, the fresh gossip that has passed them by because they were in here instead of on the street.

'What is it?' Mr Brown asks. 'Is Mr Barney all right?'

'He is.'

'Hooray!' Everyone cheers.

'I have more news,' Charity says, once again meeting Divya's gaze. What is she trying to convey? Try as she might, Divya cannot read her friend's expression.

When the room has quieted down somewhat, Charity says, 'Mr Barney's throat was too burnt to talk louder than a whisper and he has to stop constantly to sip water – his mouth gets very dry...'

'What did he say?' Mrs Kerridge clucks impatiently.

'He insists that the fire was an accident.'

'What?' Divya's hand goes to her heart. Dare she believe it?

'He heard that Raghu had been arrested. And he did not want the boy hanged. He said Raghu hadn't been near the public house.'

There is absolute quiet in the room, everyone's attention fixed upon Charity, Divya's included. The great big knot of agonised anxiety weighing down her chest loosening slightly even as tears prick her eyes.

'The sailor, the one who set upon Raghu, didn't like the chips served with his drink. It seems he and his mate stormed into the kitchen to complain to the chef. The publican, sensing a fight brewing, asked the chef and servers to leave the kitchen and tried to assuage the situation, keep the peace. But the sailor could not be placated, in his rage, overturning a vat of oil.'

Charity takes a breath even as Divya tries to absorb what she's just heard. The rest of the room is doing the same.

'He was always hot-headed, that one.' Mr Stone breaks the silence.

'Mr Barney evacuated the pub as soon as the fire started. But the sailor who had overturned the vat of oil, and his friend, got burnt,' Charity says. 'Mr Barney was trying to get them out when he lost consciousness. He is emphatic that Raghu had nothing to do with the fire.'

And now the room erupts in noise, everyone speaking at once.

Divya sits down heavily on a chair someone has pulled out.

Charity comes and puts her arms around her, gently wiping Divya's wet cheeks with a napkin. That is when Divya realises that she is crying.

'I'm sorry,' Charity whispers, 'for doubting Raghu. For not believing you.'

But Divya is too happy, too relieved to care. She holds on tightly to her friend and smiles through her tears.

61

Four days on, Jack arrives to breakfast at the curry house with grim news. 'The Royal Navy has proceeded to war stations,' he says. 'Now we just wait for the official declaration.'

The curry house, which was buzzing with conversation, falls silent, identical sombre expressions on everyone's faces.

Mr and Mrs Rosenbaum are sitting at a small table by the window, Mr Rosenbaum clutching his mug of tea as if his life depends on it. Mrs Rosenbaum is very pale. Most of their family managed to get out of Germany just in time. They are travelling to safety but then so is everyone else. 'We haven't heard from them. We fear the worst,' Mrs Rosenbaum had said, blowing her nose with her handkerchief.

The few of their relatives who couldn't escape Germany... 'I dread to think of their fate. My sister. Her children. She has three.' Bright tears shimmering in Mrs Rosenbaum's cocoa-brown eyes. 'I saw them last three ago when I visited Germany. Hitler had already started discriminating against us Jews then. I begged her to leave, to come with me. "Why should I? This is my country, my children's home," she said.' Mrs Rosenbaum sniffed, smiling sadly. 'She is very stubborn, my sister. I hugged them extra tight when leaving. Perhaps I knew, even then...'

Divya had listened. Patted Mrs Rosenbaum's back. Given her a fresh cup of tea. Not knowing what to say. What *could* you say?

Divya has not heard from Raghu. He has been released, she knows. Jack brought the news back.

But he has not come here.

She understands why. He does not want to trouble her, or bring trouble to her. Which is what he thinks, she knows.

And yes, it was hard and lonely when most had ostracised her but she would do it again in a heartbeat – she *would*.

You did nothing wrong. I am happiest when with you. I miss you. I would rather you were with me and I suffered than if you weren't, for when you are not with me, I suffer more from missing you, worrying about you, wanting you, she would tell him if she could.

She has been tempted a few – well, if she is honest, more than a few – times to go to his billet.

But she has her pride.

She wants to shake some sense into him. *We are plunging into war. Tomorrow is uncertain. Please, let me have today with you.*

She goes to bed aching, yearning, wanting him. When she sleeps, her dreams are of him.

Her days are busy with running the restaurant – it is back to full capacity. The vendors at the market are once again giving her the best bargains. When she went there with the other matrons of West India Dock Road and stood in the queue, instead of turning away from her and calling the next customer forward, or pointing to a bunch of wilting coriander and quoting astronomical prices, they had smiled as if they had always done so and said, 'Coriander and mint, plantain and okra, hugely discounted just for you.'

It was as if they were never angry, rude, discriminatory towards her.

She will take it. It is better than the alternative and at least her worries with regards to the restaurant are at bay.

During the day, she has become skilled at keeping thoughts of Raghu away.

It is at night when she struggles to fall asleep despite having been incredibly busy and on her feet all day, one ear peeled for a gentle knock at the kitchen door opening onto the alleyway, that she misses him, longs for him, worries about him.

Does he have work? Perhaps not. Was he mistreated in prison? Without a doubt. Is he eating enough? Perhaps not.

She wishes she didn't care so very much.

But she does.

She does and it hurts.

Love hurts.

PART VII

62

September. A new month and more news, all grim.

Nazi Germany, under Hitler, invades Poland.

Here in England, blackout is imposed, and the army officially mobilised. A four-day evacuation of children from London and other major cities begins.

'We are not going,' Charity's brothers declare when Charity muses that they should consider it.

'It's safest.' Charity wrings her hands. 'I will make sure you are together.'

'We are staying right here.' The boys are insistent.

'But the docks will be the first under fire,' Charity cries.

'When it comes to that, we'll see, won't we,' Mr Brown soothes.

'At least your brothers aren't old enough to sign up. My sons are all going to,' Mrs Kerridge cries. 'I know they have to do their bit and all, but... I lost my brother and my pa to the first war.' A melancholy, faraway look in Mrs Kerridge's eyes. Then, pushing her shoulders back, although her eyes still carry that maudlin sheen, she says, firmly, 'But we must all band together to defeat that power-crazed man.'

'I want to sign up,' Fergus says, yet again.

'Not a word, Fergus. You're too young,' Charity snaps once more.

He scowls, looking furious.

'She's right you know,' Divya tells the boy gently, Mrs Kerridge nodding assent.

But Fergus is not listening. He storms out of the restaurant, his brothers following.

Charity sighs and Divya places a plate of bread and butter pudding, Charity's favourite, before her. 'Eat up. You'll feel better after, I promise.'

Charity squeezes Divya's hand and smiles. 'Food is the cure, is it?'

'Always,' Mr Stone, busy tucking into his third helping, says.

* * *

At 11.15 a.m. on the 3rd of September, everyone in Divya's curry house listens to Prime Minister Neville Chamberlain announce on the BBC home service broadcast that Britain is at war.

They are just digesting the news, ashen-faced, Divya supplying tea and pakoras and cardamom-spiced biscuits when, merely ten minutes after the broadcast, an almighty screeching shatters the stunned silence.

'What's that?' Divya cries.

'Air raid sirens,' Mr Stone whispers, face pinched.

'Jesus, Mary and Joseph, the war has started already.' Mrs O'Riley makes the sign of the cross.

'Quick, get pans and pots from the kitchen!' Mr Brown cries.

Divya distributes pots and pans to everyone in the restaurant.

They place them on their heads, crouch down and wait for the bombs.

Twenty long and tense minutes later, there's a cry from the street, 'False alarm!'

They breathe sighs of great relief, hugging one another.

But in each other's wide, bloodshot eyes, they can see that this is a sign of times to come.

'We will keep on keeping on,' Mrs Kerridge firmly declares. 'Let Hitler come. We'll show him what's what.'

With Divya's rice pan on her head – she has forgotten she is wearing it – she cuts an earnest yet slightly comic figure.

But nobody is laughing.

63

England is at war.

And Divya is at war with herself. Should she try and contact Raghu? Or wait for him to come to her?

But for how long?

And will he?

Please come, Raghu. I miss you.

If only yearning, wanting, needing, believing made wishes come true...

He does not come.

It makes her angry. So angry.

If he ever does visit, she will shout at him, *You think you're doing me a favour by staying away? Think again. I don't even find joy in cooking any more, because of missing you, loving you, even when I hate that you're staying away.*

But however much she shouts, argues, rants in her head, he does not come.

And then, one morning, the postman, who hardly ever stops at her door except to drop off post for some of the regulars – Divya herself never gets any – hands her a letter.

'For me?' she asks stupidly.

'Yes, Miss Ram.' He grins, this young man who has told her he too has signed up and will be leaving to fight for England soon. 'It's your name on the letter.'

It is from Raghu. He has written in English.

'This is why I was promoted,' he had told her, 'because like you, I can read and write in English.'

'I can do so thanks to the missionary nuns in our village who set up a free English-speaking school,' Divya had said. 'I'm so grateful to them. Because of them, I got the job as ayah.'

'I too have the priests in my village to thank,' Raghu had grinned. 'They tried very hard to convert me to Christianity. But my mother tried just as hard to root me in Hindu tradition and values.'

'I think,' Divya said, 'as long as you live a good life, do the right thing, are kind to your fellows, that is the best religion. You can find God through being kind.'

His eyes had sparkled then. 'You are so wise.'

'Ah, I don't know about that. I also often find God in a delicious dish. Your rasmalai for example takes me straight to heaven.'

And he laughed, bringing to mind celebratory bells tinkling in the warm, fruit-scented summer breeze.

The memory hurts now, as she touches his letter – this is the first time she's seeing his handwriting. Big, careful letters sloping gently to the right. She pictures him writing it, head bent, face scrunched up in concentration.

My dear Divya.

She tenderly runs her hand over his words, addressed to her, imagining she's touching him.

She hears Charity's voice in her head: *You've got it bad.*

What is it about him that draws her? His smile. His gentleness. How he has treated her with respect from the first time they met on board the ship.

He owns her heart.

I am sorry I haven't come to see you. I wanted to, very badly. But I... I have caused you so much trouble already. I don't want to cause more. You are amazing. I admire you. You have achieved so much.

Divya, that night I would never have opened my heart, bared it to you, confessed my feelings if I had an inkling I would be spared the gallows. I was convinced I was going to die and that is why I shared how I felt about you.

But you are too good for me, Divya.

Let me be the judge of that, she thinks.

His letter:

You deserve better.

Raghu, don't you see? I want you.

His letter:

Please. I ask this one thing of you. Forget me. Move on with your life. Go on to even more glorious things. Marry Jack Devine. He loves you. He will look after you. He's a good man.

Don't tell me what to do, whom to love, whom to marry, she yells at him in her head. *How dare you.*

His letter:

This is my last communication with you. I dithered about whether to write this letter but I thought you deserved to know. I have signed up. I will be leaving for France for training soon.

Take care, Divya.

You are always in my heart.

I am cheering you on from afar, praying for you, wishing you the very best.

Raghu

She sets the letter down before it gets soaked with her tears. Folds it carefully and tucks it gently, tenderly, inside her blouse, right next to her heart.

Then she rubs her eyes and washes her face so there is no sign she has been crying.

It is mid-morning, the lull between elevenses and lunch, which she has already prepared.

There are the usual suspects in the curry house. The residents of the street are passing time with chai and snacks – spiced egg puffs and Divya's special cinnamon-spiced fruit cake.

'I've run out of salt. Just popping out to get some. I will be back to serve lunch,' she says.

'All right,' they call.

And, before she can change her mind, she walks out of the curry house and to Raghu's billet, his letter nestling upon her heart, keeping time with its urgent beat.

64

Divya had asked Raghu where he lived but he was vague. After much pressing from her, 'Shadwell,' he'd said.

'Where in Shadwell?'

'Oh, the lascars' barracks.'

As Divya walks past the docks, she sees groups of lascars, haggard faces on malnourished bodies hoping for work.

Further along, there's a skirmish between a group of white sailors and a couple of lascars.

Fear creeps up her chest, rooting her to the spot, even as she looks about her for help.

'You are not to use our toilet blocks. Don't you see the sign: "No Lascars"? Right there.' One of the sailors is shouting in the lascars' faces.

They fold their hands in supplication, meekly edging away. 'Pardon, sir. Sorry, sir. No read English, sir.'

The sailors calm down, even as they shake their heads. 'Dunno what you lot are doing 'ere if you can't read signs. Your toilet block is over there.'

Divya shrugs back tears all the way to Shadwell, the more so when she encounters lascars hawking everything from Tiger Balm: 'make ache and pain vanish', to worse-for-wear crockery and parts of bicycles and radios, which they have no doubt collected from some junk yard, and others begging, desperate eyes in emaciated bodies.

Now she understands why Raghu has always felt himself lesser to her, not good enough. It is reinforced every day, at work on board ships – if they are lucky enough to find jobs, where they are paid much less wages than their white counterparts and have segregated toilets – and elsewhere, with the dearth of jobs, reduced to begging and hawking junk in the hope of making a few bob.

When she finally arrives at the lascar barracks, she's shocked afresh.

It is a lean-to, shabby, falling apart, several lascars packed into one small room. The door broken and flapping in the frisky breeze.

Raghu has been making do, living here.

Of course. The lascars are paid so little, they get by in the hope that they will be able to obtain a passage back. They are paid in full only once they return to India, Raghu has told her.

The lascars look her up and down, a woman in an all-male conclave.

She feels conspicuous, assaulted by stares and glares and leers and whistles, but she keeps her head up high.

'I'm looking for Raghu.'

Please, she has prayed since she left the curry house. Since she read his letter. *Please let it not be too late. Please,* she prays now, his letter cradled next to her heart.

'Raghu, eh?' The lascars smirk. 'That man has all the luck. But sadly, he's left. Will one of us do instead?'

She ignores their lascivious advances, asks, 'Left for where?'

'Signed up to fight this war that is none of our business.' They spit. 'He always had ideas too big for his status. He's on the train now, with the other fools who've signed up.'

She turns away, ignoring their catcalls, their cries of, 'Where are you going? We can show you a good time.'

She walks back, roughly wiping her tears away.

He posted the letter just before he boarded the train, she's sure of it, knowing that even if she came in search of him, it would be too late.

I hate you, she rails at him in her head. *But I love you more. I wish I didn't care for you so. You have ruined me, Raghu.*

65

Jack is waiting for her at the curry house.

He takes one look at her and says, 'What's the matter?'

'Nothing's the matter,' she mumbles, walking right past him and into the kitchen, not wanting him to see her so upset.

He follows. 'Divya, what's wrong?' His voice soft with concern.

'Nothing's wrong.' But her voice breaks.

He holds her as she sobs her heart out.

'It's all right. It's okay, my love.'

He does not press her. He just holds her, soothes her. She weeps against his solid chest, listening to his heart beating steady and firm as her sobs die down to hiccups, and she is grateful for him.

'Now then,' he says, gently leading her to a chair. 'You sit down. Let me make you some tea. I cannot promise chai but I can make tea.'

'I'm all right,' she manages.

'You will be,' he says, smiling fondly at her, 'once you've had my tea.'

And now she smiles.

'That's my girl,' he says.

The tea is strong and sweet. 'Just what I needed, thank you Jack,' she says.

'Now not the time for more gloomy news?' he asks.

She looks at him, her heart beating frantically against her chest. 'What is it?'

He sits opposite her and his eyes are serious, no longer twinkling. 'I've signed up. I'm leaving for France.'

'Oh.' Her hand on her heart upon which rests Raghu's letter. Both the men she cares for in France, fighting for God and country.

Jack is her rock. She will miss him. But the country needs him. She swallows, finds the words she must say in her salt-clogged throat: 'You do what you have to do.'

He takes her hands in his. 'You must know, Divya, that I love you.'

She looks into his eyes and sees the truth shining there.

'I know...' He takes a breath, sadness shimmering in his eyes, the colour of the sea after a summer storm. 'I know that you don't love me in the same way.'

'I... I care for you, Jack,' she says.

'But your heart is promised elsewhere.'

She nods. 'Yes.'

The ache in his eyes, the pain...

Why can't she love this man?

She hears her parents' voices in her head. *Who will you choose? The Indian boy who has no way of providing for you or this man who makes you feel safe? We'll tell you who we would choose for you – this man, without question. Your life would be so much easier, smoother with him. You would never have to worry again. And neither would we, about you. We died on our way to find someone who could provide for you. This man would do that. He will look after you.*

But Ma, Baba, Divya protests, in her head, *I don't need a man to provide for me, look after me, any more. I can provide for myself.* It is the truth, Divya realises. She is confident enough now, even in England (which doesn't feel strange any more), even while they are at war, to stand on her own two feet, rely on nobody but herself. She will have to, with Jack and Raghu both signed up. But whatever comes her way, with war on the home front, she will face it.

She has already been through so much – she was kicked out of her childhood home and again, abandoned here, in a country on the other side of the world from all that was familiar. But she has managed, despite it, to make a life for herself. With the help of this man of course, and Charity and others on West India Dock Road, but nevertheless, she has proved to herself that she can do it. She will weather whatever life has in store for her next with confidence, her head held high. After all, she did not break, even when most of the street was against her, even when the brick came through the window. Instead, she stood up to everyone and for Raghu.

Raghu...

'Jack, I'm not right for you,' she says.

'Let me be the judge of that.'

She understands. It's how she feels about Raghu deciding that he's not right for her.

If she were to choose Jack, she would drag him down with her. Jack belongs here, effortlessly. Divya has had to work to belong and although accepted by many, there are still a fair few who will take against her just because of how she looks. And if she is with Jack, they will take against him too, judge him, mock him, and she couldn't bear that. It would hurt her to see him made fun of and derided because of her.

And she understands now that this is how Raghu feels too, about being with her – he does not want to drag her down, her to be made fun of, punished, her business suffering because of him.

'The heart wants what the heart wants.' Jack sighs and his voice is as melancholy as the wind howling through denuded trees on a snow-choked winter's night. 'From the first time you collided with me, literally, in that street, I have loved you, Divya.' He takes a breath. 'When I am away, will you write to me?'

'Yes,' she says.

'That will get me through.'

He brings her hands to his lips. Kisses them.

'Be safe,' she says.

'I will try.'

'Come back. Come home,' she says. 'I will have your favourite curries waiting.'

'If that's not incentive then I don't know what is.' He smiles but his eyes are sad.

'I will write every day, keep you up to date on the goings on here,' she promises.

'Thank you,' he says.

'No, thank you for everything.'

'You take care and stay safe,' he says.

And then he's gone, leaving her alone in the kitchen scented with spices and ache and loss.

She hears him outside saying goodbye to the others.

She goes to the door and waves as he leaves.

Her last glimpse of him is a jaunty wave and a smile even though his eyes don't twinkle, shadowed with the pain of their parting.

Raghu gone. Jack gone. She doesn't know, with the country at war, when, if she will see them again.

But in the meantime, she will keep the home fires burning. Fight the war here, on the home front. Together with the other residents of West India Dock Road. And hopefully when Hitler has been packed off, they will all be together again. Safe and well.

EPILOGUE

Once upon a time, not too long ago, Divya had wanted to go back to India before the war started and the ships were requisitioned for military purposes.

When she came here to this street, with Jack, whom she had serendipitously bumped into, all she'd wanted was to earn enough to go home.

Her first morning in West India Dock Road, she'd looked at the women washing clothes together chattering among themselves and vowed that one day, she'd find herself a community where she belonged unquestioningly. She thought she would find that in India, even though she had been ostracised for bad luck and shooed out of her childhood home. For when she arrived in this street, England too had treated her badly – she was destitute, and had been reviled for her colouring.

But now, she realises that while taking with one hand, this country has given with the other. It has shaped her into the adult she has become. She is now a businesswoman who has started her own curry house, an accomplished cook dishing up feasts involving various cuisines, catering to clientele from all corners of the world. She has found love and friendship. She has carved an identity for herself.

She looks around her, at Mr Stone and Mr Brown playing chess, Mr Lee and Mr Rosenbaum and Munnoo (looking gaunt and weak, in his threadbare suit, which is now hanging off him), watching and adding their two pennies' worth, Mrs Kerridge and the other women of West India Dock Road gossiping as they drink chai and help themselves to Divya's honey cake and cinnamon biscuits, Charity's brothers weaving between tables.

These people who have become family, gathered in her curry house.

And she realises that she is home.

Charity comes up to Divya and puts an arm around her. 'It's all changing, isn't it?' she says, sighing deeply. 'Jack and the other men on the street signing up, leaving. Soon only the women and children and the men too old to fight will be left.'

'Yes,' Divya says. 'But we have each other.'

Charity rests her head in the crook of Divya's shoulder. 'That we do.'

Divya doesn't know what the future holds. How their part of the world will change with the country, the world, at war. She tells Charity, 'We will face whatever is to come, whatever Hitler, the war, or life will throw at us, together.'

'Hear, hear,' Mrs Kerridge says.

And everyone cheers.

Since Divya was chased out of her childhood village, she's wanted to be part of a community, to belong.

Now she does.

She had come to this country as a naïve girl.

Now she is a woman. She is Divya Ram, the proprietress of the curry house on West India Dock Road, and she is right where she belongs. On West India Dock Road, she has found her place, her voice, her vocation, her community, her home.

* * *

MORE FROM RENITA D'SILVA

Another book from Renita D'Silva, *The Secret Keeper*, is available to order now here:

https://mybook.to/SecretKeeperBackAd

AUTHOR'S NOTE

This is a work of fiction set around and incorporating real events.

In 1938, there was an Ursuline convent in Forest Gate with a school attached to it. For the purposes of this story, I have not included the school or made mention of it.

I have taken liberties with regards to the Indian setting, picking characteristics, such as food, vegetation and customs, from different parts of India to fashion my fictional villages and cities; the areas I have set them in may not necessarily have places, cuisine, flora and fauna and rituals like the ones I have described.

I apologise for any oversights or mistakes and hope they do not detract from your enjoyment of this book.

ACKNOWLEDGEMENTS

I would like to thank my wonderful editor, Francesca Best – I don't know how I got so very lucky but I am beyond grateful to have you as my editor. THANK YOU for all you do.

Thank you to all the amazing team at Boldwood for helping make this book the very best it can possibly be, and for making it travel far and wide.

Thank you, Emily Reader, for your eagle eye and wonderful suggestions during copy edits for this book. Thank you, Rachel Sargeant, for proofreading this book.

Thank you, Ben Wilson, for overseeing the production of the audio version of the book.

Thank you to my lovely author friends, Angie Marsons, Sharon Maas, Debbie Rix, June Considine (aka Laura Elliot), whose friendship I am grateful for and lucky to have.

An especial thanks to Rob Downs for helping with the locations in this book.

A huge thank you to my mother, Perdita Hilda D'Silva, who reads every word I write; who is encouraging and supportive and fun; who answers any questions I might have on any topic – finding out the answer, if she doesn't know it, in record time – who listens patiently to my doubts and who reminds me, gently, when I cry that I will never finish the book: 'I've heard this same refrain several times before.'

I am immensely grateful to my long-suffering family for willingly sharing me with characters who live only in my head. Love always.

And last, but not least, thank you, reader, for choosing this book.

ALSO BY RENITA D'SILVA

Standalone Novels

The Secret Keeper

The West India Dock Road Series

New Arrivals on West India Dock Road

ABOUT THE AUTHOR

Renita D'Silva is an award-winning author of historical fiction novels. She grew up in the south of India and now lives in the UK.

Sign up to Renita D'Silva's mailing list for news, competitions and updates on future books.

Follow Renita on social media here:

facebook.com/RenitaDSilvaBooks
x.com/RenitaDSilva
instagram.com/renita_dsilva
bookbub.com/profile/renita-d-silva

Letters from
the past

Discover page-turning
historical novels from
your favourite authors
and be transported
back in time

*Join our book club
Facebook group*

https://bit.ly/SixpenceGroup

*Sign up to our
newsletter*

https://bit.ly/LettersFrom
PastNews

Boldw☾☽d

Boldwood Books is an award-winning fiction publishing company seeking out the best stories from around the world.

Find out more at www.boldwoodbooks.com

Join our reader community for brilliant books, competitions and offers!

Follow us
@BoldwoodBooks
@TheBoldBookClub

Sign up to our weekly deals newsletter

https://bit.ly/BoldwoodBNewsletter

Printed in Great Britain
by Amazon